POETIC
JUSTICE

POETIC JUSTICE

FILMMAKING
SOUTH
CENTRAL
STYLE

John Singleton
and
Veronica Chambers

FOREWORD BY
Spike Lee

Delta

A Delta Book
Published by
Dell Publishing
a division of
Bantam Doubleday Dell Publishing Group, Inc.
1540 Broadway
New York, New York 10036

Photographs by Eli Reed

DESIGN: Stanley S. Drate/Folio Graphics Co. Inc.

Library of Congress Cataloging-in-Publication Data

Singleton, John, 1968–
    Poetic justice / John Singleton and Veronica Chambers.
        p.   cm.
    Includes the original screenplay by John Singleton, with poems by
Maya Angelou.
    ISBN 0-385-30914-7
    1. Poetic justice (motion picture)   I. Chambers, Veronica.
II. Angelou, Maya.   III. Title.
PN1997.P5433S55   1993
791.43'72—dc20   93-16383   CIP

RRH

BVG 01

*This book is dedicated to my first born daughter,
Justice Maya Singleton,
born on October 17, 1992.*

The blood line continues.

ACKNOWLEDGMENTS

John Singleton and Veronica Chambers would like to thank: Maya Angelou, Sheila Ward, Audrey Morgan-Smith, Cassandra Butcher, Janet Jackson, Regina King, Tyra Ferrell, Robi Reed, Fatima Robinson, Josie Harris, Stephanie Allain, Brad Smith, Dwight Williams, and Mark Gill.

Veronica Chambers would also like to extend a special thank you to: Cecelia Ortega, Michael Trotman, Pat Sharpe, Arthur and Louise Hillman, Retha Powers, Joe Wood, Eric Huang, Martha Southgate, Alex McGregor, Harold Chambers, Sr., Cassandra Butcher (again!), Faith Childs, Jackie Cantor, Marcy Granata, Chris Davies, and John Singleton, who saw the writer in me and gave me complete access to the making of this film. Thank you.

CONTENTS

FOREWORD

December 8, 1992

Dear John,

Thank you for asking me to write the foreword for your book on the making of Poetic Justice. *I hope you don't mind it being in the form of a letter.*

As we enter into the nineties, there has never been a better time than now to be an African-American filmmaker. It's not unheard of someone being in film school one year and writing and directing a feature film the next. You yourself are the best example of that. The question I continuously ask myself is Is this New Black Wave in Cinema a trend or a fashion? Are we the flavor of the month, or are we gonna stick around awhile? I've come to the conclusion it really rests on our shoulders, the African-American filmmakers—it's on us. We, the filmmakers, will determine the outcome of our fate, by the subject matters we choose and by the creativity of our work, which brings me back to you.

When I had just finished She's Gotta Have It *and you came up to me outside the theater in Santa Monica and introduced yourself and said that you were gonna be a filmmaker also, I didn't doubt you. You looked and sounded like a very confident high school student, you had that look in your eye. It's hard to describe, but I know it when I see it. When you come across that look, never bet against that person because whatever it is that they are aspiring to do, they'll do it. So it was no surprise that every time I was in Los Angeles, you somehow hooked up with me, and it was no surpirse when I heard Columbia Pictures had given you the green light to* Boyz N the Hood.

Now John, here comes the hard part. As we all know, you rocked the house with the first joint, two Academy nominations

(Best Original Screenplay and Best Director, the youngest ever at twenty-four years old), they gave you props. On Poetic Justice, the same critics and people who championed you are gonna be after your ass. Why!? Human nature. When someone new and talented arrives on the scene, it's a time for all to rejoice. The first time out, everyone is your friend. The second time out, forget about it, and I'm not talking about the sophomore jinx, either. This happens in film, music, and sports all the time. The same people who said you were the second coming of Orson Welles will now say, "What happened?" They'll feel it's their duty to "knock you down a peg." So if you can understand that going in, you'll be prepared. Just let that stuff slide right off your back, and keep on keeping on. One or two films does not make a body of work. You are in it for the long haul, and that's what counts. The pretenders and the contenders will soon fade out of the picture.

I'm looking forward to Poetic Justice, to seeing Janet Jackson in a dramatic role, the poems of Maya Angelou, your take on young African-American women in South Central L.A. and the rest of the stories you want to tell. The many stories about Black folks you know how so well to tell.

Peace and Love,

Spike Lee
Brooklyn, New York

POETIC JUSTICE

POETIC JUSTICE

FILMMAKING
SOUTH CENTRAL
STYLE

1

From Boyz N the Hood to Poetic Justice

*I*t's April 1991. An unknown director named John Singleton is sitting in an editing room, cutting an equally unknown film: *Boyz N the Hood.* The movie, shot on a modest $6 million budget, is about three guys growing up in the gang-torn community of South Central L.A. Although others have made movies about the area before, this is one of the first to be told from an African-American perspective. At this point, Hollywood insiders know very little about the film or its director. They know that twenty-three-year-old Singleton is a graduate of the University of Southern California's filmic writing program and that he won two prestigious Jack Nicholson Awards for his writing. They know that before he even graduated, he was signed to Creative Artists Agency, or CAA, one of the most powerful agencies in Hollywood. And they know that, based on the strength of his script, Singleton was given the opportunity to direct his first film for Columbia Pictures. But at this point, nobody knows yet how Singleton's "big break" will pan out.

This is before the Cannes Film Festival, May 1991, where Singleton will debut *Boyz N the Hood* and the film will be trumpeted, all over the world, as a red-hot discovery.

This is before the July 12 opening, when it will make ten million dollars in its first weekend.

This is before Singleton is nominated for two Academy Awards. His script for *Boyz N the Hood* will be nominated for Best Screenplay and Singleton will be nominated for Best Director, making him the first African-American ever nominated for the award as well as the youngest person. (Orson Welles was twenty-five when he was nominated for the now-classic *Citizen Kane*.)

This is well before the movie becomes not only a sensational debut directing effort for Singleton but a cultural landmark that will quickly make him a revered and much-sought-after spokesman for his generation and culture. With this one film, he will become something that transcends the film business. It takes most directors much longer to achieve similar status.

Singleton's work will also change the industry's perceptions of black film. *Boyz N the Hood* will make $57 million domestically and ultimately make more than $100 million around the world. Spike Lee has been making successful commercial films for the last six years. The Hudlin brothers' *House Party* has also done extremely well. Such efforts are the building blocks of Hollywood's new deal with African-American cinema; *Boyz N the Hood* will put it over the top. By the end of 1991, nineteen films will be released by African-American directors, more in one year than in the entire previous decade. All of a sudden, African-American writers and directors are the people being sought after.

As its name suggests, *Boyz N the Hood* is very much a man's story. As compelling as the story is for Singleton, before *Boyz* is even released, he will already be thinking about redressing the balance. In particular he's captivated by this character in his head that he's starting to get down on paper, a woman named Justice. He's so taken with her that she'll become the basis for his next movie, which will start shooting in April 1992, to be released in the summer of 1993—*Poetic Justice*.

February 17, 1992

*I*t is a warm southern California winter afternoon. Director John Singleton is picking up a visitor at the airport. Despite his new celebrity status, he comes by himself, *sans* entourage. He is gracious and unflinching when other arriving passengers recognize and greet him. He is just as down to earth as he was before the release of *Boyz N the Hood*, almost a year before. For dinner, he takes his guest not to Spago's or Hugo's or Muse but to one of *his* favorite eateries: Aunt Kizzy's Back Porch, a soul food restaurant nestled in the affluent community of Marina Del Rey. Aunt Kizzy's is something like the West Coast equivalent of Sylvia's, the world-renowned soul food restaurant in Harlem, New York.

Outside the restaurant, a small crowd sits, stands, and chats, waiting for a table. An older woman sits at a table, hawking her wares: beautiful handmade dolls with sweet chocolate faces. Inside, the restaurant's walls are covered with autographed eight-by-ten black-and-white photographs of its famous proprietors. One thinks of Sal's pizzeria in Spike Lee's *Do the Right Thing* and knows that this is a place Mookie would have loved to hang out in: puh-lenty of brothers and sisters on the wall. Which is why, before Singleton is shown his table, the maître d' engages him in a lengthy discussion about when the restaurant will receive its autographed *Boyz N the Hood* poster and where exactly this poster should hang.

When he is seated at last, it becomes clear how hungry Singleton is—hungry to sit in the director's seat again, that is. "I hate people who do one film and talk about it for the next three or four years," he says, holding up a menu that he hasn't even glanced at. "I started writing *Poetic Justice* while editing *Boyz N the Hood*, while working on the sound. I knew I had to get my next picture going."

In a way, *Poetic Justice* is just as much a "make or break" film as *Boyz N the Hood*. The incredible success of *Boyz* raises the ante for Singleton considerably. Along with the dap and the duckets comes this: the challenge of making a second film just as strong as the first. As Singleton and the slowly expanding crew of *Poetic Justice* begin the rites of preproduction, there is a heavy sense of expectation in the air.

"After *Boyz N the Hood*," Singleton explains in between bites of fried chicken, "I wanted to do something street, but something different. In Doughboy [one of the main characters of *Boyz N the Hood*], I dealt with the insecurities of black men. Why not do a movie about a young sister and how all the tribulations of the brothers affect her?"

Pulling up closer, his brown eyes engaging and unshifting, Singleton explains, "The strongest women have the softest sides. One of the rules I live by is to write what I know. Some of the most complex, sexy, diverse, three-dimensional women I've ever seen in my life all came out of my neighborhood. They all had a certain mold of substance." This is no idle boast; Singleton has matured greatly in the mere nine months since *Boyz N the Hood*'s American premiere. He has sunned at the French Riviera at Cannes, toured America's largest cities, and has even taken his movie to the Far East. But in the end it is home that stays with him, and the women he has known here in South Central Los Angeles.

"Brothers have to go through some shit," Singleton says, his voice angry. "The way society drop-kicks on us, unfortunately, the first recipient of that backlash is going to be our women. For four hundred years, black women have been raped, murdered, and disrespected. They bear children and take care of the men, as well as the children.

"My attitude is you get a real, real strong black woman. She can be tearing everyone up, but if you gain her trust and confidence, she'll do anything for you. Once you betray that, it's over with. That's what Justice is like in the beginning of the movie. She's distrustful and closed. Her mother has died; her grandmother has died; her first love, Markell, has died. When she meets Lucky [the romantic lead in the movie], she's afraid to care about anybody again.

"What Justice did to make money was also important. A regular sister is usually not thinking about going to college. If she wants to think about making it, she'll go to cosmetology school. Hairdressers are the professionals of the black community; they're artists. But like all black women they sacrifice. Sometimes they don't even do their own hair, they're so busy making other people look beautiful.

"I wanted Justice to be a down-to-earth woman. Think about L. L. Cool J's 'Around the Way Girl'—so many sisters loved that song because it spoke to them, not some bourgie, stuck-up Black American Princess. The song spoke to the regular sister in Compton, Watts, Harlem, South Side Chicago, Atlanta, Mississippi. That's what I wanted to do with *Poetic Justice*."

Movie titles are often chosen after the movie is in the can and edited, with heavy marketing influence. Working titles change when test audiences don't respond well, or when it's too similar to the name of a film that's being released in the same quarter, or when some higher-up decides it simply does not work. On a studio picture, the title need not elucidate the work or even describe it with any degree of accuracy; it must simply sell the film. But when Singleton began writing *Poetic Justice*, he started with a title that is so intrinsic to the story of the film that, later, no marketing person or studio exec could even suggest a change.

More like a painter than the Hollywood player he now is, Singleton draws you into his thought process, fleshing out the picture for you. "Start with the characters—you got to have a back story. Justice is a tragic figure, nineteen years old. Her mother was in law school when she was pregnant with Justice; her mother committed suicide. Her grandmother died two years before the movie begins. In a lot of ways, she's raised herself."

Singleton pauses and then, in a somber tone: "The media sensationalized the death at the drive-in in the first day of *Boyz*'s opening. I come back to that in this movie. There's a death at a drive-in, but it means two things: the death of a love and the death of the drive-in as a venue."

It is hard to forget the violence that surrounded the opening weekend of *Boyz N the Hood*. When the final count came in, it was two dead and thirty-three wounded in and around theaters screening the film. That similar incidents had happened during the release of such gang-related films as *Colors* and *New Jack City* was no consolation. "I was very disappointed," says Singleton, his voice pained, "because that's not what my movie was about. It's a sad reflection on what's going on in our society right now. But I'm not responsible because I didn't create the conditions in which people just shoot each other."

At the time of the shootings, producer Steve Nicolaides expressed a similar sentiment: "Random violence exists not only in Los Angeles but all over the country. It predated the opening of *Boyz N the Hood,* and sadly, it almost certainly will continue into the future. The film tries to expose and explore this issue and to offer a better—peaceful—alternative. . . . We cannot interpret these terrible acts of violence as a reason for artists to stop looking at the problems of our society. The problems will not somehow magically go away if we ignore them."

Singleton has a way of disassociating, talking about his films as if he were a film student or a professor and not the director himself. "*Boyz* was successful because it had a straight-up Afrocentric perspective; it was uncompromising, and it had a good story." Yet in the very next breath, he says, "I'm my harshest critic. *Boyz* wasn't a particularly great film, but it had a beginning, middle, and an end. There is no African-American renaissance in film; most of those films are whack. Now they want to make musicals, but we've been singing and dancing too long. We need something with depth to it. People have to love what they do, not just do it for the money. I didn't grow up with a lot of money, so I'm not in it for the money. Nor am I in it to right the wrongs of American cinema. I love movies. Period. Classic structure. Classic characters.

"I'm just now finding myself as a director," Singleton says now, as preproduction on *Poetic Justice* begins. "And I think a lot of the strength of *Boyz N the Hood* came from the fact that I didn't know what I was doing, but I had a focused vision. It's like everything seemed to fall on me. So I was in everybody's shit, I was in everybody's face telling them exactly what I wanted and when I wanted it. . . . I've always been able to put myself in a position of leadership, in front. Not in a very structured way, mind you, in the matter of class president or whatever. But my father used to ask me when I was a kid—I put that in *Boyz N the Hood* too—are you a lion or a sheep? A lion or a sheep? A leader or a follower? And I would say I'm a leader."

That said, Singleton calls for the check and leads the way to his "favorite spot." Along the way, he's stopped by a college-age brother who says, "You know who you look like?" Singleton looks bored and asks, "Who?" The guy, still unsure, says, "John Singleton." It is just a few weeks after Singleton directed the Michael Jackson video "Remember the Time," and the attention surrounding that has put him back in the headlines again.

Soon Singleton reaches his "favorite spot"—not the old-fashioned movie house or store of African-American film memorabilia, as one might imagine. Instead, in this southern California minimall, Singleton marches eagerly into your run-of-the-mill American arcade. Playing video games, he claims, is one of his favorite pastimes. Right away, he starts racking up points, while a small circle of kids gather and watch. None of the kids seem to recognize Singleton as a director; it's his talent as a video impresario that impresses them.

Video games, Singleton says, help him direct because as a director you've got to concentrate on so many different things at one time. His fingers go: shooting missiles with one hand, dropping bombs and dodging shots with the other. At the same time, he carries on a full, intelligent conversation with you: What are you reading? How long have you lived in New York? Could you go get him some quarters, please?

Maybe more film students should be trying their hands at Stunt Runner rather than engaging in pretentious, long-winded conversations about what "the cinema" is all about. Singleton whips the game just as he made his smash writing and directing debut: intelligently, with focus and creativity and a valuable wellspring of confidence. Walking around the arcade, you can see that several games list "John Singleton" or "John S." or "J.D.S." as the top scorer (sometimes several times on top ten list). His name flashes in cartoon colors and space age graphics, and it echoes his current clout in Hollywood. Like Luke Skywalker, the Force is with him.

February 19, 1992
Las Vegas, Nevada

at five in the morning the Academy Award nominations are to be announced. John Singleton, along with an array of Hollywood glitterati, is in town for the annual Showest convention. At Showest, *Boyz N the Hood* has earned more praise (previous honors include an NAACP Image Award), but what the whole industry is waiting for is Oscar news. Singleton harbors a secret hope that he will be nominated for Best Screenplay. It was the strength of the twenty-four-year-old USC graduate's script that landed his deal at Columbia Pictures.

Not usually an early bird, today Singleton is up before the crack of dawn watching CNN. As the Academy announces its picks, the hoped-for nod for Best Screenplay is announced, but there's more.

Singleton is pleased, but tired. He tries to get back to sleep, but the phone calls start soon after and never stop.

There are many press reports that link Singleton's Best Director nomination with the fact that Barbra Streisand did not receive a nomination for her work with *The Prince of Tides.* Some of the news reports suggest that there is a de facto "minority" slot, and it's either a black or a woman (a black woman director not even being a consideration). Singleton tells of Oliver Stone (who was also nominated for Best Director, for *JFK*) and Stone's backhanded congratulation: "Oliver Stone was like, 'Congratulations, Barbra was real upset.' Like it's my fault that Barbra didn't get nominated. I have nothing but love for Barbra Streisand. She helped get me into the Director's Guild. But Oliver Stone—everything for him is Vietnam this, Vietnam that. He's really got to come to grips with the present, or it'll sneak up on him and bite his ass."

Even more publicly, Singleton's nomination was compared with the Academy of Motion Picture Arts and Science's consistent snubs of director Spike Lee's work. "It's all political," Singleton says. "Spike should have gotten it first for *Do the Right Thing.*"

Lee's controversial position in Hollywood is no secret. While millions of American moviegoers look forward each summer to the new Spike Lee joint, Lee is not exactly a darling of the movie industry. He lives in Brooklyn and doesn't play on Hollywood's social lots. He doesn't attend their parties or join their unions. (Lee is not a member of the Director's Guild.) Spike Lee is never more than a visitor in Hollywood; he "takes a few meetings," gets his money, and goes home.

Singleton, on the other hand, is L.A. born and bred. As an alum of USC, he's privy to an exclusive group of filmmakers that includes such directors as Steven Spielberg and George Lucas. He's a union man, and his company, New Deal Productions, is housed under the rubric of Columbia Pictures.

Before *Boyz N the Hood,* Hollywood had all but ignored its neighbors in South Central. While Singleton was still an undergrad, a film about L.A. gangs called *Colors* was released. That year, the film's producer, Robert Solo, visited Singleton's class. In front of five hundred fellow students, Singleton stood up and let Solo know what he thought of his film; "I told him he had no right to make a movie about this 'cause he knew nothing about the culture. He was marketing it as a film about gangs when actually it was a film about two white cops. He said, 'Well, Ice-T wrote the music,' and I said, 'Well, Ice-T didn't write the fuckin' script.' And everybody clapped."

Despite his outspokenness, the film industry feels that they know Singleton, they like Singleton. If nothing else, they like the fact that he made a movie for $6 million and that it made $100 million. Politics, racism, and class struggle go over a lot of these people's heads. Money does not.

"It's not a matter of whether or not they like you as a person," Singleton says. "They know me through the work. Some of them will never get past the fact that I'm a brother, right? But there are some people that are open-minded and are not so insecure as to not give respect to good, quality material."

In some ways, the Best Director nomination is an anomaly to Singleton, who has always considered himself, first and foremost, a writer. "I direct to protect my vision," he says. "I'm a storyteller consummate. I can't let some asshole direct a movie that I put my heart into writing. . . . I direct just to protect my shit. What I'm saying is I didn't expect anything and that's consistent with history. When a black person does something significant, you're not supposed to expect established groups like that to acknowledge your creativity. If we get mired in trying to do that, then we get in trouble.

"I was happy when I received the NAACP Image Award because I thought the bourgeoisie, the black bourgeoisie, was never going to acknowledge me. But the only reason I did get it, as you're aware, is because it went out to the national body to decide—it wasn't a political thing.

"I'm the first black filmmaker to receive the Best Picture honor from the NAACP. Isn't that ironic? I mean, when *Do the Right Thing* came out, they didn't give the Best Picture honor to that film, and it sent a message that they didn't think the things Spike was talking about in that film were significant or that he was significant as an artist. Which is a disrespect. I'm more critical of disrespect from my own people than anywhere else. And I haven't received any, so I have nothing to worry about. The only disrespect

I've received from black people has been from the ones who are too concerned with their Mercedes-Benzes and how their hair looks and whether or not they got blue veins." He laughs at his own vitriolic comment. "You write that? Black people worrying about blue veins."

February 20, 1992
Culver City, California

*S*ingleton drives onto the Sony Pictures lot in his Pathfinder, blasting Leaders of the New School. "Do you know why brothers play their music so loud?" he asks, then answers his own question: "In order not to be ignored." I notice that he increases the volume a few extra decibels as we pass through the studio gates. The brothers at the security guard post shout out "Wassup?" to Singleton and congratulate him on his Academy Award nominations. "These are the people I make movies for," he says, "the regular brothers and sisters on the street." Inside Thalberg, an imposing white stone building that houses Columbia's executive offices, Singleton is greeted warmly by a sister sitting at the front desk.

Several critics spoke harshly of the women's roles in *Boyz,* but their comments were most often packaged in a sweeping commentary about the pervading sexism in the all-male-directed African-American film bonanza of 1991. *Poetic Justice* restates and redefines Singleton's commitment, respect, and affection for black women. The script is populated with the black women that the community knows and loves: mommas, aunts, and grandmas; best friends and sisters; chitchats, divas, and hootchies. These roles, especially Justice, will be the goal, dream, and prayer of every black actress in town once Singleton begins casting.

February 22, 1992

Saturday afternoon, Singleton and Peter Ramsey are meeting in Singleton's living room in Baldwin Hills. Ramsey, an alum from *Boyz N the Hood,* is the storyboard artist and second unit director for *Poetic Justice.* Also a young black Californian, Ramsey and Singleton have a good rapport, and their conversation shifts easily from the work at hand to favorite movies to comic books. Ramsey is here to show Singleton his sketches of the various scenes. Later, once shooting begins, Singleton and his director of photography, Peter Collister, will refer to these almost cartoonlike drawings as visual references for the camera. (Collister's job as director of photography, or DP, is to set up the lights and camera angles for the director.) As Ramsey sketches out a scene from the family reunion, Singleton talks it out, aloud: "Lucky and Justice walk away, pull backward from Iesha and Chicago."

"I write it like I want to cover it," he says, motioning to the script on the coffee table. "Basically every shot is here. You've got to have a sense of touch, concentrate on the subtleties. Never be afraid of the material, and let the material tell itself. People need fancy effects because they don't have a story. You notice people don't use a lot of opticals like dissolve. It's MTV, it's all cut, cut, cut."

He and Ramsey discuss the shots in a language that seems almost like Morse code: P.O.V.'s, reverse P.O.V.'s, cut to the right, foreground, background, V.O.'s. On laserdisc, Scorsese's *Taxi Driver* rolls, without volume. Singleton catches a glimpse of a scene he likes, pauses the movie, and rewinds. "This is the shit," he says, referring to the close-up on a glass of bubbling Alka-Seltzer. The conversation segues from the storyboards of *Justice* to the character-driven themes of *Taxi Driver.*

"In *Taxi Driver* you see the madonna/whore images played against each other. Even the city is a character in the film," says Singleton. "Nobody makes this shit anymore. This is what's happening on the street." Fast-forwarding the film to his favorite parts, he becomes momentarily more engrossed in its story than in the film he is about to direct. "It's all about studying movies," he insists. "If you don't love them, then you can't make them, not good ones."

March 9, 1992

*S*ingleton and crew pay a visit to the Crenshaw Post Office, not far from where the same team shot *Boyz N the Hood* two summers before. The U.S. government won't allow a movie crew to shoot in an actual post office, so production designer Keith Burns and the art department team will re-create a post office on a sound stage. Our "tour guide" is Darren K. Royal, a friend of Jacques Beaver, the art assistant. Royal, a young, handsome brother in his mid-twenties, comes from a family of successful postal workers. His dad, this station's postmaster, takes a minute from his duties to compliment Singleton on his work.

As Royal takes the group through the back room of the post office, it becomes immediately apparent to everyone who's read the script how well Singleton has captured this particular slice of life in his script: the tensions between the black and Mexican workers, the black Nikes that pass for regulation shoes, the mail sorters listening to Walkmans. Royal confirms further details and explains that "ninety percent of the time, the most fucked-up employees end up becoming the supervisors. Their job is to push you, and your job is to push them back." At this basic element of working-class life, the demonic supervisor, Singleton lets out a healthy laugh. In his college years, he worked as an airport shuttle driver. He has run into his share of ball-breaking supervisors.

March 14, 1992

a night off. We're at the Ahmanson Doolittle Theatre in Los Angeles. As the audience makes their way to the seats, there's the sort of antsy excitement that only live theater can bring. A few fans approach Singleton and congratulate him on his work. He is, as usual, gracious, patient, soft-spoken.

We are here to see August Wilson's *Two Trains Running*. Singleton is a big fan of Wilson's work. But there's an even more personal connection to this evening's performance. This Broadway-bound production stars a member of Singleton's *Boyz N the Hood* ensemble: Larry Fishburne, or Fish, as he is affectionately called, who played Furious Styles in *Boyz*. As the house lights dim, Singleton whispers, "This means a lot to me 'cause I'm getting ready to see the third August Wilson play I've ever seen. Before I wrote my first script, I saw *Fences;* before I wrote *Boyz N the Hood,* I saw *The Piano Lesson;* now I'm about to shoot my second movie and I'm seeing *Two Trains Running.*"

As Wilson's drama about a small, sleepy fifties black town evolves, Singleton points out the similarities between his work and Wilson's: "I admire August Wilson because he has kept alive the tradition of oral storytelling, the way he chronicles the past through our language, music, mannerisms, and so forth."

As he peruses the room, Singleton points out that the audience is predominantly white. "It is for this reason that we need both black theater and black cinema. The majority of black people can't afford to go to black theater," he says. "The tickets cost too much. A seven-dollar movie ticket is a lot more affordable than a forty-five-dollar theater ticket."

He is impressed with Fishburne's performance, and it's clear that the actor is not only a friend but someone Singleton wants to work with again. "That's good acting," he says. "Look at his *energy*. It's not up to us to build someone up who doesn't have shit. They have to bring something to the table. The director's job is to just help them over."

When the performance is over and the audience, Singleton included, gives the cast a standing ovation, he recollects the first time he met August Wilson in person. "He told me that line," Singleton says, "from the play. The first time I met him he said, 'If you walk around carrying a ten-gallon bucket, you'll never be happy. But if you get yourself a little cup, then when you have a few drops, it'll be full. You'll never fill a ten-gallon bucket.' "

March 16, 1992

*t*he rites of preproduction continue. Singleton, Steve Nicolaides (who is producing *Justice,* too), and first AD Don

Wilkerson work on the film's budget, hire the crew, scout locations, and start planning the shooting schedule. The three men worked together on *Boyz N the Hood* and know each other well. While *Boyz* propelled Singleton into the spotlight, it was also an important career move for Nicolaides. After a long career as a line producer, including work on such Rob Reiner films as *When Harry Met Sally . . .* , *Misery,* and *A Few Good Men,* Nicolaides received his first solo producing credit on *Boyz.*

As first AD, Wilkerson wields considerable power. The first AD is the director's mouthpiece and strong arm—he or she basically runs the set. When they yell "Quiet on the set!!!" there is absolute silence. When they ask for something, production assistants scurry. Wilkerson also wears the hats of unit production manager and associate producer on *Poetic Justice,* earning *his* first producing credit on the film.

The success stories behind the scenes are almost as fantastical as the ones in front of the camera. Joe Dougherty, the director's assistant, left *Poetic Justice* halfway through, with Singleton's encouragement and blessing, to write the Scott LaRock story for HBO and to begin a career in screenwriting. During the shoot, he was courted by Singleton's agency, CAA. Dougherty has since signed with CAA.

Storyboard artist Peter Ramsey was given his first directing gig as second unit director on *Justice,* thereby earning his membership in the Director's Guild of America. Production designer Keith Burns got his first shot as captain of a movie art department with *Justice.* And at the tender age of thirty-two, Burns became not only one of the youngest members of his first union but the first African-American in the production designers' union.

Twenty-three-year-old Rae Haun, the camera PA, took an important step toward becoming a black woman cinematographer. (She knows of none working commercially in Hollywood.) Cassandra Butcher went from being an assistant at Paramount Publicity to being a unit publicist. Butcher quite literally went from answering phones to conducting business on a mobile phone, that true sign of status in L.A. Singleton's director of development, Dwight Williams, like Don Wilkerson, earned his first producing credit as associate producer of *Poetic Justice.* And the list goes on. As preproduction intensifies, these people who have been given the opportunity to strut their professional stuff add a layer of excitement, spirit, and a circulating flow of fresh ideas that keeps the 8461 Warner Drive production office abuzz.

Bobby Thomas, best boy grip and a pal of Singleton's from USC days, talks about the impact the director has had on the old-boy network movie unions. "*Boyz N the Hood* was a litmus test for a lot of the black crew and technicians," he says. "Having an all-black crew meant that we were under the microscope. It was a union show *and* an all-black show—which had never been done before. It got a lot of the young black technicians into the union. If it wasn't for John pushing for that, it wouldn't have happened. *Boyz N the Hood* opened a lot of doors for a lot of people. The ones that didn't do well weren't asked back for this movie, which is fair. This isn't an all-black crew, and because of that there isn't as much of a family atmosphere. It's a good crew, but there's a different energy. John's commitment hasn't wavered, though. He understands the struggles that we go through. Sometimes I have to remind him, but he understands."

Although most movie audiences are unaware of it thanks to the seamless editing done on studio films, there are actually two directors on most films. The director directs the main sequences, all the scripted dialogue and scenes. But the second unit director, with his own crew, goes out and shoots the visual imagery that is needed to tell the story fully—the sunsets, the windmills turning in the breeze, the driving sequences shot with doubles. Watching a roll of second unit photography, take after soundless take, can seem like the visual equivalent of elevator music, but it's these images that add credence to scenes that are shot on sound stages and in other movie-artificial environments.

Peter Ramsey was sitting in Singleton's living room one afternoon during preproduction, showing him storyboards for *Justice,* when "John started talking about how he liked the work I was doing, my visual style," Ramsey recalls. "He said, 'Man, if you ever want to direct . . .' I said, 'If?' He asked me if I was writing [a script], and I said yes. He told me I should try to get on second unit somewhere. Then he turned to Don [Wilkerson] and said maybe I could do second unit on *Justice.* A few days later, John called and said he'd talked to Steve Nicolaides and they all thought it was a good idea. From all the different films I've done, I knew what the second unit director had to do," Ramsey continues. "As a storyboard artist, you're one of the first people on crew, so I'd been watching the process. I always knew that second unit could be a stepping stone to actual directing. So when the opportunity came up with this film, I was pretty well prepared."

But Ramsey admits to being rattled in the early days of his central and northern California film shoot. "We were completely surrounded by fog," Ramsey says, shuddering. "The weather dogged us the whole time. The first couple of days we were sweating for a while, but the sun usually came out at the right spots. As for the actual directing, it took some getting used to being in charge. I didn't have a hard time making decisions or communicating with people. But the biggest thing was getting used to being in charge, realizing that my opinions mattered, that my choices had weight. All the things you know you know really kick in when you're at the helm."

March 20, 1992

*I*t's seven o'clock on a Friday morning. Several members of the crew pile into a van, with coolers of juice and snacks, on one of the many location scouts that will come to be known as the *Poetic Justice* field trips. The group includes Singleton and Ramsey, Steven Nicolaides, Don Wilkerson, Peter Collister, Keith Burns, and location managers Kokayi Ampah and Elisa Ann Conant.

Wilkerson not only worked with Singleton on *Boyz N the Hood* but has since become a close friend. Such a close friend that Wilkerson spent a few weeks of preproduction camping out at Singleton's house as he negotiated a difficult and expensive divorce. He is a tall, muscular red-skinned man, who carries his Native American and African-American heritage with an almost regal posture. Knowing Singleton both personally and professionally, Wilkerson is well aware of the harsh criteria to which *Poetic Justice* is being held, even before principal photography has begun.

"Is *Poetic Justice* '*Girls N the Hood*'?" he wonders aloud. "Yes and no. I think it's a continuation of something John started with *Boyz*. 'Once upon a time in South Central L.A.—' a ghetto fairy tale. Much more like the Brothers Grimm than Hans Christian Andersen."

"What holds your interest," Wilkerson explains as the van ambles on, "is that it's referential. *Boyz* would have been an art film twenty years ago, because it talks to you from the heart. We were thinking about Italian neo-realism, films like *Open City* by Roberto Rossellini." I admit that I never saw the film and ask Wilkerson to explain the story. *"Open City,"* he says "is about the killing of a priest by Mussolini. The story is told in the streets, there's no glamour, it's raw stylistically. Put the camera on the ground and record. Treat it like a documentary. In *Boyz,* we used the point of view of each person so you can see how these kids live. When you're getting young Tre's story, it's all told at his eye level." Steve Nicolaides reminds us that the hocus-pocus of filmmaking is really quite simple: "The camera only sees what you point it at."

Who Singleton will point the camera at is of critical importance. A film's stars can make or break a movie. For a love story, it is especially critical that the two leading actors have the right chemistry. Although he hasn't told anyone yet, Singleton is thinking of casting two prominent musicians in the lead roles.

Singleton wrote the role of Lucky with rapper Ice Cube in mind. Cube had given a visceral performance as Doughboy in *Boyz N the Hood,* and Singleton was looking forward to a chance to work with him again. But Cube could not accept the part, due to his commitment to the action film *Trespass.* Still, one wonders: Could Ice Cube, this former "Nigga Wit Attitude," have played Lucky? Could Cube have reached past his "bitch-ho" definition of women and interacted with a female as complex as Justice? Could the rapper-actor have revealed the softer, more unsure, even romantic sides to himself that we only glimpsed in Doughboy? Rapper Tupac Shakur, who made his feature film debut in Ernest Dickerson's *Juice,* became Singleton's first choice. Once a member of the rap group Digital Underground, Shakur landed a smooth one-two in the winter of 1991. First, there was a successful movie, *Juice,* followed by an incredibly popular solo album, *2Pacalypse Now.* Shakur was determined to win the role of Lucky, he says. "I knew this role was for Cube and it was a mission for me. I wanted to take the role over, make them feel that they could never get anybody else to do this. There was nothing major about Lucky—no fighting, no drugs, not a De Niro role. You had to add dazzle. Lucky's a regular brother, responsible."

In the end, that Singleton chose one rapper to replace another was not terribly surprising. What *would* shock many people was Singleton's first choice for Justice—singer Janet Jackson. Jackson was no stranger to acting. As a child and teenager, she appeared on such television shows as *Good Times, Diff'rent Strokes,* and *Fame.* Singleton and Jackson had become good friends during the year since the release of *Boyz N the Hood.* Singleton began considering Jackson for Justice without telling even her. "I had her look at Sophia Loren's *Two Women,*" he says. "Sophia is a really beautiful woman, but in that movie she played an unglamorous role and it made her even more beautiful. I thought Janet had so much beauty that playing Justice, where her looks would be deemphasized, would do the same thing. . . . I gave her a book of Maya Angelou poems and read "Phenomenal Woman" to her. . . . Everybody in town wanted her to do a movie. One prominent studio executive told her not to do any black movies, but I thought she could do more than just sing and dance. I thought in her first movie she shouldn't play herself." While Singleton had his heart set on casting Jackson, not everyone was convinced that the singer could realistically play a girl from South Central Los Angeles. Singleton agreed to audition other actresses "just in case."

In the end, however, Jackson was Justice and Shakur would play Lucky. In a way, the film is as much about two very different young adults from South Central Los Angeles as it is about the three "stars" of the film: Singleton, Jackson, and Shakur. The once-homeless Shakur is the son of a Black Panther from Oakland, California. Jackson is the youngest of a superstar musical family, raised in Encino, an affluent suburb outside Los Angeles. Singleton is a prodigous young director from the gang-torn streets of South Central Los Angeles. These three diverse backgrounds challenge and defy the stereotype of "black" film; they are all black, but their experiences are so different. In part, the story behind the story is about what happens when you take a rapper from Oakland, a singer from Encino, and a director from South Central Los Angeles and put them all together on a movie set.

2
Casting:
"No Maids, Prostitutes, or Welfare Mothers"

On February 18, 1992, the casting breakdown for *Poetic Justice* went out, and it looked something like this:

To: ALL TALENT REPRESENTATIVES
Re: COLUMBIA PICTURES
"POETIC JUSTICE"
FEATURE FILM

Producers: John Singleton
Steve Nicolaides
Writer/Director:
John Singleton
Casting Director: Robi Reed
Casting Associates: Cydney
McCurdy, Andrea Reed
Start Date: April 1992
Locations: Los Angeles,
Northern California

WRITTEN SUBMISSIONS ONLY TO:

ROBI REED
8461 WARNER DRIVE
CULVER CITY, 90230

PLEASE NOTE: No scripts will be issued for this film. Please do not fax submissions unless requested.

STORY LINE: A contemporary love story involving an African-American man and woman from South Central Los Angeles. Having been thrown together during a road trip, they find their initial opinions of each other are not as different as they had thought them to be. Through poetry and violence, these two learn how to cope with their inner-city lives, responsibilities, and coming of age. . . .

Seeking:

JUSTICE: A beautiful brown skinned African-American girl, age 17 to 22 years. A poet working as a hairstylist, still looking for her place in the world . . . LEAD

LUCKY: A 22-year-old post office mail carrier whose true desire is to write rap lyrics. Limited to the inner city and his responsibilities, including his 6-year-old daughter Keisha, he longs for a way out of a violent environment. This young African-American male with a gangster past becomes more attracted to Justice during a road trip to Oakland, California . . . LEAD

IESHA: An African-American 17–22-year-old girl. She's Justice's friend and encourages Justice to go on a road trip with herself, her boyfriend Chicago, and Lucky. During the trip, she rules Chicago, putting him down, threatening to leave him, which only puts a strain on everyone's "good time." At such a young age, she has already acquired a drinking problem . . . CO-STAR

CHICAGO: An African-American male in his early 20's. He works with Lucky at the post office, and is Iesha's boyfriend. His inability to communicate with his feelings allows Iesha to ridicule him; however, his temper gets the best of him and he gets into a fistfight with Iesha and Justice during their road trip. As a result, Lucky leaves him on the side of a highway . . . CO-STAR

JESSIE: An extremely shapely, beautiful African-American woman in her late 20's. She is the owner of "Jessie's Beauty Salon and Supply," where Justice is a hairstylist. Her attire puts the "E" in ethnic, wearing the hottest, most expensive outfits. She, along with the hairstylists from her shop, caravans to a hair show in Oakland, California . . . SUPPORTING

HEYWOOD: An openly gay African-American male, mid to late 20's. Working at Jessie's as a hairstylist, his effeminate ways continue to disgust his co-worker, Dexter . . . SUPPORTING

DEXTER: An African-American male, mid to late 20's, working as a hairstylist at Jessie's. His lust for women has brought him to this world of cosmetics. He constantly locks horns with his co-worker, Heywood . . . SUPPORTING

MAXINE, COLETTE, LISA, GENA: Four African-American women, all hairstylists, working at Jessie's. NOTE: Maxine has blood-red hair and a large lower physique. She is Jessie's friend . . .

ANGEL: A beautiful, innocent-looking 22-year-old African-American woman. She looks as if she's headed toward a hard life. She has a daughter by Lucky and a son by his friend, J-Bone . . . 8 lines, 3 scenes

And so the breakdown continued, listing every character in *Poetic Justice,* from the leads to the supporting roles, from the "day players"—actors whose contracts are negotiated on a per-day basis—to the "under fives," actors who have under five lines. The script was kept under wraps until the beginning of rehearsals, but the word was out long before the casting breakdown was faxed to agents, managers, and the like all over Los Angeles. The rumor was that it was a sort of *Girls N the Hood.*

To the thousands of African-American actresses struggling for the few scraps of tasty roles that are written with them in mind, the name John Singleton means one thing right now: work. A job and the opportunity to work with an Oscar-nominated director. "The nominations were out yesterday," explains casting director Robi Reed. "I had a stack of messages from agents today. Everybody wants to be involved with a winner." Every black actress in town, from Lisa Bonet to Robin Givens to Rae Dawn Chong, wants the role. Singleton shakes his head. "They're saying there are forty roles for black women in *Poetic Justice!* There aren't forty roles. I wish there were, but there are not."

Reed has earned respect in her field by casting all the Spike Lee movies since *School Daze,* along with such television shows as *Roc* and *In Living Color.* She concurs that the hype over *Justice* is huge. "John does the same thing to me that Spike does," she says, laughing. "He tells all the actors, 'Casting, see Robi Reed.' They started calling me weeks before I'd officially negotiated my deal."

Singleton starts discussing the 1991 feature release of *Fried Green Tomatoes* and how Cicely Tyson, a prominent African-American actress, played a servant in that film. Singleton, incensed, says, "It is safe to say there will be no maids, prostitutes, or welfare mothers in my movie." The dearth of roles available to black actresses is felt even more severely because so many of those roles that do exist fall into types mired in racial and economic prejudice. Not that such women don't exist in the African-American community, but they represent a limited spectrum of black women's lives. Still, these roles are like roadblocks on Hollywood Boulevard, and it seems nearly impossible to avoid them, if one wants to work, if one needs to eat.

The actresses and actors turn out in droves for the *Poetic Justice* auditions for the opportunity to play romantic leads. Despite whatever bit part they played in this soap or that film, they want to show that they can play a three-dimensional character; they want to enact the drama and humor of romantic relationships. It seems like an odd takeoff on the *Field of Dreams* scenario: "If you build it, he will come." For these African-American actors, their Field of Dreams seems to be, "If you write it, we will come." Write roles that have dignity and humor, that allow them to stretch dramatically and have a good time, write them a John Singleton role, and they will come.

The first few weeks in February are for prereads. Robi Reed and her associates, Cydney McCurdy and Andrea Reed, will try to see any actor that wants to audition. From the quality of some of the auditions, it is clear that a lot of these people aren't actors. Reed says that's okay. She takes the time to explain to actors lines they may not understand. She lets them start over when they mess up.

Again and again, the actors read from "sides"—one or two pages of dialogue, chosen from the script. We hear lines such as Chicago's, "You can't make your mind up whether you wanna kiss me or hit me, huh?" repeated over and over again, by actor after actor. Sometimes the lines sound exactly the same, flatter with each read; sometimes two actors read the same line, and it sounds like it's from two different movies.

Interspersed with the many actors and actresses are a group of street-smart young men whom Reed ID's as members of Jim Brown's organization. "They're former gang members," she explains. "I read about the group in the paper and got the idea to read some of these guys. I'm always looking for new faces; I thought maybe I'd find a diamond in the rough. It was an idea I had since they are guys from the community. I'm always looking for nonactors, people who have natural ability like Rosie Perez." Singleton has had luck before with talented neighborhood kids. In *Boyz N the Hood,* both young Doughboy, played by Baha Jackson, and the pacifier-sucking gangsta Dookie, played by a teen called VW, went straight from the street to the screen, giving memorable performances.

Reed herself has been responsible for bringing more than one unknown out of the wings and onto the stage, like actors Wesley Snipes, Darryl Bell, and Robin Harris. But when the movie is released and a star is born, most people credit the director, not the casting director. Says Andrea Reed, casting associate and Robi's sister, "The casting director is a thankless job. Actors rarely say, 'When Robi Reed brought me in . . .'" It's always, 'When Spike put me in his movie.' They always forget that they have to go through us before they even get to the director."

During prereads though, as the actors sweat it out in the front office, the casting director is the most important person in the world. Actors mumble lines to themselves, size each other up, bite nails nervously, and knock back bottle after bottle of Evian. So deep in concentration are they that once or twice John Singleton passes right by them and they don't even notice.

As the actors come in, you see the range. From those who are unknown to those who are simply untalented, from commercial and sitcom actors to the actors who are household names. "As casting director," Reed says, "I don't just look at the obvious actors, the ones you always see working. That gets boring. I always try to find fresh faces, even if that means going through twenty actors who don't have a clue about what they're doing."

Nicolaides explains that one of the exciting, albeit unfortunate things about casting a black film is the abundance of available talent. "You see all these fabulous, great, incredible performers who should be giant stars, and you've never heard of them. Look at Regina King or Monica Calhoun—the talent is incredible."

"*Poetic Justice* is a film about a young man and woman," says Reed. "There's an interesting mix of teen actors and older actors who can play young, meaning play younger characters. With young people there's less time for them to have any life experience. They're green. You find yourself casting older people to look younger, and that's hard too."

As some of the actors come into the casting room, they greet Reed by her first name: "Robi!" Many come over to kiss and hug her. It's obvious that a lot of these actors have read for Reed again and again. "I always leave room for them to have improved from the last time," she says. "I see people over and over again." Of the auditioning process, she says sympathetically, "It's not easy. People think, 'I can do this.' They think they can just come in and read. It's harder than it looks."

From the beginning, it looks like casting Heywood, the gay hairdresser, will not be easy. Singleton is adamant that Heywood not be a stereotype, that he not be a parody of black gay life like *In Living Color*'s skits on "Men on Film" and "Men on Books." "I said I wanted Heywood to be androgynous. I don't want him to be blatantly homosexual, 'cause a lot of people do that in film. I wanted there to be some mystery about the dude. I think that's what makes him real. So if I've got to have a homosexual character, I've got to have him be real so that if they attack me, I can say this person is real, he's not a caricature. It's like all my other characters, you see what I'm saying? And all the sisters are real, too, you know? So that if people attack me I can say, they're real." There's a little bit of defensiveness in Singleton's voice, cynical traces of his tumultuous first year in the public eye. But it's also clear that in Heywood, Singleton is seeking to avoid caricature because deep inside, he feels this is the right thing to do.

Reed agrees with Singleton that in Heywood, they want an actor who can explore the subtleties of sexuality, not just play up the campy queen stereotype. "He's not a flame," Reed says. "He is who he is." Is homosexuality a tough issue to broach in the black community? Singleton shakes his head. "It's a tough issue to deal with in *any* community."

That is why Robi Reed has a free fifteen-minute slot in her afternoon auditions. "We had an actor who was scheduled to come in and read for Heywood," Reed says. "And he's not sure he wants to." Reed refuses to push. "If they don't realize on their own that this is just a movie, then I'm not going to try to convince them. Because there are plenty of people who are willing to do this role."

One of the actors who comes in to read for the role of Heywood is Roger Smith. A stage actor who has appeared in such films as *Deep Cover,* Smith is probably best known to film audiences as Smiley in *Do the Right Thing,* the stuttering postcard vendor whose "MMMMMalcom" and "MMMMMMartin" not only hawked his wares but held up two black ideologies for the film audiences to ponder and eventually choose.

A tall, fair-skinned black man with low wavy hair, Smith comes in dressed for the part: earrings in both ears, a stylish suit with colors that make your gay-dar buzz but not so much that you'd want to bet money that this brother isn't straight. Smith flirts with androgyny with the aplomb of pop stars like Madonna and Annie Lennox—playing with his voice, gestures, facial expressions. But certainly, what distinguishes Smith from the other actors who audition for the role is the improvisations he does during his callback. When the character Dexter calls Heywood "a bitch" for borrowing his brush, Smith refuses to let his character take such a diss with no retort. He sizes Dexter up and says, "I was all-star wrestling champ at Dorsey High School."

Everyone in the room looks at each other, wondering at the unscripted line for a millisecond, then collapsing in laughter. In improv after improv, Smith changes sports and schools. He is boxing champ at L.A. High, karate champ at Jefferson, even *lacrosse* at Beverly! And then the finishing stroke: Smith as Heywood warns Dexter that he should be careful whom he calls a bitch because "I'll give you your ass, Sexy Dex, and *not* the way you want me to." Not only does Smith win the role of Heywood, when the movie is finally shot, the script has changed to incorporate his improvisations.

Sitting on the steps in front of the production office, nineteen-year-old Keisha Jones is nervous about her audition. She really wants to be in this movie. Even at her young age, she's frustrated with the roles she goes up for. "Every time there's a role for a black woman, she has to be physically exploited," she says. "But if you say something, then you're out the door. Because they know they can get someone else to do it. If only all the black actresses would say, 'We're not having it.' Maybe something would change. I want to be in this movie because John Singleton is a great filmmaker—he depicts black women as we are. He's not afraid to write us as positive."

Monica Calhoun is a beautiful young actress with that larger-than-life, movie-star presence. Best known for her work in *Baghdad Café,* her commitment to the television show kept her from playing Brandy in *Boyz N the Hood.* She's the front runner for the lead role of Justice. Besides the fact that the part could ignite twenty-year-old Monica's career, she wants to be in *Poetic Justice* because she wants to be in a John Singleton movie. "He has a clear mind and a clear vision of what he wants," she says. "He brings to film the issues and concerns of my generation."

After Monica's callback, John Singleton, Robi Reed, and producer Steve Nicolaides are all impressed with her work, and all agree that she would be a wonderful Justice. But in the end, the difficult decision is made to give the role to Janet Jackson. Singleton shakes his head, "This is the second time I've missed a chance to work with Monica. I've got to write a role for Monica Calhoun."

The newest member of the popular television show *A Different World,* actress Jada Pinkett is also twenty years old. She met Singleton when he visited the set of *A Different World.* He congratulated her on winning the television role and told her that he admired her work. Sitting in the front casting office, Jada waits for the opportunity to meet John again and hopes he'll be impressed enough with her work to offer her a film role. "I loved *Boyz N the Hood,*" she says. "One thing I really like about John is he's real. He writes real stuff—he doesn't front on what's going on in our community. People have no idea of what the real deal is. I respect and appreciate that. I don't think older people really understand what's happening with us and our generation. It's a whole different time, it's a whole different set of circumstances, and situations that are coming up. I want to be in this movie because I want to be in a black film, and I want to be part of the history that I think John is making."

Connie Marie Brazelton has been acting for eleven years, appear-

ing on such television shows as *China Beach* and *Knots Landing*
and in films like *Nuts* and *Hollywood Shuffle.* She's itching for a
better selection of roles, though she says, "It's getting better. I
haven't been called for too many hooker roles lately. I did play a
drug addict a while ago." She thinks for a second and shakes her
head. "Girlfriend, I'm about playing a doctor, lawyer, psychiatrist,
nurse—people I can relate to. The media makes it seem we're all
out on the streets."

Brazelton is intrigued by the romance in *Poetic Justice,* and
when asked to describe her dream role, she says, "A 1990s black
woman—someone who falls in love with a tall, black, knight in
armor. We don't get to see this. Her occupation could be anything,
an actress, a nurse. . . . I was going to say anything but a welfare
mother, but if it's a welfare mother, why can't she go to a club one
night after work, meet a nice guy, and fall in love? That never
happens in the movies."

Brazelton, who has cocoa-brown skin and delicate features, also
wears her hair in Senegalese twists, a popular West African style.
She is one of the few black actresses who has come in who hasn't
straightened her hair. Brazelton says that while her Afrocentric
hairstyle may have hurt her career, she's sticking with it: "I did
four projects with the Senegalese twist, and I'm very proud that I
got away with it. I also did a commercial. European directors tend
to appreciate our beauty more than American directors. Here,
you're lucky if you can be the way you are—natural—and work."

Ta-Tanisha is an older black actress who despite the fact that
she's out of the ingenue age range has still found work. "I've never
played a hooker," she says. "And that's against type because I'm a
dark-skinned black woman. But I've always said Hollywood doesn't
owe me anything because I came in as an artist and I've stayed an
artist. Probably for all actors, not only black actors, there's a
certain way casting directors expect us to be like. What gets me is
casting directors who say, 'That's not black enough.' It's like, how
do *you* know that's not black enough?"

When asked when was the last time she saw a black love story
that she really enjoyed, Ta-Tanisha goes back forty years in film
history. *Carmen Jones,* she says, referring to the 1950s Dorothy
Dandridge film. "There was a real passion there."

She also enjoyed Reva and Furious's relationship in *Boyz N the
Hood:* "The relationship in *Boyz* was nice. Even though they were

divorced, they were civil. In film and on TV, we're always hating each other. It was wonderful to see us as we really are."

Jonelle Allen is one of the few African-American actresses to work consistently in daytime television, but like most black actresses, she's found it difficult to break into film. "I think that yes, there are roles that are stereotypes," she says. "I've been very lucky. But because I didn't want to play certain roles, I didn't work all the time. On *Generations* [a now-defunct black soap opera] I got to play the diva. That's always been the domain of white actresses on daytime television."

Her favorite black love story? *"Paris Blues,"* she says, "with Diahann Carroll and Sidney Poitier. That was really lovely because they were simply two people in love and in Paris." Yet judging from some of the critics' responses to the black corporate background of *Boomerang*, the recent Eddie Murphy romantic comedy, part of the white audience still finds films with affluent blacks to be "inauthentic."

Regina King is the favored choice for the role of Iesha, Justice's best friend. King is a beautiful black women in her early twenties with skin the color of brown sugar and cat-shaped eyes that make one think of divas of yesterday: Eartha Kitt, Ava Gardner, Marlene Dietrich. Singleton wrote the role of Iesha with King in mind, yet she still seems nervous. She knows how capricious this business can be.

Formerly a classmate of Singleton's at USC, Regina appeared in *Boyz N the Hood* and before that spent three seasons as Brenda on the television series *227*. Having worked with Singleton before, she says, "John's the type of director who lets you know what he's looking for, but he's so open, he lets you run with it. Sometimes you watch a movie or a show, and you can tell that a certain person directed it because everyone is acting just like the director. John gives you a chance to really develop the character into what you want her to be, which is something I like and appreciate. I think that, in addition to the writing, is what made *Boyz N the Hood* a fabulous movie."

Theresa Randle had just wrapped a co-starring role in Spike Lee's *Malcolm X* when she came in to read for *Poetic Justice.* She's more optimistic about Hollywood's ability to accommodate black actors and filmmakers. "It's a little too early in the new game to talk about stereotypes," she says. "There's so little to begin with.

You can complain for the lack of roles—a few lines here and there, and even that's so far in between. I'd just like to see a script that's really well written, like *Steel Magnolias,* but about black people. You don't want to complain because at least we're in the movies now. But I feel like, somebody, please, write me a full story!" Then with a mischievous look in her eye, Randle pauses and says, "And as for the stereotypes—every black actress in town would want to be a hooker if they were making a black *Pretty Woman*. It's just that nobody wants to be a ho."

As the actresses file in and out of casting sessions, it's amazing how many shades of black there really are. The women range in skin tone from Lena Horne tan to Diahann Carroll brown to Grace Jones ebony. Since antebellum days, fair skin has been the most valued in both the African-American community and in the larger American society. But time is wreaking a slow but definite change in attitude. Black has become beautiful, and many proclaimed that "the darker the berry, the sweeter the juice." Hollywood is a good thirty years behind the times, and American movies have yet to portray a full spectrum of black women.

Singleton wrote the role of Jessie in *Poetic Justice* for actress Tyra Ferrell. Ferrell played Ms. Baker in *Boyz N the Hood,* then went on to play John Turturro's love interest in *Jungle Fever* and Wesley Snipes's wife in *White Men Can't Jump.* Still she finds that it's a struggle to beat the barrier of colorism; "When I went to audition for *White Men Can't Jump,* my insecurities rose. I thought, 'He'll never think I'm pretty enough, he'll never like me.' But what I've learned in this business is that it's a collaboration. You have to show a part of yourself to people so they'll know that they have something to work with. . . . I represent a minority who haven't seen themselves onscreen, and that's black women who look black."

Singleton is deeply aware of the beauty myth that most black women have grown up with. That's why in *Boyz* and now in *Poetic Justice,* he wanted to see all types of women. "No matter what anybody says," he claims, "the women in any movie reflect the director's standard of beauty. Directors cast women they are screwing or aspire to screw. In any one of my projects you'll see the type of woman I'm attracted to. I don't think there's any one specter of Afrocentric beauty. How could there be? There are more shades between black and white than there are in the whole rainbow."

Aspiring actress Chandra Brody is startlingly beautiful—big round eyes, Marie Osmond white teeth, and the darkest, smoothest skin you've ever seen. It is three weeks into casting, and Robi Reed and her associates have narrowed down the talent to the top contenders. These select callbacks are known as producers' reads. In John Singleton's office, Andrea Reed videotapes the actors, while Reed, Nicolaides, and Singleton watch, listen, and assess the auditions. Chandra Brody has not been preread. She has no professional experience, no head shot, no résumé. She gets to do a producers' read because she has flown all the way from Dallas at her own expense to audition for *Poetic Justice.*

Reed explains that she does her best to dissuade would-be actors from wasting valuable time and money for an audition that may very well lead to nowhere. But Brody is twenty years old, headstrong, and starstruck, she wouldn't take no for an answer.

Like Tyra Ferrell, Brody hopes to change Hollywood's standard of beauty. "It's hard to be a black actress," she says. "Especially my being of dark complexion, it's even harder. Black men have more opportunities to get roles, whatever color they are. Look at Wesley Snipes. You see him everywhere. They often cast dark-skinned men in roles. Being a darker-skinned woman, when you see all the light-skinned actresses you think you'll never get a chance. As a kid, I only saw light-skinned actresses, and so I thought that's what beautiful was. Me and my best friend used to say 'White is right' and 'The lighter, the better.' "

As Brody speaks, her voice gets smaller, more childlike, and you can tell the hurt isn't very deep under the surface. She says, "This is going to sound really corny, but I want to be the black Marilyn Monroe. I don't think beauty is just white. Like Josephine Baker, I want to leave a mark on the world. I'm scared sometimes that I won't fulfill my dream. I'm afraid of failure, that I'll come and go and no one will know Chandra Brody was here. I wasn't born with my looks and my talent for nothing—God gave me this for a reason."

Brody's strong mix of ambition and naïveté is a combination often exploited in Hollywood. You admire her chutzpah, you worry about her youth. Steve Nicolaides says sympathetically, "That girl needs to go home before the sharks get to her. Depending on who the agent is and who the client is, *agent* is just another name for pimp." After her audition, which consists mostly of nervous giggling, Brody hangs around the casting office. She knows no one else in L.A., and she has nowhere to go. She says, again and again, "he [Singleton] said I was pretty." When asked how she plans to spend her evening, she explains brightly that she is "waiting for John." He has made no plans to meet her. On the contrary, Singleton has an American Film Institute black-tie dinner that evening. Given the bad news, Brody asks for a ride over to Singleton's production office. She wants to visit Tina, John's assistant, with whom Brody has "become friends" through her many calls to Singleton's office. For the rest of casting, as Polaroids and home-made head shots pour in from young girls across the country, Brody will be distinctly remembered as Miss Texas.

By mid-March, all the adult roles have been cast. Janet Jackson is playing Justice. Tupac Shakur will play Lucky. Tyra Ferrell is Jessie. Regina King is Iesha. Comedian Joe Torry is Iesha's lover/sparring partner, Chicago. Roger Smith will play Heywood. The only roles left to cast are the children.

Singleton loves kids. Whenever he sees cute kids in restaurants or on the streets, he tells their parents to call the office. But it is Robi Reed who must wade through *Romper Room* and pick the ones who'll work. She says, "You have to see kids all the time. They never look like their pictures. Parents don't spend money to get pictures done often, and kids change almost daily."

Out in the front casting office, it looks like a meeting of the PTA. Parents mill about, sometimes with kids in tow, sometimes not. There are what seem like hundreds of children just running around, doing whatever they feel like. Some of the parents obviously know each other. They meet, greet, and chat. Many stage mothers and fathers take their children into corners and coach them intensively.

Robi Reed's brother, Doran, was a child actor, so she knows the scenario and just shakes her head. "It's really hard to cast kids; it's the hardest thing to get them to be natural. The parents just make it worse. They teach them gestures, words, and intonations, and it's so hard to break them out of that. What we do with Spike is, we give them a scene to improvise and we ask the parents not to work with them."

One by one, the little girls come in, all dressed up with everywhere to go. Red is a favorite color—red sweaters, red plaid skirts, red ribbons in their hair. And of course, there's the de rigueur black patent-leather shoes. Even the older girls dress young, Shirley Temple style.

Surprisingly, few of the young girls seem nervous. The ones that are nervous, though, wear their hearts on their sleeves. Reed says, "You can tell when they don't want to do this." Knowingly, she says to one little girl, "Do you want to be an actress?" The girl shakes her head no. Reed says kindly, "You don't want to be an actress?" The little girl shakes her head no. Reed asks, "Who wants you to be an actress?" The little girl says, "My daddy." Reed sighs. "You can't force them. They'll tell on you every time."

Most of the girls tilt to the other end of the spectrum: they seem extremely well-schooled, cool, mature beyond their years. One five-year-old darling walks in and responds to Reed's hello with: "I want this part. Are you going to give it to me?" Another girl, who doesn't look a day over eleven years old, refuses to give her age. She asks first, "How old am I supposed to be?" When Reed tells her that her real age is fine, the girl bats her lashes and says flirtatiously, "How old do you *want* me to be?"

Minor setbacks and bug-outs aside, Reed is a pro and quickly casts the children's roles. Young Justice, it is decided, will be played by Janet Jackson's niece, Autumn. It has been hoped that the decision to cast Jackson can be kept a secret, at least until production starts. All those in the know have been referring to the actress who will play Justice as Ansara. But the first day of the location scout a couple of hundred miles up the coast of California, the news comes as news in show business does, over the cellular phone. The first page of *Variety* has leaked Singleton's casting coup: "Janet Jackson Said Doing Columbia's Justice." A couple of weeks later, before the ink on the contracts was even dry, *Variety* will receive a leak that Tupac Shakur has been cast as Lucky along with the names of the actors cast in supporting roles. It is clear: *Poetic Justice* is hot, and everybody wants to know who, what, when, where, and why. And they won't even wait until the contracts are signed to find out.

March 25, 1992
Screen Test

*i*t is eight o'clock on a Wednesday morning. Singleton, after weeks of auditioning actresses, has decided to give the
role of Justice to pop superstar Janet Jackson, and today she is
here for her screen test. There are those who have their doubts.
Can the singer act? And if she can, can this soft-spoken young
woman from Encino convincingly play Justice, a nineteen-year-old
graduate of South Central's School of Hard Knocks? This screen
test is make-or-break time for Jackson. If she doesn't come
through, Monica Calhoun is waiting in the wings. Later, many
will assume that Singleton cast Jackson because of her name, but
those who are at the screen test know that she won the role because
she was the best person for the job. Singleton was perfectly willing
to cast an unknown actress if Jackson did not work out.

The studio is also anxious to see the chemistry between Jackson
and the movie's romantic lead, Tupac Shakur. But ultimately,
Shakur and Singleton made a fine match. Holding an infant in his
video "Brenda's Got a Baby," about a desperate, inner-city teenage
mother, Shakur reaffirmed two Singleton tenets: that a real man
isn't afraid of being sensitive and that black men must be fathers
to their children.

Today we will see if Jackson can pull off the role of Justice and
whether she clicks with Shakur's interpretation of Lucky. Singleton is more than a little nervous. "If she doesn't test well, I'll have
to decide if I should give it to my second choice, Monica Calhoun. I
don't have any reservations about Janet, but she has to do her
research."

Scurrying around the director, a small army of film technicians—PA's, lighting and sound people, transform X, Y, Z hair
salon in Ladera Heights into the fictional Jessie's Salon. The scene
that will be acted out today involves Justice, played by Janet Jackson; Lucky, played by Tupac Shakur; and Jessie, played by Tyra
Ferrell.

The first time Ferrell met Jackson, Singleton says, "Tyra was
pressing her buttons. The first thing Tyra asked her was, 'Can you
be hard?' Janet shyly replied, 'Yes.' Later Janet was thinking about
it and she said, 'I should've said, Fuck yeah.' I was telling Janet

that in her character, being hard isn't just where you're from. There's a certain amount of pain and tragedy that Janet has been through that she can draw from. If I wasn't aware of this, I wouldn't have cast her."

The first glimpse of Jackson is convincing. She wears a black baseball shirt and baggy jeans, homegirl style. She sports a head full of box braids and a floppy black hat. Watching her, you realize that she's an expert at using costumes, environment, and her own inimitable style, to create different personas for herself. In your head, you wish her luck; and along with all the other bystanders, you hold your breath as the cameras roll.

In between takes, Steve Nicolaides explains what they're looking for in the screen test. "If the chemistry isn't there, if his or her performance isn't up to par, that's what we're looking for. What you see on set isn't always what you see onscreen." Singleton eyes Ferrell as she prepares for her scene. "Tyra's one tough woman. A lot of directors don't like actors who have some fight in them. I like an actor who's going to speak up, bring something to the table. 'Cause then you can pull back. They can be guided. People who don't have images have nothing to work with."

The next day, at the first of what will seem like endless weeks of dailies, we watch the outtakes of the screen test. The scene being played out is one that Jackson and Singleton actually wrote together. It is the first time Lucky and Justice meet. Lucky enters the salon, delivering his mail and trying to charm the beautiful Justice. She is, at first, cold to him, unable to relate or respond to him outside the enclave of sadness she has made her home. Then we see a shade of the old Justice. With a mischievous gleam in her eye, she flirts with him, asking him what he really wants, asking him if he wants to smell her "poonani." Lucky swoons, smitten, *sprung*. Justice suprises him by calling Jessie over. She tells Jessie that Lucky wants to smell her poonani and asks whether she should let him. Jessie sizes him up, says yes, and breathes in Lucky's face. In the scene, both Shakur and Jackson are powerful, entertaining presences. Ferrell as Jessie is sexy, smart, sardonic. Those three, at least, can make this movie happen.

When Jackson, as Justice, opens up her baseball shirt, just a little bit, and seductively whispers to Shakur's Lucky, "What do you really want?" there are catcalls from the men in the audience, the loudest voice being Singleton's. "I can hear the guys screaming in the audience," he says. "It's a whole different side of Janet. She knows how to do that tease."

March 31, 1992

*i*t's the Tuesday morning after the Academy Awards. Singleton won neither of the two awards he was nominated for, but he is proud to have been nominated. It's early, and everyone is in various stages of waking up. We are gathered in a warehouse room, down the block from the production office, for the first cast read-through. Most of the actors know each other—the circle that is Black Hollywood is really quite small. Hugs are exchanged, along with news and congratulations.

Singleton begins by saying, "Since I didn't win last night, I'm going to give y'all the acceptance speech I had prepared." The whole group laughs at his joke, then he continues: "Filmmaking is not an exact science, there's no set path to follow. All I'm going to ask of you is that each and every one of you get into who you are as characters and don't worry about what other people are doing. If you come up with something that you think is integral to the scene, don't be afraid to come up to me. I'm open to suggestions—I think only fools are not. I just want to cut through all that mire. We're going to have a great time, and in the end, I think you'll all be satisfied with the work we've done."

The read-through begins; the cast laughs at the funny parts. At a certain point, early on, Singleton pipes in, "I'm trying to get permission from Columbia to play with the logo and make the Columbia lady a black woman"—that gets a round of approval. From Jackson's sweet "Markell, do you love me?" to Ferrell's sassy "I know I'm fine, but damn," the dialogue sings. Singleton's script is real, funny, and coming to life. The ensemble reflects the energy and diversity of the African-American community.

Twenty-odd people in the room, and the script goes through the first steps from being words on paper to becoming a movie. During rehearsals, the actors quickly develop history for their characters and form relations with each other as characters. In one improvisation, the actors go into therapy as characters. One by one, they sit alone in the circle and answer questions from the other characters who are sitting around her or him.

Already, singer-actor Keith Washington has established himself as a flirt and ladies' man—it's hard to see where Keith ends and Dexter begins. In the circle of "character therapy," he reveals a certain vulnerability and professional focus. "I'm separate from the rest of the stylists in the salon," he says of Dexter. "I'm to myself. Everyone in the salon gets a certain kind of treatment, and that's unfair. My purpose is to satisfy my customers to have them leave the salon feeling like Jessie's Salon is the shit, and Dexter is a hell of a hairstylist."

It was only a couple of weeks ago that the crew visited Hollywood Curl, the Baldwin Hills salon that will become "Jessie's" when production begins. A friendly but quiet hairdresser named Leigh had made a comment not dissimilar to Dexter's: "Sometimes in the salon, I isolate myself. I'm from the South, and I can't be anything but who I am. I can't deal with the cliques." In creating Dexter's character, Singleton has represented Leigh and the men and women like her, who sit at the outskirts of the hustle and bustle of a busy salon.

In character, Crystal Rogers, who plays Angel, is also surprisingly forthcoming and vulnerable. "I don't love myself," she says. "I could say that I do, but I don't. The pipe helps me forget." There is an eerie silence in the room when she speaks. Perhaps it is because crack has so devastated the African-American community that it has personally touched some of the actors' lives; or maybe it's her blunt admission of insecurity and self-loathing; or it could simply be that Crystal's performance is so painstakingly real. Nobody says, but you can feel a sort of invisible emotional rope connecting the group, pulling the actors closer to their characters and each other.

3

L.A., It's a Riot

Tuesday, April 14, 1992

*I*t's the first day of principal photography, and the air is tense with excitement. Some of the crew have known each other and Singleton since *Boyz N the Hood* days, but this is a very different production. There was very little attention from the studio or the media to the then-twenty-two-year-old director's low-budget, first feature-length project. The actors, with the exception of rapper Ice Cube, were all veritable unknowns.

The budget on *Poetic Justice* is double the very modest $6 million spent on *Boyz N the Hood*. Although she won't begin shooting for another couple of weeks, everybody now knows that the film stars Janet Jackson. Rapper Tupac Shakur, the male lead, is also well known in this urban community. When production begins, "Brenda's Got a Baby," the sec-

39

ond single of his debut album *2Pacalypse Now,* is topping the charts. Keith Washington, who plays Dexter, has just been nominated for a Grammy for *his* R&B album *Kissing You.* And of course, Singleton has become a celebrity himself, especially here in his hometown.

On the set, everything is brand new, including the director's chair. The logo on the back of the cast and crew's chairs reads: POETIC JUSTICE: BACK TO THE HOOD. Singleton is dressed in his usual B-boy uniform of a T-shirt, baggy jeans, and baseball cap, a Malcolm X pendant dangling from his neck. Although it's the first day, Singleton is unbelievably calm. He shrugs when you mention the pressure. He's deeply aware that no matter how difficult it is to be a young African-American director in a cutthroat Hollywood, on these streets brothers are going through a hell of a lot more just to survive. "I was really intense in film school," he says, "a lot more intense than I am now. Whenever someone foils a person's ability to be creative, they make that person dangerous. A lot of people should be glad I'm making movies. I could be out somewhere robbing cars."

We're in a predominately black Los Angeles community, not far from the Culver City production office. We're so deep in the hood that rapper-actor Tone Loc, who plays J-Bone, is surprised as we get out of the van. In the extra-deep voice that made him famous, Loc says, "This is *ridiculously* close to my house. I could've walked." He looks around and laughs. "Coulda *skateboarded.*"

It's a street scene: Lucky is driving up to his ex-girlfriend's apartment. He is here to see their child, Keisha. In the street, he sees a car of gangstas, pauses, then recognizes them as friends. While that encounter unfolds on the blocked-off street, nonactor neighbors peer out of windows and stand around the corners of buildings, out of the camera's range. The street is full of cars and people. But it's hard to tell which people are the actors and which live in the neighborhood, what cars are "picture" cars brought in for background, and what was actually parked on the street before the movie crew arrived.

It is this blurring of the line between fiction and reality, between Hollywood and the black community, that sets Singleton apart. It is a new era in film, where romanticized Norman Rockwell visions of American life fight for attention and credibility with street movies like *Boyz N the Hood.* Reality is in, particularly African-

American reality. Singleton knows his strengths, and surveying the scene, he says repeatedly, "This is *it*, this is the real *shit*." The scenes go off without a hitch. It is a confident beginning.

What Singleton is not confident about, however, is his decision to cast first-time actress Crystal Rogers as Lucky's ex-girlfriend, Angel. When Rogers auditioned, Singleton was impressed with how heartfelt her reading was. Yet he could see the roughness, the actress's insecurity, her lack of polish. "There's a real problem with giving people responsibility when they're not ready," he says. "It's going to be tough. We're shooting Angel's scene partially on location, partially on set. It's got to be a perfect match." In the end Singleton decided to take a chance and give her the role. A thin, light-skinned girl with suicide-blond hair and a penchant for bright pink lipstick, Crystal is a twenty-one-year-old mother of one. Like so many, she came to Hollywood to be a star. After this movie, she may very well be on her way. But right now Singleton has to direct her so that all she feels will come across on screen. Rogers is drawing on minimal technique and experience. All she really has going for her is her natural rawness. Today we will find out if that is enough.

Shannon Johnson, the little girl who plays Keisha, Lucky and Angel's daughter, is five going on twenty-five. She really looks like she could be Crystal's daughter with her baby-smooth fair skin and golden-colored hair. Already an experienced child actress, she seems unfazed by the drama of the scene. That's good—a crying child at this point would be a nightmare. But getting a child, any child, to act on cue, to follow her marks, to deliver memorized lines, is another thing entirely.

Take after take, Angel curses out Lucky, then goes after J-Bone. The little girl looks on dispassionately as the adult cast yells and screams; she seems to really understand that this is pretend. Nevertheless, after five or six takes, barely enough to get thorough coverage on the scene, the set teacher pulls her out of the scene, afraid the child will burn out. "After all," she says, "there *are* child labor laws." There are child labor laws, but the production is nowhere close to breaking them. Although it is early on in the production, there's already a growing tension between the set teacher and Don Wilkerson, the first AD; it's nothing professional, a very clear personality difference and struggle for power. The first AD is not unlike the hall monitor at school: the director is the one with the title, but the first AD's the one who really runs the show. When the teacher pulls the little girl out of the scene, she is exerting what little power she has. Then, not unlike the five-year-old in her charge, she makes a face at Wilkerson as she walks away.

Crystal, her hair up in curlers, her black roots showing prominently, walks back to her trailer in a bright yellow robe and pink slippers. How does she feel after her big scene? Not like going to Disneyland. "I feel all right," she says, tired. "I'm just trying to calm down. I feel like I've been fighting somebody."

At the end of the day, Singleton feels the same way. "I could always be working at Super Shuttle," he mutters. "What?" I ask him as we walk back toward his trailer. "I could always be working at Super Shuttle," he repeats. "That's what I tell myself when things get hectic."

Tupac Shakur, on the other hand, doesn't feel pressed at all. But it's still early on in the shoot—that will change. Right now, he's still riding the high of his hit album and the fact that he won the role of Lucky. "I feel good," he says. "We've been rehearsing and discovering all these good things so I'm ready to go. It makes it easier that John and I are friends. I don't have to worry so much about what I'm doing. Directors want to be so mysterious. John lets me know what's going on in his head. He explains what the shots mean, why they crane up, so I understand what's going on. And John listens to me. When I have something to say, John listens and that means a lot to me. We have a real give and take. Just because he wrote it doesn't mean I don't have anything to contribute. We work together. Changing stuff, adding things."

A few days later, we are out of the hood and back in Culver City on a sound stage. The art department has created a fancy New York loft apartment here. It looks more like Woody Allen's New York than John Singleton's L.A.—and that's the point. The scene is a gag, starring two of the movie's few white characters: Brad and Penelope, played by actors Billy Zane and Lori Petty.

It's a mock seduction scene, riddled with highfalutin drama, that will eventually play as a movie within the movie. It actually helps that Billy Zane has showed up for his first day of shooting bald. It could've cost him his job, but Singleton took it in stride, asking the hairdressers not to give him a wig: "Leave him bald, it's funnier that way." Singleton is also amused by Lori Petty's comedic timing. "Lori's facial expressions are so funny," he says. "She has such a raw sense of humor. She's going to be a star once this Penny Marshall movie [*A League of Their Own*] comes out. She's going to be big." Six months later, Singleton's call is right. *A League of Their Own* is a summer 1992 hit, and the critics praise Petty's performance.

Twice, Petty breaks character and bursts out laughing. Take after take, she gets tired of chug-a-lugging the grape juice that the prop guys have substituted for wine. Before the fifth shot, she looks up pleadingly and says, "Oh, God, if I don't vomit . . ." Singleton smiles like a maniacal elementary school teacher. "You can go pee after the next shot." The shot works, he calls "New Deal" (which is a call to the crew to set up the next shot), and Petty rushes off to the bathroom.

Between takes, Singleton sits amidst the hustle and bustle of cast and crew and imagines how surprised audiences will be when they see this scene. "I don't know what possessed me when I was writing this." He laughs aloud. Then more seriously, he states, "I think what's gonna start happening with my work is I'm going to have characters who aren't African-American, but my work will always have an African-American focus. It'll always be from the perspective of a black man."

Right now, though, Singleton is mainly concerned with keeping up the fast-paced shooting schedule set for him. "I'm a half a day behind, and people at the studio are getting nervous. It's not anything gratuitous—I'm shooting what's necessary. A lot of people think I shouldn't spend a lot of time on this because it's going to be in the background, but it's an element."

As he speaks, a swarm of hair, makeup, and wardrobe people attend to Petty with combs and makeup brushes, hair spray and lint pickers. Petty's dressed in an electric blue lace dress; Singleton sings "Blue Velvet" as she approaches. Her short black hair glistens, and her skin glows. It's amazing how one can envy the beauty of movie stars. As the small army of people whose job it is to make the stars look good do their work, it's obvious that this is a sort of glamour vigilance that no one could keep up in real time.

To make Petty's character seem even more like "a deadly diva," the wardrobe people have put falsies in her bra. Between takes, uncomfortable, Petty tugs at them. Singleton spots her and laughs. "Come here, Lori—let me check them for consistency."

Then, aware that he's sitting next to a journalist, he makes sure I know: "I say that shit just to be controversial." He looks around at the beautiful women both on crew and in the cast, and continuing the joke, he says, "*Somebody* said I cast the whole movie by making the women bend over." Rene Elizondo, Jackson's boyfriend, walks by and, hearing Singleton's line, quips, "That's how I got my job."

Elizondo is actually in the film. He plays E. J., a Mexican post worker with only a few lines. Another Hispanic actor had originally been cast for the role, but when Singleton heard Elizondo read, he recast it. By then, Elizondo had already earned a reputation as a set clown.

As the scene begins, Lucky looks at his paycheck and is clearly not pleased. Then his supervisor adds insult to injury by arguing with him about his route. Lucky has complained about the dogs on the route, and the supervisor asks, "Did you not once think about using your Mace?" Lucky looks at him in disbelief. "Mace? That shit is like Binaca to those Rottweilers. You don't *pay* me enough to go through this shit."

The scene also shows the very real tensions between black and Mexican workers. Elizondo was concerned when he first read the script and saw that Chicago (played by black comedian Joe Torry) says: "What's up? Hey you know, they put two more Buddha heads on mail carrier. Still got me waiting, sorting with these Mexicans." "Being Mexican," Elizondo explains, "I thought, 'That's kinda fucked up.' And later, when they say E. J. can't get the ZIP codes right because he's Mexican . . . That's why I made the character the way he was—high, screwed up, saying crazy things. That way it's clear that they're talking about this particular guy, not all Mexicans."

It also helps that Elizondo improvises lines that aren't in the original script. Instead of allowing his character E. J. to be told off by these brothers, he talks back, poking fun at African-American culture. When Lucky and Chicago talk about going out with "yamps" (young tramps) and refuse to include E. J. in their conversation, he says: "Why don't y'all go have your yamps with some cornbread and watermelon and whatever else y'all eat." Singleton burst out laughing, and the whole crew laughs with him. To make jokes like this it is important that one feels that she or he is in the atmosphere of friends, Elizondo points out. "I saw it as a racial thing between friends. If you and I go way back, and I make a joke about your being black or you make a joke about my being Mexican, then it's a whole different ballgame than if we were strangers."

It's nearly ten o'clock, and everyone is beginning to feel the strain of a long day. (They started at eight that morning.) Singleton, however, is determined to get back on schedule. "They think I'm a day behind, but I'm not if I finish this. I heard from my agent that they plan to pull a 'Spike Lee' on me if I go over budget." Last winter, when Lee's *Malcolm X* went over budget, Warner Bros. pulled the plug on his funding, forcing him to make drastic cutbacks, borrow money, and work under the tight supervision of a bond company. "I hate that shit," Singleton continues. "But I'm trying not to get stressed. If I preplan everything, if I keep my shots to three or four takes, then I'll keep up."

All of a sudden, the ground begins to vibrate and an earthquake hits, shaking the whole set. This is not the wrath of the studio "gods" or the personal effects guys acting up, but the real thing. Everyone stands absolutely still, and the grips nervously eye the heavy lights and weights that are rigged to the ceiling. In a few seconds, the tremors stop, and it's back to work with barely any mention of the quake. It's typical California and straight-up Hollywood; Neither rain nor sleet, neither a tight schedule nor an *earthquake* will keep this picture from finishing on time.

April 23, 1992
Rehearsal

*t*he cast and crew have moved to a different location, a residential block in a more upscale neighborhood. This neighborhood is also predominately black, but it has bigger houses, pretty gardens, and lavish, rolling lawns around back. Several members of the crew, Singleton included, walk around singing lines from the hit of the moment, "Tennessee" by Arrested Development. Singleton and some of his boyz went to see the group perform the night before at Jamaica House, an L.A. club. Singleton is talking about one of the members of the group: "Soon as I got in the club, they were doing an interview with an underground video show. There was one, she had orange hair and a body like a marble statue. She looked like she just walked off the savannah! I went crazy." One remembers that although Singleton is a very serious-minded director who writes projects with strong social messages, he is still, after all, a twenty-four-year-old guy.

The setting is Justice's house, and we are rehearsing the scene with young Justice and her grandmother. Justice and her grandmother get out of the car with bags of groceries and enter the house. Once inside, Justice will call her mom, go looking for her, and discover her dead body. Her mother has committed suicide. It's a scene the movie audience will see in flashback, to show them why Justice is so cold and closed.

Don Wilkerson calls, "Rehearsal's up," and there is quiet on the set. As the girl and her grandmother get out of the car, they see the neighbors—not actors, but the actual neighbors. The people next door, not realizing what is going on, wave and say a friendly, "Hi, how are you?" Singleton laughs, calls cut, and decides to put the people next door in the movie. The extras are ordered, and the locations staffers are sent to find the owners of the house. So much of moviemaking depends on making on-the-spot decisions. There are the initial elements—a good script, talented actors, a capable crew. But when you put it all together, you've got to figure in a heavy dose of the unexpected and be ready to improvise. As Singleton walks up the steps of the house, he turns to Peter Collister, the director of photography, and says, "Only a fool isn't open to change." Singleton is wearing an official Public Enemy tour jacket and a newly adopted French director's black beret. The PE jacket is a symbol of Singleton's undying love for rap music, but the beret is a mark of distinction and his desire to be taken seriously as a filmmaker and an artist.

April 27, 1992

*S*ingleton is doing his best to keep a tight rein on the schedule, and a difficult decision has been made: the scene with young Justice and her grandmother has been cut. Sitting outside

Justice's house, Singleton is quiet, intense, studied. He's thinking about his relationship to the studio, and his eyes show both resolve and uneasiness. "They're really afraid to cross me," he says. "Right now, they're trying to decide who's going to tell me what to cut. I've already cut four scenes, but I'll decide what goes. No one's going to tell me what to cut."

As the first shot goes up, Janet Jackson is in frame, feeding her cat. Rene Elizondo stands talking to her. Singleton looks up and laughs, "E. J. Get out of the shot!" He turns to Don Wilkerson and explains that he wants the cat on the porch when Justice and Iesha leave "so when Iesha comes out, she'll say, 'I'm gonna kick one of these cats' to exhibit the difference between Iesha and Justice." Singleton, as the crew has learned, loves cats and thinks that the fact that Iesha hates them show how ornery she is.

Despite the pressure of cutting scenes and keeping to a schedule, Singleton remains confident—it's his calling card, his ace in the hole. "I love shooting this stuff because it has rhythms like a good song. It goes up and down. It's funny, it's dramatic." Then, right before he yells action, he remembers something funny and whispers, "Do you know what Arnold Schwarzenegger said when he saw *Boyz N the Hood*? He said, 'You know what this means, this means the American system works.' " Singleton laughs, then yells, "Action!"

The morning's shots go up without a hitch. But after lunch things are stalled. About fifty people, cast and crew, stand disconsolately inside and around the comfortable house, doing nothing, burning up studio dollars and valuable production moments. Singleton sits outside, quietly fuming.

The trouble is, an important video segment hasn't arrived as scheduled. Today's scene can't be shot without it. It's a scene in which Justice sits in the living room of her home watching television; the missing segment contains the images that are supposed to be played back on television. "Somebody forgot the video remote," Singleton says. "It should've set us back an hour, but it's taking most of the afternoon."

While many directors habitually rant and rave, Singleton is not known for blowing up. He admits to getting frustrated and says he often wants to vent, but he doesn't believe overt anger has ever made something happen more quickly on a set.

His mom, Sheila, is on the set this afternoon. She is a petite, shapely woman who doesn't look old enough to have a twenty-four-year-old son. Like Singleton, she has a private funny side; her dimples show when she laughs. But she is serious now and watches Singleton from a distance, concerned. "He takes a lot," she says. "He vents to key people. He called me to the side and said, 'Someone fucked up.' He'll throw a tantrum at home if someone eats his bean pie, but on set, he's real mild-tempered. You have to push him real far for him to blow his top. I wanted to go home, but I can't. I can tell he's upset, and I want to be here for him."

Today's delay has raised the tension on set to an all-time high. It's still relatively early in the shooting schedule, and the crew has yet to settle in. Everybody looks uncomfortable. Trying to chill, Singleton locates a box. He puts on Rick James's "Super Freak" at block-party decibel level. A few of the crew members start dancing around, and everyone seems much more relaxed. "I should have thought of this sooner. Play some music when things are getting tense. We used to do this all the time on *Boyz*." The earlier film was shot in six furious weeks; then, every delay was much more problematic. On *Boyz*, Singleton had only two takes to get a shot. On *Justice*, he has anywhere between three and five; while it's nowhere close to the forty-five takes Warren Beatty is rumored to average, it does give Singleton some breathing room.

April 28, 1992

a twelve-year-old girl visits the set with her mom and two brothers in tow. She wears a key on one of her hoop earrings and a Rhythm Nation World Tour T-shirt. Looking around anxiously, she explains that she is "Janet Jackson's biggest fan." Her little brother pipes in, "You should see her room. Janet Jackson *everything*."

The girl explains that she met Singleton last year when he visited her elementary school. When she heard Jackson was co-starring in his new film, she wrote him a letter asking to meet her. "John liked the letter and invited me to set," she says. The girl keeps one eye cocked, looking for Jackson at all times. She spots

Jackson's chair and squeals, "Oooooooo! She's here! This is her chair!" Like Goldilocks at the Three Bears' house, the girl and her two brothers take turns sitting in Jackson's chair.

Singleton comes out and greets the family as respectfully as he would any studio vice-president. Then Jackson comes out to meet her fan, trailing two bodyguards, who try to stay unobtrusive. She looks like any of the very pretty black women on set, the sort of girl who's always told she should be a model or an actress. Face to face, not projected larger-than-life on a video screen or dancing around a stadium stage, even her biggest fan can see that she's a real person. It's both comforting and reassuring.

Although she is not very tall, Jackson has an almost regal grace and posture. Perhaps the most-avoided subject on the set is the fact that she is the youngest member of America's First Family of Soul. Clearly, to this little girl, meeting Janet Jackson is like meeting the Queen. After burbling a few comments, the girl and her family are shuttled off set so that the actress and director can continue their work. The meeting is a rarity—fans are rarely granted access on any movie set. On most movies, the cast and crew quickly become a closed circle of people, gathered to do one very difficult job—making a movie. Every interruption afterward, be it from fans or press or studio heads, breaks their concentration and the rhythm of the work at hand.

As the cameras roll, Rene Elizondo is talking about the fanfare that surrounds someone as well known as Jackson. "Even before John had told Janet he wanted her to play the role," he says, "the press named her as one of the many actresses hounding him for a part. The *Enquirer* said that there's no way that Janet could be believable as a 'girl in the hood.' It bothered her because she felt that she hadn't even started in films and the press was shooting her down. Do you know how Janet and John met? After *Boyz N the Hood*, Janet and I invited John over to dinner. Janet was telling a story about how these four girls approached her. Three of them were really nice, saying they liked her music. But one of them—there's always one—was saying how 'she ain't all that, she ain't all that,' meaning Janet wasn't such a big deal. John was surprised to hear Janet slip into street slang and imitate the girl's voice. He realized that there's a side to her that most people don't see, and he began writing the role with her in mind. John's smart. He realized that when you're dealing with someone like a Michael Jackson or

Janet Jackson, there's so much bullshit. It's better to deal with them directly."

It is days away from the announcement of the Rodney King verdict. The case is this: Four cops are on trial for the brutal beating of a black man, Rodney King. But what differentiated this case from hundreds like it was that this beating had been videotaped and replayed on television news programs hundreds of times. This was no local trial, but a national event. Perhaps the most salient issue of the trial was how differently the black and white communities viewed the case. For most white people, it was the first real awareness that police brutality and racial violence still existed. For the black community, the Rodney King trial was the last chance for the criminal justice system to prove itself. Singleton had Rodney King on his mind the year before, when he began writing *Justice*. He'd planned to have a scene where several cops are beating up a black man, and Singleton, in a cameo appearance, would videotape it with his camera. He paces, worried. "If those cops don't go to jail . . . if they don't, when I'm with the video camera, I'm going to have one of the cops say, 'What's *that* going to do?'"

In the meantime, though, Singleton has to shoot a series of shots of Justice in her house, alone at night. Rene Elizondo comes out from their trailer and asks when the mirror scene is coming up: "Janet knows she's going to have to dig deep for this scene, and we want to be prepared." In this scene, we see Justice in her bathroom, burning the tips of her braids. She hears a noise on the first floor and descends the stairs in fear. She lives alone; the noise could be a burglar or a rapist or anybody. She peeps out the front door, and it's her cat, White Boy, scratching to be let in. She makes popcorn, splashes it with Tabasco sauce, takes it and lies down in her dark living room. She tries to call Iesha to talk, but Iesha is busy with her boyfriend, Chicago. She puts on an old record, Stevie Wonder's "I Never Dreamed You'd Leave in Summer." She stares at her reflection in the mirror. She starts off admiring herself then changes emotions: she makes faces at herself, gets angry, and wraps her braids around her throat. She reveals a little bit more of her sadness with each changing face, finally ending the scene in tears.

Standing outside, the crew crowds around a video monitor watching the scene. It's been another long day; it's cold, and they are standing in the dark. But there is a hush over the group. This has never happened before. There are tears on many faces. Over the radio, we hear a quiet "Cut." The few crew members inside the house are crying as well. Movie-making is such a controlled medium that the fragmentation of the script into shot after shot and take after take can obliterate any emotional continuity. Often that continuity doesn't come until much later, in the editing process. But this scene, in the three or four minutes that it runs, has the poignancy and power of live theater. The next day, in dailies, Singleton sits quietly, nodding his head in approval. He knows that her pain and loneliness are of the ilk that thousands of black women will be able to identify with. With each day that Jackson continues to prove her talent as an actress, Singleton becomes more confident that he made the right choice in casting her. "She has a lot of pain," he says empathetically. "She has to go through her [music] career being all happy." *Poetic Justice,* in contrast, is a perfectly acceptable artistic outlet for Jackson's pain.

April 29, 1992
Simi Valley, California

The roof, the roof

The roof is on fire.

We don't need no water, let the motherfucker burn.

Burn, motherfucker, burn.

—popular house party song, circa late 1970s, early 1980s

as the old folks would say, it is the Day of Reckoning. Today an all-white jury in this predominately white community has found a group of police officers who were charged in the beating of Rodney King innocent. Generation after generation of African-Americans in Los Angeles have grown up saying don't trust the police, and finally the videotape of King's beating showed millions of people outside the inner city just what they'd been talking about. President Bush will later declare on prime-time

television that he finds the verdict "hard to understand." For blacks
in Los Angeles, the verdict is many things: a slap in the face, a
mockery of their rights, a grotesque imitation of justice. But hard
to understand? No, this is the final confirmation.

Hard thoughts run through Singleton's mind as he hears the
verdict on the radio in his Pathfinder all-terrain vehicle. Coinciden-
tally, the *Poetic Justice* crew has moved to Simi Valley—the location
managers rented the local drive-in theater for the drive-in scenes.
When that decision was made, no one connected the location with
the site of the King trial. The location staff were unable to rent a
drive-in theater in Los Angeles, mostly because of the cost involved. But the drive-in owners were also reluctant to host Singleton and his movie crew in the wake of the violence that surrounded
the release of *Boyz N the Hood* the summer before. So Singleton is
heading out of L.A. toward the Simi Valley set when he hears the
news. Angrily, impulsively, he switches direction and heads to the
Simi Valley courthouse.

Singleton and his assistant Shorty, who just happens to stand
over six foot seven and weigh 360 pounds, make their way through
the racially mixed crowd. Most are there to protest the verdict;
many are reporters. Singleton's goal is single-minded; to express
his disappointment at the results of the trial. He keeps his comments to the media succinct, knowing that he might very well be
misquoted or that what he says can easily be misconstrued. But it
is a sign of his stature that everyone listens closely to what he has
to say. On the fuel of one film and in one short year, Singleton has
become not only a voice of his generation but a representative of
South Central Los Angeles in the nation's eyes.

Passionately, Singleton addresses the small crowd in front of the
courthouse: "By this verdict, the jury has lit the fuse to a bomb
from which many innocent people would feel the shrapnel. It is
almost impossible to believe that this verdict could happen in the
wake of the Latasha Harlins case [when a storekeeper who shot to
death a black teenager was sentenced to five years' probation,
raising tensions in the African-American community]. It's the sad
state of the American judicial system that it always seems to work
against African-Americans rather than for them."

When two of the police officers exited the courthouse, the crowd
swarmed them, but Singleton stood back, wishing in the back of
his mind that he could "have my hands around any one of their

necks or hit them upside the head with a baton, like they did Rodney King."

Back on the set, everyone tries to carry on business as usual, but their hearts are in a different place. All eyes remain glued to Singleton's state-of-the-art Watchman, a tiny hand-held television. In what will become only the first of many media distortions, in the early hours the rioting is reported as minor. But as more and more footage comes in, it becomes clear that L.A. has turned into a tinderbox. It is as James Baldwin, Malcolm X, and a hundred rappers predicted—the fire *this* time. As setup progresses at the drive-in, Singleton watches the drama and shakes his head. He looks at the tiny images of people, the sparks of fire, the cop cars, ambulances, and helicopters interacting across the urban jungle, and he says, "It's like *Apocalypse Now.* The judicial system feels no responsibility to black people—never has, never will."

For the next couple of days, the crew will be shooting nights. Night shoots are particularly harrowing: the cast and crew begin at about five or six in the evening and work until dawn the following morning. Many of the crew members are distracted and worried about their family, friends, their homes. Some say they feel a schism between whites and blacks on set, though there are no overt incidents. It seems as if the blacks are visibly angry and the whites are either silent or apologetic. The racial split on this crew is about fifty-fifty, unusually integrated for a big-studio production. But holdovers from *Boyz,* whose crew was almost entirely black, feel the added white presence. It doesn't help that, only a few yards away, a dozen police are patrolling in full riot gear. It's almost as if they think Singleton might lead a riot then and there.

The Simi Valley drive-in sign has been replaced by an art department sign that says COMPTON DRIVE IN. It's almost funny and the only physical sign of the black presence in this small, almost entirely white town. Simi Valley is a lower-middle-class bedroom community, like many similar American suburbs, in the northern San Fernando Valley. Its very existence epitomizes 1980s white flight from and fear of the increasing minority populations in major cities. Tonight, as black and Korean communities burn, Simi Valley remains untouched. The cast and crew are perfectly safe in Simi Valley. At about eight o'clock, the dusk-to-dawn curfew in Los Angeles is announced. Steve Nicolaides tells the crew that anyone who can't or doesn't feel safe returning home that night should stay at a Simi Valley hotel at the production's expense. Many do.

Finally, the drive-in is set up and the filming begins. The mise-en-scène is an old-fashioned open-air drive-in theater. Because the initial shot is panoramic and doesn't involve any of the actors, most of the crew, including Singleton, aren't directly involved. They spend their time crowded around Singleton, who's sitting in his director's chair holding a small television on his lap. As the evening goes on, the two dramas unfold concurrently—one starring Janet Jackson, the other starring the angry throngs of Los Angeles. On the small television the riot looks surreal, a Hollywood concoction of burning buildings, cars on fire, helicopters circling, and people on the streets.

For three days filming continues in Simi Valley as the riots rage on thirty miles away. Although the physical violence never reaches Simi Valley, a real mental and emotional outrage does. By the weekend, the worst of the riots have passed. But upon returning home, many of the cast and crew find that their neighborhoods have been hit hard. Later, the burned-out buildings, the black and hollow structures that gape like holes in the community infrastructure, and the amputated community morale will be incorporated, with second unit photography, into *Poetic Justice*.

As haunting as the pictures are, they could never fully convey what it is like to be there: the paralyzing fear, the sense of utter chaos, the smell of smoke so strong, you can't leave your window open. It will take weeks for the blunt anger to dull and the miasma to lift. To many on the set, the whole idea of making a movie amidst all the destruction of property and spirit seems an aberration. Singleton is aggresively sought out by the full gamut of the media for comment on a community he has proven he knows well. On television and in newspaper and magazine articles, Singleton urges people to learn from this experience, to look into the eye of the tornado, not just at the destructive aftermath: "Anyone who has a moderate knowledge of African-American culture knows this was foretold in a thousand rap songs and more than a few black films. When Ice Cube was with NWA [Niggas Wit Attitude], he didn't write the lyrics to 'Fuck tha Police' just to be cute. He was reciting a reflection of reality as well as fantasizing about what it would be like to be on the other end of the gun when it came to police relations.

"Most white people don't know what it is like to be stopped for a traffic violation and worry more about getting beat up and shot than about getting a ticket. So imagine, if you will, growing up with this reality regardless of your social and economic status. Fantasize about what it is to be guilty of a crime at birth. The crime? Being black. Think about how a mother feels when her fifteen-year-old daughter is shot in the back of her head and her murderer goes free on six months' probation.

"You are told to believe in the system—a system that was not created to serve you and your own. Sometimes you believe in the dream; other times you catch reality. Many people caught reality when the jury found those four officers not guilty of beating Rodney King. Maybe if the verdict had been different, it would have stood as a testament to the possibility of true justice in this country. By issuing that verdict, the jury not only violated Rodney King's civil rights and the rights of all African-Americans, it showed a lack of respect for the human rights of every law-abiding American who believes in justice. The bomb that blew up in the wake of that verdict existed beforehand, as another one does now. The fuse is waiting to be lit by the next gross, inconsiderate action by the powers that be. No justice, no peace."

As difficult as it is, Singleton eventually returns his complete concentration to the production of *Poetic Justice*. Through his own success, Singleton is living a new brand of the American dream. But he knows that should the wrong cop catch him on the wrong night, he will be just another black man, just as vulnerable as Rodney King. Singleton is motivated, in large part, by the incredible injustices suffered by the black community. If the riots don't show why he's making movies, nothing else will. As Ice Cube said at the end of *Boyz N the Hood*, "Either they don't know, they don't show, or they don't care what goes on in the ghetto."

4
Phenomenal Woman:
The Poetry of Maya Angelou

Alone. Lying, thinking. Last night. How to find my soul a home. Where water is not thirsty. And bread loaf is not stone. I came up with one thing. And I don't believe I'm wrong. That nobody. But nobody can make it out here alone.

—MAYA ANGELOU

When John Singleton was writing *Poetic Justice,* he initially toyed with the idea of writing the poems in the film himself. Later, he decided to use the work of a black woman poet who had influenced his life, Dr. Maya Angelou. There was a large array of black women poets to choose from: Nikki Giovanni, Gwendolyn Brooks, Rita Dove; but Singleton was drawn to Angelou's verse because "she's so real. She speaks about the people, to our people."

*   *   *

> Alone, all alone. Nobody, but nobody. Can make it out here
> alone. There are some millionaires with money they can't use.
> Their wives run round like banshees. Their children sing the
> blues.

Angelou is perhaps best known for the first volume of her auto-
biography, *I Know Why the Caged Bird Sings.* In it, she bravely
speaks of her battle to overcome abuse, rape, and poverty. For
thousands of young black women reading the book is a rite of
passage; for those who have been similarly victimized, it is a salve,
a soothing ointment that helps heal the wounds. Angelou gives
voice to the voiceless; she says, "You're not alone. It happened to
me, too. You're not to blame. You *will* survive."

In many ways, the character of Justice is one of those voiceless.
A young black woman from the streets who has known more than
her fair share of pain, Justice has seen everyone whom she loves
die. The anguish has squeezed all the joy out of her young life, and
the ink in her poet's pen is black with grief. But Justice is a
survivor and has not closed herself off entirely, not yet. With eyes
wide open to the tragedy of real life and a heart open to all the
goodness the world has to offer, Angelou's poetry too is neither
cynical nor rose-tinted. Her verse strikes the delicate balance that
is at the core of Justice's character.

> They've got expensive doctors, to cure their hearts of stone.
> But nobody. No nobody. Can make it out here alone. Now if
> you listen closely, I'll tell you what I know. Storm clouds are
> gathering, the wind is gonna blow. The race of man is suffer-
> ing, and I can hear the moan. Cause nobody. But nobody. Can
> make it out here alone.

"Most of the girls I knew growing up," says Singleton, "their main
creative outlet was writing poetry. Whether they were good at it or
not. From the beginning I had to think about where the poetry
was coming from. Maya's poems speak to the heart. Their message
is social; they accomplish all the emotions that we go through
without being soft."

Angelou's hard edge matches Singleton's own. The poet states in
typical Angelou boldness, "I have no modesty, none. It's a waste of

time. It's a learned affectation stuck on from without. If life slams the modest person against the wall, he or she will drop that modesty quicker than a stripper will drop her G-string. What I hope I have and what I pray I have is humility. Humility comes from within."

By the time Justice reads Angelou's poem "Phenomenal Woman" at the end of the film, we have seen her confidence and humility in many different scenes. This is a girl who can put a guy like Lucky in his place, but at the same time she can respectfully and lovingly interact with an elder like Maya Angelou. Justice has lost her mother, grandmother, and first love, but she finds the courage to love again, to make herself vulnerable again. She is a phenomenal young woman. . . .

PHENOMENAL WOMAN

Pretty woman wonder where my secret lies
I'm not cute or built to suit a fashion model's size
But when I start to tell them,
They think I'm telling lies.
I say,
It's in the reach of my arms,
The span of my hips,
The stride of my step,
The curl of my lips.
I'm a woman
Phenomenally.
Phenomenal woman,
That's me.

I walk into a room
Just as cool as you please,
And to a man,
The fellows stand or
Fall down on their knees.
Then they swarm around me,
A hive of honey bees.
I say,
It's the fire in my eyes,
And the flash of my teeth,
The swing in my waist,

And the joy in my feet.
I'm a woman
Phenomenally.
Phenomenal woman,
That's me.

Men themselves have wondered
What they see in me.
They try so much
But they can't touch
My inner mystery.
When I try to show them
They say they still can't see.
I say,
It's in the arch of my back,
The sun of my smile,
The ride of my breasts,
The grace of my style.
I'm a woman
Phenomenally.
Phenomenal woman,
That's me.

Now you understand
Just why my head's not bowed.
I don't shout or jump about
Or have to talk real loud.
When you see me passing
It ought to make you proud.
I say,
It's in the click of my heels,
The bend of my hair,
The palm of my hand,
The need for my care.
'Cause I'm a woman
Phenomenally.
Phenomenal woman,
That's me.

—MAYA ANGELOU

In the original script, the poem narrates an almost dreamlike sequence in the film, when the characters are on a road trip in northern California; and we *see* Justice walking through a field of zebras, escaped perhaps from Hearst castle. The down-to-earth grittiness of the poem roots the surrealistic visuals of the scene. The zebras could almost be a foil for Justice herself; she is an amazingly complex young woman, at once solemn as she is in the cemetery, but also mirthful, as when she and Jessie tease Lucky the first time he enters the salon. And like a zebra, she won't change her stripes—she's a real black woman through and through.

Later, in postproduction, Singleton will cut the zebra scene from the film and move the poem to the end of the film. As Justice's final words, the poem will represent all that Justice has suffered, her steely strength and her blossoming into womanhood. Through the poem her will to live, to survive, testifies to the beauty and strength of all the black women who have been through so much and still carry on. The film also features Dr. Angelou's poems "Alone," "In a Time," "A Kind of Love, Some Say," and "A Conceit."

Dr. Angelou fears that too many young people are giving up too soon. "It is imperative that young people be told that we have come a long way," she says. "Otherwise they are likely to become cynical. A cynical young person is almost the saddest sight to see because it means that he or she has gone from knowing nothing to believing in nothing."

May 4, 1992
Griffith Park

there is nothing close to cynicism the week that Dr. Maya Angelou arrives to film her cameo in *Poetic Justice*. During early drafts of the script, Singleton considered casting the poet as a fortune-teller who reads Justice's palm. Later, he decided that she should play one of three chatterbox aunts at the Johnson family reunion. The aunts are wittily named Aunt April, Aunt May, and Aunt June; together they form a Greek chorus for the community, commenting on the past, present, and future, as well as narrating the drama between Iesha and Chicago. Angelou is to play Aunt June. A stage actress with such credits as *Cabaret for Freedom* with Geoffrey Cambridge and Jean Genet's *The Blacks,* Angelou is a tall, big-boned black woman with a regal posture and a definite grace in her gestures. At the same time, her gaze is so intense, her husky voice so cutting, that nobody dares cross her. She is perfect for the role of Aunt June.

In storyboarding the scene, storyboard artist Peter Ramsey good-naturedly drew the three aunts as triplets of Aunt May of Spiderman comic book fame. The day of the shoot, that is exactly what the three women look like. Sitting on a park bench in Los Angeles's Griffith Park, the three actresses chewed the fat about everything old and new. Aunt April is a cameo appearance by casting director Robi Reed's mom, Ernestine Reed. Aunt May is being played by veteran thespian and still grand diva Norma Donaldson. Dr. Angelou rounds out the group. Dressed in a navy blue dress with lace trim and a pink Sunday church-style hat, Dr. Angelou looks like a mature "around the way" woman that would do L. L. Cool J's song justice. She looks like the sort of woman you might see sitting on the porch on the block you grew up on, sure to let your parents know if you are behaving badly. She looks like the church matron who heads the choir, teaches Sunday school, or is the treasurer of the Ladies' Auxiliary (or maybe all three). Her expressive face soaks in the hustle-and-bustle of the busy crew, the nervous restlessness of a hundred extras, and last, but not least, the approving glances of the young director.

"Look at her face. Look at her *face*," Singleton says excitedly as Dr. Angelou runs through her scenes. Her diction rolls and flows with the eloquence of one who is a scholar, a writer, and an actress. A woman who knows the power of words.

It is in this wonderful voice that she recommends a reading list for the young writer who is interviewing her. Have you read Coco Abe's *Women in the Dunes,* Wole Soyinka's *The Man Died,* Sean O'Casey's *Juno and the Paycock*? A Tony Award nominee as well as a Pulitzer nominee, Dr. Angelou holds a lifetime appointment as Reynolds Professor of American Studies at Wake Forest University in Winston-Salem, North Carolina. It is May, and she has just come from school. "I love teaching," she says. "It's a good thing I started writing first, or I might have never begun." The list of books and plays continues . . . *Rar's Fire* by Hans Bald, *A Room of One's Own* by Virginia Woolf, García Lorca's *The House of Bernarda Alba* . . .

It is with the same authority that she "reads" the character of Iesha, played by Regina King. In the scene, Iesha and Chicago unwittingly sit at the table of the three nosy aunts. The aunts get all in the young couple's grill, and Iesha, a fast girl with a smart mouth, tries to lie her way out of the hot seat.

A writer through and through, Dr. Angelou wastes no time in rewriting the script. Her improvisations are dead-on. "That ain't no family," she proclaims upon first sight of Iesha and Chicago. When Iesha tries to snow her into believing that she and Chicago are married, Dr. Angelou comes up with a different line each take:

"That girl ain't a bit more married than the man in the moon."
"I was young, but I wasn't flirty. Not like this one right here, trying to tell me, she's married—hummmph."
"Married? You have to get up *early* in the morning and stay up all night to fool me."

After each take, Singleton jumps in the air and yells "Whoooo!" His highest compliment; the admiration is mutual.

Sitting on a stone stoop in the park where cast and crew hope against hope that it won't rain (eventually it does), Dr. Angelou explains how she and Singleton met. More like a Hollywood player than a poet from Missouri, she says, "His agent had been talking to my agent. I had not seen *Boyz N the Hood*. Columbia had a private show for me in my little town. I took my sister, friends, my secretary, my housekeeper—all black women. We all loved it. We were all moved by it."

"Maxine Waters [a Los Angeles congresswoman and one of the most powerful black women in the Democratic party] told me that I need to talk to this young man myself, not through agents. She gave me his number. Then I met him, and I saw at once the intelligence of the man. Everybody born is born with talent. They may not know it, they may not show it, but they are born with it. But it's the rare person who has the intelligence, the discipline, the forthrightness, and the perseverance to architect a dream. I could sense this in him."

What gave Angelou the confidence to entrust her poems to be incorporated into a script that she had not read nor would ever ask to improve, was the strength of writing in *Boyz N the Hood*. "John was able to capture something very real," she says, "an element in black American life, maybe all of American life—the duality of our life, the ambiguity, the schizoid nature of our life. And that is that we are loving people who become destroyers; we are destructive people who become love. Quite often, we are portrayed as things with no redeeming qualities, or Martin Luther Kings with no chicanery, no cruelty. John had the courage to give lie to those falsehoods. And I respect him for it."

Dr. Angelou explains that she wrote the movie's first poem, "Alone," because "I am always fascinated with the difference between being alone and being lonely. One of the reasons black people have survived is that we've managed to create a human system—the church, the fellowship of sisterhood, barbershops, street corners, Elks, Masons. In our gathering place, we've been able to find some solace. We've been left alone, neglected, ignored by the larger society, and we've always been able to come together in some sort of group. Maybe we've been without desirable food or shelter or the benefits of the larger society, but we have not been alone. What is so desperate and frightening to me is the preponderance of songs that say 'Don't trust your best friend,' 'Don't turn your back on your man.' Somebody's setting us up, because the only way we can be wiped out is if we are alone."

Dr. Angelou sees the poem as "a warning, advising, counseling to others, not to allow themselves to fall prey to some of the problems the larger society has." She says that the kids who do fall prey to the perils of larger society are the casualties of an oft-begrudging integration: "Their parents did them a serious disservice by making them think that by having things, they will provide an entrance into white society. There's no way they can enter the white society, and they should be glad about it. We must treasure those things that have kept us alive. If we enter white society, we would be imitating white people and not being ourselves."

As for Singleton's place among the so-called Black Pack of filmmakers, she says, "Black film may be something that slipped through the cracks. But if *Boyz N the Hood* hadn't been so good, we'd have seen the end of a new phase, a new trend. However, not only was *Boyz N the Hood* good, it made money. Nothing so powerful as something whose time has come, and it's time."

While she is optimistic that black films will continue to be made, she is not naïve about the role black culture plays in the larger society. Dr. Angelou is no stranger, after all, to the world of film. She wrote the original screenplay and musical score for the film *Georgia, Georgia,* and she was a writer/producer for *Assignment*

America. She has brought to the screen televised versions of both *I Know Why the Caged Bird Sings* and *The Sisters.* She is also one of the few women members of the Director's Guild.

"A white society always needs exotica to enrich its life," she says matter of factly. "It needs black America, it needs the Spanish-speaking Americans in the barrios. The Native Americans, of course, they want to forget; although they will be interested in the people of Puerto Rico, Thailand, or India. You can see how they relish the presence of these cultures in their world because they say, 'What's for dinner? Tex-Mex, Mexican, Thai, Szechuan. Shall we go for the true Szechuan or modern Szechuan?' *Please,* we are needed for the fashion, music, and for film."

It's the last day of a difficult week. Rain has interrupted the flow of things on more than one occasion. Handling a large number of extras in a new location has taken some logistical juggling. All throughout the week, Dr. Angelou has been patient, retreating to her trailer when it pours. It's a true sign of Dr. Angelou's status that she has her own trailer for only one week's work. Canvas director's chairs with the director's, actor's, or crew member's name are for short rests between takes. A trailer, for those who rank high enough to earn one, is for longer breaks and lunch hours. Dr. Angelou socializes, good-naturedly, with her aunt co-stars while different shots are being set up. In a rare sunny moment, she sits on her star chair and jokes, "What I nee-eed is a mint julep." But her character is about to wrap, and she is tired.

Singleton, ever the energetic one, even late on a Friday afternoon, keeps telling the actress to say a certain line over and over again, urging her to try it different ways. While he *is* the director, Dr. Angelou is old enough to be Singleton's mother and eventually she has had enough. She says to him, as sweet as can be, "I'm writing it for you. I'm not writing this for Columbia Pictures because you know what it would take for me to write this for them. Now chile, *please.*"

And on that note, she stands up, unpins her hat, and starts to walk back to her trailer. Singleton takes it all in stride, laughing at his comeuppance. The whole crew follows suit. Don Wilkerson, first AD, yells out, "May 9, 1992. Dr. Maya Angelou, wrapped."

The next night in dailies, Singleton laughs just as hard when he sees her exit replayed on the screen. "Maya is too cold, boy," he says with a smile. "She is *too* cold."

5

Midproduction:

Scratching the Surface

May 6, 1992
Griffith Park

a bunch of extras are riding in a shuttle van from crew parking to set. Extras are a phenomenon unlike any other on the set. They are human decoration, and yet if they can't "act," the film is wasted. Nothing ruins a shot faster than an extra staring into the camera. Today we are shooting the Johnson family reunion, and extra casting has hired a real family and assorted others to play members of the Johnson family. In the van, the women talk:

"Is this a comedy?"
"I think it's supposed to be a love story. Why do you ask?"
"I just want to know if I'm s'posed to laugh."

"Who's in this movie?"

"Working on a movie and don't even know who's in it."

"Regina King."

"I thought her name was Regina Harlem."

"Nah, her name is King, and she's from Harlem."

"What a mix, Regina King and Maya Angelou."

"I want to see this movie, if I heard about all the things we're doing, I would be dying to see this."

The extras *are* doing a lot, but right now, not a hell of a lot is going on. We're being plagued by bad weather, and Peter Collister, the director of photography, is afraid that the film from the day before won't match the overcast on today's shots. Singleton is stalwart. "Rain, sun, sleet, riots," he says. "We're still shooting. Push comes to shove, we're going to need more days." In the end, the art department rushes and finishes the mock mail truck so that some of the interior mail truck scenes can be shot while we wait for the sky to clear up. For the time being, the family reunion is on hold.

Regina King and Joe Torry have great energy together; onscreen they are pure fire and ice. King as Iesha is clearly the fire and Torry's Chicago is melting quickly. The two actors prove themselves to be not only talented but quick studies. The mail truck scene wasn't scheduled for another two weeks, but they went in their trailers, quickly studied their lines, and came out and did it. As the crew sets up for the next shot, Torry's close-up, Singleton laughs out loud: "It's about to get *real* hot in here." He's referring to the fact that because of Torry's dark skin, they'll need extra lights in order not to lose the definition of his features. Joe Dougherty, the director's PA, says that they had to do the same thing on *Boyz N the Hood* for Morris Chestnut. "Not everybody knows how to light black skin," says Singleton. As the camera crew moves lights and the heat comes down on Torry, Singleton's mom gets in on the ribbing: "Go on, child," she says. "I like to *see* my black men."

Norma Donaldson, who plays Aunt May, sits under a tree and waits for her scene to come up. Others are annoyed at the change in schedule, but she's a veteran actress and a consummate professional. She keeps her cool. "I wouldn't care if I had just one line— just to be working with John Singleton is a thrill. People tend to write about all the negative stuff, but they don't write about this. There's a lot of love on set, and I think it comes from the top."

If people are able to retain a sense of humor about all that has gone on in the first half of production, that also comes from the top. Tupac Shakur says the best thing about Singleton is the side he rarely shows in public; his humor. "We went to see *Deep Cover,* and John screamed in the theater, 'Linc, Linc, Mod Squad,' when Clarence Williams III came onscreen. I couldn't believe he called the brother out like that. I told him, when this movie comes out and he has his cameo, then I'm gonna be in the theater screaming 'John' 'John-John.' " Word has gotten around on set about Singleton's love of animals. The pet of the week is a Burmese python given to him by Carlos White, a stand-in. Singleton has named the snake Justice. It can be seen slithering in and out of his Public Enemy jacket, in between takes.

Singleton sits in his trailer one afternoon during lunch, discussing the day's scenes and coverage. He lies on the floor, resting. It is during these rare moments of repose that the age shows in his eyes, the fact that he's not just a twenty-four-year-old wunderkind but an often-tired, hard-working black man with more responsibilities than most men his age. He asks, in a groggy voice, for a mudcloth pillow that is on his trailer bed. A guest reaches for the pillow but gets a handful of snake—*hissssssssssssssss.* She screams and screams. Singleton laughs and laughs with all the glee of a practical-joke-playing schoolboy.

What's not so funny is this: the two white men standing near the truck. Suits. On location the crew wear casual clothes: shorts, T-shirts, and jeans. These men walk onto the set with their designer suits, stiff white shirts, and print ties, and it's as if somebody came in a clown costume. They could be anybody: agents, lawyers, accountants, or Columbia executives coming to check up on their investment. While any suit is an obvious intruder, there's always a tension of not wanting them there but having to make them feel welcome at the same time. As it turns out, they're not studio guys; the Columbia executive in charge of the project is Stephanie Allain. A young black woman, Allain doesn't don suits but vintage-style dresses and skirts with a backward baseball cap over her short, curly hair. While Singleton describes their working relationship as a "love-hate relationship," it's the love part that makes the difference. The suits on set today are talking to one of on the camera crew; the camera guy is also white. The suits, who obviously haven't read the *Poetic Justice* script, ask the camera guy what the movie is about. "It's a love story—they meet and then fall in love on this car trip," the camera guy says. The suits pause, considering this.

"So it's a nice story?" one of them asks.

"Did you see *Boyz N the Hood*?" the camera guy says, looking at them dubiously.

"No," the suit says, shaking his head. "But I saw *New Jack City*."

It's a minor moment, but a telling one. There will always be those who throw Singleton's work into that big grab bag called Films About Black Folks. Those who will never be able to tell the difference between *Superfly* and *Lilies of the Field*.

May 13, 1992

*f*resh from their week with Maya Angelou, the cast and crew of *Poetic Justice* head out of Los Angeles and over to the Disney ranch, about an hour outside of the city. Once the set of such classic television Americana as *Little House on the Prairie,* the ranch, with its wide expanse of green fields and tall oak trees for shade, has been recast as the African marketplace.

Production designer Keith Burns and his team have organized teams of real African vendors and Afrocentrically dressed extras. With a huge Ferris wheel at its center, along with many amusement park games and contests ("Test your strength! Test your aim! Hit the bull's-eye and win a prize!"), it has the feel of a genuine African-American carnival. It is hard to believe that only a century ago black women stood in cages at such carnivals in Europe, their bodies the subject of both amused scorn and surprise. And even today, as Singleton makes a movie that celebrates black women, the genitalia of a black woman that poet Elizabeth Alexander calls "the Venus Hottentot" floats in a pickling jar in the Musée de l'Homme in Paris, testament to what a freak show black women once were and, in some sectors, still are.

Here on the Disney ranch our minds are far from the horrors of modern science. We are eagerly awaiting the arrival of this week's guests, the Last Poets. They will be performing as part of the festival. For those who grew up with the Last Poets in the sixties and seventies, either seeing them live or hearing them on our folks' old albums, it's a moment of pure inspiration. This isn't fashion-statement Afrocentricity or dance-floor dogma by half-baked hip-hop artists—it's the real thing.

When the Poets arrive, decked out in dashikis, it's like a continuation of the family reunion. Singleton is also dressed in a dashiki, a beautiful blue batik. He could be one of the musicians' sons or neighbors. And in the most Africanist sense, he is. Although the black cast and crew members are a motley mix of suburban and inner-city blacks, today the emphasis is on togetherness. There are lots of references to that "brother," and the fellas call all the women "sister." It is definitely the *poetic* influence. The Last Poets are here, still as vibrant and relevant as ever.

Pauletta Lewis, the lead hairdresser on the film, looks around the marketplace in a daze. "Maya Angelou and the Last Poets," she says reverently. "This is like heaven. I found out today that I have their first album. I was describing it to them, how it was yellow with blue writing. And they said, yeah, that's their *first* album. It's a collector's item."

These are the genuine legends in their own time, people like Dr. Maya Angelou and the Last Poets. By inviting them to appear in *Poetic Justice,* Singleton pulls together a common history and a sense that history provides inspiration for the present as well as a continuum for the future.

As the African drums give lead to the melody of the Poets song "Niggers Are Afraid of Revolution," various extras, young and old, mouth the words. Singleton jumps onstage, smiles, dances around, mouths his favorite lines: " 'Niggers are lovers, Niggers are lovers of lovers . . .' "

The lead Poet wears a No Justice, No Peace hat, giving play to what has become the anthem of these postriot times. (Shorty, John's assistant, has NO JUSTICE, NO [peace symbol] shaved into the back of his haircut.) Yet as the Poets continue to sing about "niggers," some of the white members of the crew seem both captivated and curious. Some of the white crew members cluster together and whisper to each other. Others stand apart, with their arms folded, staring straight ahead.

"Nigger," said by either blacks or whites, seems particularly hard-edged and touchy in these politically correct times. But that is part of the magic of it all; even after four white cops were found innocent of a crime that was videotaped, even after neighborhood upon neighborhood burned, there is still a tendency to cling to the illusion of racial harmony. By inviting the Last Poets here today, by letting them sing this song, Singleton avoids what is comfortable or pleasant for the more salient goal: that which is real. While the "nigger" may be off-putting, at the core of the song is an assertion of black pride and a call to activism.

May 15, 1992

*a*t lunchtime, the catering crew wheels out a huge cake that reads "Happy Birthday Janet." Jackson approaches the crowd shyly, as they begin to sing. She gives the first piece of cake to Singleton, and he smiles. As the musicians start to play the drums and people eat and dance, one feels transformed, not back to the Africa one knows but to the Africa that most African-Americans have created in our heads—a long-lost place where community and love reigned supreme and the people were one with the land and each other. A dream perhaps, but on a forty-minute lunch, on an increasingly hectic set, it's not a bad place to be.

> Talkin' bout good and bad hair
> whether you're dark or fair
> go and swear
> see if I care
> good and bad hair.

—bill lee, *school daze*

Is hair still political? If you're a black woman, chances are the answer is yes. The history of hair in the black community and the way it delineates social class and political belief is hundreds of years old. While *Poetic Justice* does not address the subject of "good" (that is, straight, Anglo-Saxon) hair and "bad" (kinky,

Afrocentric) hair, the fact that part of the film's drama takes place in a beauty salon is significant. And when it comes to references to hair, much of the dialogue works on two levels. For example, in the salon when Jessie is telling Justice she needs to stop mourning for the love that has left her, it's no coincidence that she comments on her hair: "You still in mourning? Sporting black, don't make time to do your own hair. Looking tore up from the floor up." It's not a matter of pure vanity, but more a matter of culture and pride. When a black woman doesn't take the time to do something to her hair, then something is wrong. Rapper Q-Tip of A Tribe Called Quest plays Markell, Justice's first love. Singleton feels a great affinity to rap music and the messages in it. The beauty shop scenes might be characterized by this Tribe Called Quest rap:

If you can't achieve it, then why not try to weave it?
If you can't extend it, then best to suspend it.
If you cannot braid it, then why not try and fade it?
I ask who did your hair and you tell me Diane made it.
If you were just you, talk to you, maybe.
But I can't stand no bionic lady. . . .

Shooting the first beauty shop scene with Justice, Jessie tugs at Justice's cap. But when she sees what's underneath, she says, "Ooow, keep it on." During one of the takes, Jackson improvises and says, "Give me my hat, girl. I got new growth." The whole crew laughs because it is so startlingly real. New growth is the kinky hair that has grown between your last perm and your next touch-up. On a properly coiffed do, it's bad form, but it's something almost every black woman has experienced. The line is funny by itself, but more so because Janet Jackson is saying it. One can't imagine Diahann Carroll or Lena Horne or any other glamorous black leading lady of yesteryear admitting to the fact that she too, like everyone else, gets new growth.

Similarly, while magazines like *Glamour* and *Vogue* herald the fashion of wigs and "falls" to accentuate a hair wardrobe, nobody knows more about fake hair than black women. *That's* why it's doubly funny when the character Rodney walks in and says, "Hey my girl need her hair and nails done. I wanna buy her a weave down to her butt." And when it's clear that she doesn't have an appointment, Heywood quips, "She ain't got no hair either!"

Doesn't matter. In African-American beautyland anything is possible, including any length of hair, the popular saying being, "Yes, it's mine, *I bought* it."

Hollywood Curl, the Baldwin Hills salon that doubles for Jessie's Beauty Salon and Supply, is the black woman's version of Elizabeth Arden. The salon was confirmed as a location early in preproduction, long after Singleton's script was completed, but the parallels between art and life are startling. Miss Fanny, the proprietor of the salon, is a lot like the character Jessie (Tyra Ferrell). A beautiful woman in her forties with long flowing hair and a love of multicolored silk pant suits and African print robes, she is a diva from head to toe. And just as Jessie has a vanity plate that spells her name, the license plate on Miss Fanny's sports car lets you know the ride is *hers.*

The salon is painted in a modern Art Deco style, with opulent yellows and greens. It features not only a clothing shop but private rooms where celebrities and other high-level women can get their hair weaves done in privacy, where a man can get a manicure without sitting in a roomful of women. The salon is soooo slick that on a crowded Saturday afternoon, when demand far surpasses the supply of stylists, Miss Fanny serves margaritas to calm the anxious customers. And if that weren't enough, the boyfriend of one of the hairstylists at Hollywood Curl is a postman. They are a real-life Justice and Lucky.

Pauletta Lewis, the head hairstylist on *Poetic Justice,* finds the script to be a lot more than vaguely reminiscent of her life. Like Justice and so many real black women, Lewis found herself looking at a quickly impending high school diploma with no idea of what to do as a career. "It seemed like my only choices were go to college or go to the service," she says. "I went to my counselor, and he suggested that I transfer to vocational school so that when I graduated, I'd have not just my diploma, but also my license. I liked it a lot. It was learning something from scratch. I enjoyed making someone look pretty, seeing the result of my work after two hours. I enjoyed the process."

Lewis is standing at the front desk of Hollywood Curl, surveying the location that will eventually be the movie salon. "Beauty parlors are like back to your culture. It's a meeting place, like church." Her youthful looks don't match her undeniable experience, but due to the head-start she received in high school, Lewis has racked up an impressive twenty-one years in the business. Along the way, she's gleaned a number of wisdoms. Among them: Black women don't like their hair cut. No "Sorry, oops," or "Dear me, I've buzz cut the top of your head." Lewis says sagely, "Black women must have their hair cut on the new moon. They say it grows faster when you cut it then." Tyra Ferrell comes out from the back room where she has been talking to Miss Fanny. Hearing the conversation, she agrees wholeheartedly: "Black women do *not* like to get their hair cut. They're saving every inch." Although her onscreen time is limited, Ferrell is excited about what she can bring out in the role of Jessie. "John was writing *Poetic Justice* around the time when *Boyz* opened. He'd call me up at night, and we'd talk about it. It's real interesting. I'm being offered a lot of roles, a lot of money's involved, but my loyalty is to John and to playing Jessie."

What interests Singleton is how the salon serves as both town hall and local bar, how it is as service-oriented as your local Laundromat, yet the bonds formed there are as tight as those of any sisterhood. "You're getting all this information here," he says with the kind of quiet awe guys reserve for when they speak of "girl" things, "In a barbershop, all they're going to talk about is sports and politics."

One of the elements of the script that is both perplexing and illuminating is the relationship between Justice and Jessie, and between Jessie and the rest of the women in the salon. Clearly, Jessie thinks of Justice as a little sister and treats her with equal amounts of care and "Get over it" impatience. But it's also obvious that while Maxine is her best friend, Jessie doesn't trust any of the women in the salon. In this way the beauty parlor scenes alternately portray images of sisterhood and images of strong disunity among black women. Lewis, the real-life expert on hairdressing as a business, says the dichotomy of the situation is natural. Yes, there is a level of sisterhood. At the same time, "When you work in a competitive sort of position, it's cutthroat. . . . You really can't trust women. You can't have women in here who are trying to take your place, trying to stab you in the back."

At the same time, a real level of trust happens between a black woman and the sister who does her hair. In a way, hairstylists are not only the professionals of the black community, they are the psychological equivalent of bartenders. There isn't much a woman can hide from her hairdresser: everything from a bad mood to the bad dye job some man talked a woman into giving herself is as plain as pie when she's sitting in that chair. If a woman starts missing visits or "letting her hair go," as in the scene between Jessie and Justice, her hairstylist will know. By the same token, if a black woman runs into problems and her money is tight, it's her stylist, not the butcher or the landlord, who will tell her to just bring the money next week or offer to work out something reasonable. On the most spiritual level, many black women won't allow just anyone to touch their hair. From the tradition of oral storytelling to modern literature such as Gloria Naylor's *Mama Day*, many black women have believed in the danger someone can cook up with their hair. It may even be as innocuous as the old saying that if a bird makes a nest with a lock of your hair, it will drive you crazy. There may be black women who lay no stock in such superstitions and will let just anybody play in their hair, but they are probably in the minority. There's a reason why Iesha comes to Justice to do her hair and why, at the end of the script, Lucky brings Keisha to Justice to do her hair. It's about love, it's about friendship, and it's about trust.

Trustworthy isn't exactly the word to describe Tyra Ferrell's entrance as Jessie in the film. Dressed in a slamming red dress and not a hair out of place (who said stylists don't have time to do their own hair?), Ferrell's Jessie is impeccable. The men on set, of course, respond accordingly. Michael Colyar, who plays the neighborhood panhandler, jokes around about trying to ask Jessie out, in character: "I just got out of jail," he says pleadingly, "so you *know* how I feel." Tupac Shakur uncharacteristically lets down his cool and says, "I think I could make some time for that." Singleton just smiles at what he recognizes as a perfect casting choice: "I have my muses. . . ."

Joining Tyra Ferrell in Jessie's Salon are Roger Smith as Heywood, Keith Washington as the homophobic Dexter, comedienne Yvette Wilson as Colette, and singer Miki Howard as Jessie's gal pal Maxine. As the other stylists in the salon—Lisa, Gena, and Deena—are Kim Brooks, Mikki Val, and rapper Dina D.

Roger Smith is definitely one strike against biological essentialism. In the time since his audition, he has done a complete character transformation—smooth face, slick Edwardian sideburns, a haircut as soft and low as a baby duck's fur. The outfit is perfect— pale yellow blazer, a white undershirt, cream linen pants, and hippie-dippie crystals hanging around his neck. He's achieved that perfect, classic androgyny—he's neither a flame nor a closet case. Regina King also stands out as a key casting coup. King is a natural actress, with a husky voice that reminds one of Lena Horne and the warmth and energy of an actress like Josephine Baker. One senses that most people won't even know how different she is from Iesha, how strong her ear is, how she works what could be a type—the B-girl—into a complex, individualistic character.

In between takes, Singleton is reading *The Rising Sun* by Michael Crichton. Never is he disconnected from the film world; at the time of shooting, the book is being made into a movie starring Wesley Snipes and Sean Connery. Book smart as well as film savvy, Singleton is always working his way through one book or another. That is, when he isn't playing Lynx, a hand-held video game system. Baha Jackson, who played young Doughboy in *Boyz N the Hood* and has a cameo in this film, is a favorite competitor of Singleton's. Once Singleton establishes a shot, he has a well-demonstrated ability to concentrate on the book or game in front of him, to the exclusion of the bustle of activity surrounding him. Grips and camera crew set up the next shot.

Another scene begins. Singleton looks up from his book and shouts, "Action!" Jackson and Tyra Ferrell cut up, almost losing their self-control in a maelstrom of giggles. Their timing is right on. But after the film stops rolling, Peter Collister says the shot was no good because one of the screens used for lighting purposes shows in the shot. "Maybe it will just show a little bit," Singleton says hopefully.

Don Wilkerson shakes his head. "John, at a drive-in that screen will look a block long." Singleton looks annoyed. "But the performance was so good. It gets no better. Damn, I hate when this happens." Seizing an opportunity to nag, Collister says, "Now if we were on a sound stage . . ."

Singleton just smiles at him, acknowledging the point. He fought for location shooting, even though Hollywood lots are much easier to work on. Defiantly, he says, "I didn't want to be on a sound stage. It's too artificial. I wanted to be on location. With my *people*." To underline his point, he turns and hugs the person standing next to him. He does this a lot.

The screen is fixed, and picture's up again. Singleton goes to the actors, whispering directions to them in between shots. After one good take, he yells from his chair, "Now that was *perfect*. Let's do it again." The cast and crew groan. They've heard the line before. And they've also heard what comes next: "I love you and I love myself. Action!"

May 21, 1992

*i*t is only the second day that the cast members who work and hang out in Jessie's Salon have performed together. There's also a whole new set of extras. The newness of it all, coupled with the scripted comedy, keeps the salon abuzz with chatter and giggles. But for the actors and crew members who are trying to concentrate, the distractions have become annoying. Tyra Ferrell is talking to Singleton, and apparently the din is drowning out their conversation. She looks up in frustration and says, "Quiet on the set, *please*." Not everybody hears her, or maybe some people think she doesn't mean them. So she says again, "Quiet, people, we've got a little bit more to go. Please be quiet."

At another corner of the room, the PA's are discussing the extras. "They don't look like they have any business," one says. The rest agree that the extras are moving around the room like robots. Deon Vines is a set PA/actor who had bit parts in *White Men Can't Jump* and now in *Poetic Justice*. He tries to explain to the extras the art of being extras, that even background players must have *verve*. "When you are crossing—it looks like you're just doing it cause we told you to," he says to one young woman. "But I am," she earnestly replies. "But it can't *look* like that," he says. "Act like you've got somewhere to go, something to do. Swing your purse. Walk like this." He goes on demonstrating, to full comedic effect, how one would be a sassy sister in a beauty salon on a Saturday afternoon. His parody evokes giggles from all—and a dirty look from Ferrell.

Another take on this scene begins. The sound guys are seated in the back of the salon. Not that they have to be sound "guys," but these are. Like elementary school Dungeon and Dragon enthusiasts, these guys are nerdy, intense, and pompous. They tend to keep to themselves. The way they wear their headphones and fiddle with the sound equipment, muttering to each other in sound-tech-ese, reveals an early love of all things technical and scientific. One of the sound guys whispers accusingly to the sound PA, "Did you see anyone wearing a digital watch?" The sound PA, Jason, a black skater kid in his late teens, surveys the roomful of people and says, "Uh, no." The other guy whispers, clearly annoyed, "*Somebody* is wearing one of those digital watches that beeps on the hour." The first sound guy takes a deep breath, surveys the room, and says to the sound PA, "Don't make a big deal out of it. But walk around and look at people's wrists." The second sound guy, who must hear this beep in hi-fi on his headphones, is truly rankled. "When I find the person, I'm gonna glue them to the floor." This sound guy is living proof that someone can actually get so worked up over a digital watch that it could ruin their entire day. Jason returns. "I found the guy whose watch is going off," he says proudly. "Did you tell him to take his fucking watch off?" the second sound guy asks. Jason says, "He said he'll stop it before the next hour." Now the second sound guy is furious: "Bullshit! He'd better take it off *now*." And he tears off in search of the offending beep. Later, when someone whispers during a take, the sound guys' tempers flare once again. "Who the fuck is *talking*?" one of them asks the other. "I don't know," says the other, "but let's give an IQ test. If you fail, you get to come work on this movie." They discuss the cast with equal scorn. Eventually they make their way to the subject of race. "Put one of us in the scene," one sound guy says. "There should be at least one white person in this movie."

In between takes, Tyra Ferrell looks thoughtfully into space. It hasn't been easy to do what she has done, to be a brown-skinned Afrocentric black actress and make a living in Hollywood. No sound editors on any big-budget Hollywood flick sat in the back of the room and said, "Put Tyra in a scene. There should be at least one black person in this movie." Ferrell and Cassandra Butcher, the unit publicist, sit and discuss their worst colorism stories. "I did a show, a two-hour TV movie, and there were two black women in the movie," Ferrell tells us. "Me and a fair-skinned, white-black girl. And an agent came up to me and said, 'You're very talented, but you won't get much work because Hollywood likes the Vanessa Williams type, and you're a nigger black.' I took him by the collar and took him into a corner and said, 'As long as you're in my presence, don't you ever say that word again in my presence. You don't know what a nigger is.' "

Outside, waiting for the next shot to be set up, Tupac and

Singleton are enjoying the southern California sun, talking about their experience in film and how they've changed over the last few years. Sitting in their canvas director's chairs, directing and acting for a living, it is refreshing to see two young brothers in such lofty positions. As hard-core as both of them may profess to be, their faces don't show the hardness that so many guys on the street have: the coldness in the eyes, the emptiness within, the downcast eyes, and the dragging gait of a broken spirit—these are inner-city symptoms that Singleton and Tupac simply do not have. One overhears bits and pieces of their conversation. Singleton says, "When I was in film school, I used to beat up other film students, kick 'em out of the editing room, curse them out. I'm a lot more mellow now." Tupac says he prefers the music industry to the film business. "Yo, if it weren't for you," he tells Singleton, "I wouldn't be making movies. I would have stopped with *Juice*."

Back inside the salon, Singleton prepares to shoot one of the last scenes in the movie. Two sisters stare each other up and down, then finally can't resist reading each other with razor-sharp diss: "You better get your soul-train-dancing ass out of here!" and "Get outta here, you cheap-weave Naomi Campbell wannabe!" Then the coup de grâce: "Bitch, just remember this. Every time you kiss him, you're tasting my pussy." Singleton and the crew bag every time the actress, Serena Mobley, gets to that line. On the fourth or fifth take, Singleton gets up and whispers to Mobley, then returns to his chair, grinning mischievously. "This one's for TV coverage," he says. And sure enough, when it comes time for Mobley's line, she delivers it with a variation: "Bitch, just remember this. Every time you kiss him, you're tasting my nookie." The nookie line is only half a joke. Just a few days before, Singleton had received a detailed analysis of his script and what would fly on network television and what wouldn't, as well as what sort of coverage the director should aim for in the future. The movie hasn't wrapped and the theatrical release is a year away, but the studio is already counting the dollars in television sales. When you're dealing with a studio system, it seems, it's almost impossible to stay ahead. There are an infinite number of planners with an infinite number of plans; almost all of them have their eyes glued to the bottom line: mo money, mo money, mo money . . .

Almost every film is shot out of sequence, some deviating more drastically from the narrative order than others. The *Poetic Justice* shoot is no different; that's why in the middle of the production schedule, the crew is shooting the last scene in the movie. Justice and Lucky are in the place where they first met, Jessie's. Lucky has brought his daughter, Keisha, to meet Justice and to ask Justice's forgiveness for the things he said and did. Again, the scene rings true to life to Pauletta Lewis, the lead hairstylist on the film. She stands by a row of curling irons and shakes her head. "I was telling John that this scene was a flashback to my own life. Fifteen years ago, my husband brought his little girl into the salon for me to do her hair. I read the scene when I read the script, but seeing it acted out brought chills down my spine."

Singleton has done a sufficiently impressive job of scripting situations so close to life, so full of clear and specific details, that for many of the onlookers the film seems, at times, an appropriation of their own lives. But a subject of running discussion among cast and crew is whether this is really a woman's movie. It's called *Poetic Justice,* but some people argue that it is really Lucky's story, his coming of age. Singleton is finally beginning to concur. "The more I look at this movie, the more I think it's about women, but it's still from a man's perspective," he says. "You still got the booty shots, the breast shots of Colette, I'm sorry. The fact is that I'm going to emphasize certain things in certain ways. I don't even know it till after I see it. It just comes from an innate part of who I am." Then, surveying the room appreciatively, he says, "But you gotta admit, you never seen so many black women in a movie in so many different sizes, shapes, and colors."

May 28, 1992
Tha Hair Show

When the crew first came here, on a location scout two months ago, this location was merely an extension of the parking lot of the L.A. Civic Center. But production designer Keith Burns and his art department have whipped up a nice batch of movie magic, transforming this space into what is supposed to be the Oakland Hair Show. Where once there was dirty cement, there is now wall-to-wall royal blue carpet; there are banners, runways, and booths; not to mention what a coat of fresh paint can do. The real-life hair professionals and beautiful models who are milling about top off the effect. It is as Singleton wrote it and, prior to that, how he might've imagined it.

Besides a competition of hairstyles, which is what brings Jessie, Justice, and crew up to Oakland in the first place, there is also a fashion show. Keith Burns, a longtime admirer of Gordon Henderson's work, invited the internationally renowned designer to design a set of outfits for the show. Henderson donated his time and labor for that piece of recognition that some would sell their firstborn child for: screen credit.

Dressed in a Gap baseball cap (an initial G embroidered on the pique), a T-shirt, and linen pants, Henderson has the relaxed stance that the truly confident, the truly wealthy, and most often some combination of both best exhibit. Far from the gunfire-fast pace of New York City and the drama and divas of the Paris runways, Henderson seems not so much a rugged individualist as a chameleon type, adept at blending into his surroundings. Tell him he's looking very California, especially for a New Yorker, and he just smiles. "Keith called and told me what he wanted, what his ideas were," he explains. "I gave it some thought. Usually, I give these calls to my publicist, but I wanted to make a supportive contribution to John Singleton, another person whom I felt was being a role model to the black community.

"Films have used my clothes before—the *Cosby* show, Spike's films. But Keith asked me to design something special for this show, inspired by my spring collection and keeping in mind that this was a hair show. I knew I wanted to do something colorful so I put all these things together on the budget they gave me. The budget wasn't much, but these are summer clothes. Summer's also when complexions get darker, so I went with brighter, more fruity colors, with black and white as a backdrop." Henderson pauses, and the conversation shifts to *Boyz N the Hood*. He is quiet and serious when he says, "I especially liked the relationship between the father and son. I thought that was significant. I thought that was a poignant expression of the relationships we need to see in the inner city that would help cure a lot of the issues of the inner city. I think he's very talented. I like what John is doing."

The hair and fashion shows go off without a hitch. The fashion show is especially popular. People cheer and whistle as the models walk out wearing Henderson's designs. Rapper Dina D, who plays Deena, is also a model in the fashion show. She puts on the most animated runway walk since Right Said Fred let the world know just how sexy, *too* sexy was. It is all in good fun.

The next day the production returns to Jessie's Salon. Because Jessie's Salon is actually Hollywood Curl, a working business, the crew must work around the shop's schedule, leaving and returning several times. The scene Singleton is shooting has an even stronger poignancy in these postriot times. Justice and Jessie stand at the window of the salon, we see police lights, we hear sirens, we see the police shaking some brothers down. Michael Colyar, playing the local indigent, reads the police, screaming at them to leave the brothers alone, daring them to treat these young men "like a King." His words aren't just the meaningless prattle of one who has fallen from the graces of society. Colyar's words resonate because in the year since Singleton first wrote the script of *Poetic Justice,* the city of Los Angeles and indeed the whole country have been reminded that the poor (and that includes the homeless) are the most revolutionary classes because they have nothing to lose by challenging the powers that be. It is Tyra Ferrell as Jessie who really brings the message home, when she looks out the window and says, "There's always another man somewheres, and out here, you gotta know sometimes you gonna lose one." It is so silent in the salon that were you listening for it, you could hear a tear drop.

6

From L.A. to
Oakland

June 3, 1992

The cast and crew have moved to a desert highway. It's hot as hell out here. The official temperature is 85 degrees, but the highway is located in the valley. Mountains all around the highway trap the heat inside like a pressure cooker. The set nurse, Mitchel El Mahdi, keeps an eye out for people who might faint or get sunstroke. He sets out buckets of Handi Wipes in ice-cold Seabreeze. Everyone from the actors to the grips and the PA's swarm the buckets for the freezing-cold strips of cloth. People walk around with different colored Handi Wipes wrapped around their heads and necks. Anything to stay cool.

Singleton is filming tow shots—shots of the inside of a moving car. It's a big ordeal, made worse by the heat and by the very real snakes that make their home in this uninhabited area. A camera is carefully secured on the driver's side of the car that the actors "drive"; that car is actually towed by a truck that houses lights, Singleton, Collister, Wilkerson, and a few other absolutely necessary crew members following in caravan cars. The rest of the crew waits at base camp.

Back at base camp, anxiety levels are rising as fast as the temperature. There is only one week left in the L.A. shoot. Next week the company will go on the road for a month, filming on location in selected areas from L.A. to Oakland. Today, the crew finds out who among them will be invited on the trip and who will have to start looking for a job.

The leads of each team—camera, art department, makeup, hair, locations—aren't worried. They are guaranteed work throughout the shoot. It's the PA's and the assistants who are worried. They are just at the beginning of their careers; their few credits are practically indistinguishable from each other. Ironically, two years before, many of the junior crew members were Singleton's peers—film school classmates, social acquaintances, young upstarts muttering their way through grungy jobs. Now these young men and women must compete with one another to accompany Singleton up the coast.

A few hours later, during a lunch break, "the list" is passed out. People search frantically for their names. There are the inevitable disappointments, made even more awkward by the excited outbursts of the lucky few who get to go. The crew have become accustomed to each other, have formed individual relationships and group jokes. They have developed a rhythm of working together, and now that rhythm has been broken. The sadness of breaking up the team, coupled with the frantic air of unemployment among those who will be let go, casts a shadow over the rest of the L.A. shoot and makes the road trip ahead seem ominous.

June 11, 1992

*t*he production has traveled several hours up the coast to Pismo Beach. The beauty of the beach—the clear blue waves met by the widest expanse of snow-white sand—has everyone awestruck, even the crew that had visited the area on an earlier location scout. Only Tupac Shakur, ever the city boy, seems unimpressed, complaining quite seriously, to a very amused crew, that he doesn't want to get sand in his brand-new shoes.

The scene being shot today includes Shakur, Jackson, King, and Torry. The four main characters have stopped at the beach on their way to Oakland, and they stare out into the waves, lost in their own thoughts. Later, in the dubbing process, Singleton will record the actors speaking their thoughts in voice over. Joe Torry, who plays Chicago, thinks that this scene is particularly key. "The relationship between these characters is so important," he says. "Janet [Jackson] said it first, the vibe between us has to be right. If any of us isn't feeling good about this, then it's going to come across onscreen. She's invited us over to dinner a couple of times, invited us to jet-ski with her on her birthday."

Jackson has displayed a similar affection for Torry and her onscreen best friend, King. "I had the most fun hanging out with Joe and Regina," she said later. "Those were the best times. I think they're doing a wonderful job portraying their characters. I hope I look just as good as them. If I do, then I'm safe."

June 13, 1992

*f*or the central California shoot, the crew has camped out in Cambria, a small artistic community that seems like a combination of Walden and Woodstock. Today they are shooting one of the most critical scenes in the movie—a grassy field, high up in the hills, with "wild" zebras running free. Singleton got the idea from the old Hearst Castle near Cambria, where there were actually once zebras on the estate.

The scene will never make it into the movie, but at this point, everyone is excited about it. Pismo Beach, the field of zebras, Big Sur—by shooting in these almost exotic locations, Singleton aims to redefine the parameters of inner-city life, show a bigger picture, a wider breadth of possibility.

As the crew sets up the shot, Singleton gets his first horseback-riding lesson from the zebra trainers (who ride on top of horses during the scene). As Singleton rides up the hill, his pals blast the soundtrack from *The Good, the Bad and the Ugly* from his Path-finder. "I learned from Westerns," Singleton explains, "that the first thing you have to do is get over your fear of the horse. The guy said that I'm a natural."

While Singleton pretends to be Clint Eastwood, Don Wilkerson instructs the cast and crew who must be down with the zebras. Apparently, there is no such thing as a "tame" zebra—you can't domesticate them like horses. So the cast and crew who must deal with them must take extra precautions in order not to be stam-peded by the herd! Wilkerson, as usual, is calm. Chewing on a toothpick, he says, "Let me give you some etiquette for down here. If a zebra rushes you, stand still and put your hands up so it thinks that you're bigger than it is."

During the first shot, Janet Jackson boldly approaches the more docile of the zebras. (Only one of them bucks wildly.) She feeds and pets them. Steve Nicolaides looks on in admiration. "She's brave, good with animals. Leave them alone. This may never happen again." As one zebra starts to approach Jackson, Singleton quips, "Maybe he wants an autograph."

In the next shot, a trainer hides behind a tree, shadowing Jackson. The zebras are feeling feisty and aren't responding to the trainers' offscreen commands. More than once, it seems they are rushing toward Jackson a little too quickly. But she simply raises her arms high and stands perfectly still. She explains that animals don't scare her, because "I've always had pets around me, ever since I was a little girl—a giraffe, a llama, a deer, pheasants, raccoons, dogs, horses. I wasn't afraid to do this scene at all."

Standing on the road overlooking the field of zebras, Tupac Shakur looks down at Jackson. "She's a star," he says. "We're not on the same level at all. But it's definitely a timeline to show myself how far I've come. I can remember when I was first beginning to write rhymes [rap lyrics] and 'Control' being on in the back-ground." While Shakur claims that "I conquered my Janet Jackson shit before I even met her" and "It wasn't nothing to be with her," in his voice is all the affection of a schoolboy crush.

As young men are prone to do, Shakur, Torry, and Singleton bounce in and out of a competition of friendly insults, "doing the dozens" even when there's work to be done. After the next take, when Don Wilkerson screams, "We got to do it again! The light changed!" Joe Torry says loud enough for all to hear, "The light didn't change. John's grandmother just flew by the sun."

Shakur adds his two cents in the Diss the Director game that has begun: "Don't come to the pool party tonight. If you come, bring Shorty *and* his brother, 'cause you're going in."

Singleton laughs, challenging: "Can you swim? 'Cause I can swim, and I'll drown your ass."

Then Torry plays turncoat, taking Singleton's side: "Now, you know you can't drown a beaver"—referring to Shakur's front teeth.

Shakur makes a break for the director's chair and, once seated, launches into a clever impersonation of Singleton. "Okay, picture's up." Then, waving to Singleton as if he were some Ken doll actor: "Go sit in your trailer. I'll call you when I need you."

Wilkerson rolls his eyes, but he doesn't stop the guys. While on location, the film is shooting six days a week, per union law. It is late Saturday afternoon, and everyone is feeling more than a little punchy. Once the sun sets, Singleton calls "Wrap" and everyone heads off for the hotel and the pool party.

June 15, 1992

*I*t is seven o'clock, and the sun is just beginning to rise on Big Sur. The crew is lined up on a precipice—ahead of them is nothing but blue waves and clouds, and somewhere out there is Hawaii. Several of the guys from the camera and electric crews pitch rocks, but the drop is so deep, the rocks disappear somewhere in midair and you can't even hear when they hit the water.

The wind makes the deceptively beautiful sight as cold as a Chicago afternoon. One of the grips walks by. Wrapping a scarf tight around his neck, he says, "It's a grip's nightmare, but I love it that it's so windy." When Collister walks along the ledge of the turnaround, Singleton yells out, only half kidding, "Peter, move away from there! I don't have time to fly Storaro in"—referring to a legendary Italian cinematographer.

In this scene, Chicago and Iesha, the ever-battling lovebirds, duke it out for real. The beautiful view is an unusual backdrop for what amounts to a truly nasty streetfight. But it almost seems as if Singleton is issuing a warning about the state of the African-American family structure. Perching their fight on this dangerous ledge, Singleton seems to be saying that black men and women have reached the point of no return. The choices are either to stick together and survive, or to separate and destroy each other and the black family in the process. Collister explains how the camera angles will emphasize the separation: "Usually, you start with a master wide shot then go in closer. I'm going to start close and move out to wide so you lose definition, see them as smaller figures in a big empty space."

Rehearsing the scene, Torry and King improvise. Their words are sharp and biting. Looking at the ocean and mountains that surround them, Torry says, "Look at all this beautiful shit. This could be us. Why can't our shit be as beautiful as this?"

Without missing a beat, King sizes Torry up with her eyes and says sardonically, "Because you ain't a beautiful motherfucker."

When King walks away from him, Torry says, "Why are you going to turn your back on me, Iesha? Why?"

King never gives him an inch. "I need to turn my back on you because I'm tired of your shit. That's why that other bitch left you—because you couldn't hang."

Torry looks seriously hurt. One can see that behind all the cursing and screaming is a real sense of vulnerability and a maligned self-esteem on the part of black men pitted against a very legitimate anger and frustration on the part of black women.

Torry pauses, then says quietly, "That's a fucked-up thing to say, 'Esha."

She looks him in the eye, unforgiving: "It's a real thing to say, Chicago."

The cast and crew are nothing short of stunned, silent, and captivated by the drama unfolding before them. It is clear that this fictional couple, Chicago and Iesha, have struck a very real chord. Having read the script and knowing that in the very next setup Chicago's going to swing for Iesha makes it all the more nerve-racking to watch.

Torry is ready for the fight scene (which will be spliced together with fighting done by stunt doubles). "I'm so locked into Chicago," he says. "He feels so much pain during the movie, it's not going to be hard to hit her. The way I want it to come off, I don't want people cheering in the theaters when I hit her. But I want people to see that she pushed me so far, she got me so fucking mad, I snapped."

Singleton has also thought about the subtext of the fight scene. "I hope people understand that just because he hit her doesn't mean that was the right thing to do. My father always used to tell me, never hit a woman. If you feel like you're going to hit a woman, then walk away."

"Do you remember in rehearsal, John?" Torry asks. "In character therapy when I was in the middle of the circle, they were asking me why I was hitting my girl, what was that all about. But my character's not a woman beater. It's just at that particular point, I've been taking so much that I go out of control."

June 16, 1992
The Fight: Chicago versus Iesha, Round 1

*b*ob Minor, the stunt coordinator for *Poetic Justice,* is a pioneer in his field. Having worked with Singleton on *Boyz N the Hood,* he also cites a long list of credits in film and on television, including such projects as *Glory, Mo' Money, Iron Eagle III, Unlawful Entry,* and *Magnum P.I.* "As late as 1968, there were white stuntmen putting blackface on and doubling black actors," says Minor incredulously. "I got in the business in 1970. A few of us black guys got together and started practicing. We knew we could do this, do anything. It was just a matter of training."

Together, Singleton and Minor work out the intricate details of the scene. "I got to figure out how she'll get slapped," says Singleton. "It's so much easier with dudes—you just hit them soft a couple of times, then hit them for real. Cuba Gooding [Tre in *Boyz N the Hood*] got slapped for real in *Boyz.*" Minor points out, "Every scene where a man slaps a woman down isn't the same. Iesha is a girl from the hood, so a fight is everyday life to her. If he makes her mad, she'll hit him back." Which is exactly what happens in the film.

Singleton seems more comfortable with the logistics of the fight than with the emotional implications of the scene. "I worry about the gender divide. So many black men feel that black women cut them down as bad, if not worse, than society. I'm always denying it, but truth be told, I know more than one Iesha—some sisters cut a brother to the quick, in cold blood." As if to illustrate his point, Singleton shoots an extreme close-up on Iesha's mouth—pretty mouth, ugly words.

There is a short break as the crew set up for the next scene. In an effort to break up the heaviness of the violent scene, Jackson, Elizondo, King, Shorty, and two of the set PA's, T-Dave and Dion, gather around Singleton's chair and start singing a medley of songs from Dougie Fresh's "The Show" to John Cougar Mellencamp's "Jack and Diane." A few months earlier, the cast and crew had been slaughtered in a softball game against the cast and crew from Robert Townsend's *Meteor Man*. Singing with Singleton, they proved to be much more talented musically than athletically!

When the stunt doubles arrive, everyone stops and stares. It's not so much that they look exactly like the four principals, but that wardrobe has dressed them in exactly the same outfits that Chicago, Lucky, Iesha, and Justice wear on the trip. The Lucky double wears his black baseball cap backward, the Chicago double has his hair cut into a fade like Joe Torry's, and the two stuntwomen sport braids exactly the same length, color, and texture as Justice and Iesha's. The two women, in particular, are such eerie replicas that Dion promptly dubs them "Justine and Myesha, Justice and Iesha's cousins from Detroit." Jackson explains, "It was funny, really strange to see our doubles. I was ready to do the fight stuff myself. But John said that there was no need to risk it. If I got hurt, I might not be able to complete the film, and it would be horrible if I held up production."

The rehearsal of the fight scene seems to take forever. Every move of the fight must be choreographed like a dance. Bob Minor decides not to use mats; the small pebbles and gravel on the turnabout are all there will be to cushion the actors' falls. Singleton and Collister opt for a hand-held camera for a more documentary effect. When at last the camera starts rolling, the takes are never long. The actors shout and scream, pushing each other, flailing arms and legs. Then Singleton calls "Cut!" and the stunt doubles come in for a few minutes of sharper fighting. Still, it is so believable that during one take Jackson's dog, Puffy, sees her stunt double being beaten up and runs into the scene, barking angrily because she thinks Jackson is being hurt! During another take, Jackson is supposed to run up to Torry from behind and kick him in the balls. She runs out of the truck, kicks him—perhaps a little too enthusiastically—and Torry doubles over, letting out a blood-curdling scream. Jackson immediately breaks character and begins apologizing profusely, "Oh shit. Joe, I'm sorry. I didn't mean to . . ." Everyone on set pauses, unsure of what to do. Torry isn't wearing a protective cup over his genitals. Seconds later, Torry jumps up laughing. "Ain't nothing. I was just acting."

June 17, 1992

*t*oday's the last day of the fight scene. But the cast and crew's mind is actually not on film but on TV. After two days of people milling about and paving the way, Oprah Winfrey is scheduled to spend the day on set, taping a segment of her hour-long movie specials. She arrives in a limo, and once introduced, Winfrey and Singleton become fast friends. They discuss their mutual friend Maya Angelou, the movie business, and today's scene. "I wanted to do something about the war between the sexes," Singleton explains to her. "Ironically, today you'll see a knock-down, physical embodiment of the strife between black men and black women."

As Winfrey observes the set and the way Singleton works, it's clear that she thinks the young director has a good head on his shoulders. At one point, she turns to her crew. "John has a great way about him, a great way," she says. "It's very calm, unlike quite a few of the sets we've been on. Like the one where the director was acting like he was having a stroke." Winfrey also congratulates Singleton on hiring so many women in key crew positions. Singleton smiles, mischievously. "I must have my muses," he says.

"Janet's an actress. She's given me no trouble. She gives me exactly what I want," says Singleton, walking away from Winfrey and her camera crew. Then looking over at Tupac Shakur, who is making a habit of being late to set, he says, "I'm always looking for a young De Niro, and it always gets fucked up. I don't think a lot of young people respect what it takes to do great work. When you have things handed to you so easily, you don't respect it. I need a palette with which to paint my ideas. You know, I see parts of myself in Lucky and Chicago. I saw parts of myself in Doughboy and Ricky [in *Boyz N the Hood*]. Doughboy was me in college—that's why it was so much fun to write him. Not that I was getting into trouble, but I had Doughboy's attitude—I thought I was the shit. But I was also a dreamer like Ricky, college bound. What makes this movie different is that it's not really about me but about the things that affect women's lives. I'm trying to grow as an artist, trying to grow beyond what's happened to me personally."

When asked if he is tired, Singleton, who has been working every minute since film school, says, "No, not really. What else would I be doing now? I might as well be doing this. It's all about putting the shit out there and seeing people's reactions to it. I just can't wait to see what people are going to say about this fight." Then, laughing, he says, "I wonder what Michael [Jackson] is going to say when he sees Janet in this movie. It's gonna be a trip. I'm telling you, Janet's the ultimate homegirl. She can dance. She can sing. She can *hang*."

June 24, 1992

*t*he production has moved to Alice's Restaurant in Woodside, California. It's a long way away from Alice's Restaurant in Stockbridge, Massachusetts, where Arlo Guthrie once made a hit movie and song of the same name. But this place is also a hippie enclave—with a Bullwinkle stuffed moose's head above the counter, more tie-dye than a Grateful Dead concert, and even a picture of Guthrie himself. The actress who plays the waitress wears a nametag that says SUSAN/FOLLOW YOUR HEART. Nestled in the woods of northern California, the restaurant really does seem caught in a time warp. Which is why, on their way to the Oakland Hair Show, Jessie and her stylists stop off there—for a bite to eat and, as Jessie says, "to stir it up, shake it up, make things interesting around here."

Miki Howard, who plays Jessie's best friend Maxine, is shaking things up before the cameras even start rolling. During rehearsal, Howard gets out of the car, looks around, and says contemptuously, "There's too many white people here." It's meant to be a joke, but no one laughs. The tension of the riots, as well as the basic day-to-day racial difference, has never really left the set. White crew members just look at each other. One of them says, annoyed, "Maybe we should just go home, and she can drive herself to set, run errands, and do all the things she can't seem to do for herself." Another white crew member claims, "If a white person said, 'There's too many black people here,' it would be racist." Rehearsal begins again, and the moment is past. Past, but not forgotten.

Howard doesn't hear the comments, and she doesn't seem to realize she's offended anybody. A popular R&B singer, Miki Howard is anxious to get back to work on her latest album, *Femme Fatale.* She's not loving the movie business these days. "I get so excited when I hear my voice on the radio, I just *scream.* With movies—I can take it or leave it. Maybe if I was the featured actress, maybe. But no more getting up at six o'clock in the morning just to be *glimpsed* at."

Tyra Ferrell, ever the diva, poses on the hood of Jessie's Lexus. Collister quips, "First there was *Boyz N the Hood.* Now there's *Jessie on the Hood.*" Ferrell picks up the joke, cooing, "From the woods to the hood. From the hood to the woods." Singleton laughs. "Sell those tickets, Tyra," he says.

A new scene is improvised where Yvette Wilson, playing Colette, won't let Dina, Kim, and Mikki, playing the other hairstylists, get out of the car on the way to the Oakland Hair Show. "No one's getting out of the car," Yvette says threateningly. "I got my man in Oakland I got to see." She takes a Polaroid out of the glove compartment, and it's a picture of Yvette and—who else?—Singleton. "Ooo, he's fine," the girls all swoon. "Yes, girl, he's all that and some Häagen-Dazs," boasts Yvette. "Is he paid?" Kim asks. "I said Häagen-Dazs," says Yvette, rolling her eyes. "What flavor?" asks Mikki, devilishly. "Rocky Road—girl," says Yvette, bumping and grinding. The girls dissolve into a fit of giggles, and Singleton laughs out loud as well. T-Dave, Singleton's assistant and friend since film school days, says, "Look at him, he loves the attention." Don Wilkerson shakes his head in agreement. "I should have never told him about *Lifeboat,* that Hitchcock movie where Hitchcock's picture is in a newspaper on the deck of the boat." "Nope," says T-Dave, smiling. "You shouldn't have shown it to him. He's young and impressionable."

Over on the side of the road, Singleton is talking to another young, impressionable man, a student from Berkeley who has

come to visit the set. "The best advice I can give you," says Singleton, "is it all starts in the writing. You hire the people you need to
help you see your vision. It was a lot more difficult in film school,
when I had to do everything—lights, camera, everything."

June 27, 1992

*t*he shoot is almost over. Today is a relatively quiet
day, shooting inside a warehouse where two sets have been built—
Iesha's bedroom and Kalil's sound lab (Kalil is Lucky's cousin). Eli
Reed, the Pulitzer prize–winning Magnum photographer, has
been shooting all the unit art for the film. In a corner he has set
up lights and a white tearsheet to shoot "specials"—special photography of the director and principal actors. At Singleton's request,
Reed has agreed to do a special shot of all the black women on the
crew. There are an unusual amount of black women involved, as
even Oprah Winfrey had noted. Stephanie Allain, the creative exec
on the project, has flown up especially for the shoot. Once assembled, it's an impressive array of talent and ability—Allain, Robi
Reed, casting director; Sherri G. Sneed, assistant production coordinator; Simone Farber, second assistant director; Elisa Ann Conant, location manager; Dawn Gilliam, script supervisor; Alvechia
Ewing, head of makeup; Pauletta Lewis, lead hairdresser; Cassandra Butcher, unit publicist; and April Hunter, wardrobe assistant.
Surveying the group, Sherri Sneed remarks, "This is something
that needs to be done. There's a lot of powerful black women in this
business that the industry doesn't know about."

The set for Iesha's bedroom is a hootchie's heaven—thanks to
Keith Burns and the art department. Decorated in red and black,
the room features among other things, balloons with "I Love You"
printed on them, numerous pictures of Iesha with assorted fly
guys, a picture of Regina on a fake cover of *Essence,* and a huge
waterbed.

It's a closed set for the love scene between Iesha and Chicago.
Although there will be nudity, even simulated seduction is best
without an audience. When the scene begins, Chicago is sitting at
the edge of the waterbed, wearing nothing but a pair of shorts and
a Chicago Bulls cap. Iesha approaches him, wearing only a robe,

winding to the rude-boy rhythm of the Jamaican Ragamuffin music that is played during the scene. But the scene is clearly more fun to watch than to do. After the second take, King asks Singleton, "Haven't we done enough of these?" Singleton says no. After the fourth take, King calls out again plaintively, "New Deal?" Singleton rewinds the takes and watches the shots on the monitor. "Okay," he says mercifully. "New Deal."

All afternoon, the production has been waiting for Tupac Shakur to show up. We are three months into the shoot, with only five more days to go. But it is a sunny Saturday afternoon, and the actor doesn't *feel* like working. When he finally gets to set, he's livid. He throws punches at his trailer, cracking a window. He yells for all to hear, *"I feel like a fuckin' slave in this dungeon."*

The scene Shakur is to shoot today is a silent walk through the basement "sound lab" of his murdered cousin, Kalil. The room is sparsely furnished with a cot, a chair, and the all-important stereo equipment. The walls are decorated with posters of popular rap groups: Ice-T, Public Enemy, Nice & Smooth, NWA. The crew is absolutely silent as Shakur makes his way around the room, touching things, looking at things, and finally listening to the tape his cousin had been working on. Shakur is at home and appropriately mournful in this young rapper's dream-room. After a few shots, Singleton has what he needs and everybody calls it a day.

June 29, 1992
Oakland

*I*t's seven in the morning, but the spectators have already lined up to see what's going on. The scene being shot today is the day after Lucky arrives in Oakland, only to find out his cousin Kalil has been murdered. Lucky's aunt and uncle give him Kalil's sound equipment, urging him to use it since their son cannot. Singleton is making a special effort to be tender to Rose Weaver, the actress who plays Lucky's aunt. "Her brother died last week," he explains, "so she's really not in the frame of mind for this role."

Weaver, in turn, has nothing but praise for Singleton. "He's the same age as my daughter, you know," she says. "He's great to work with, he's one of the most sensitive directors I've worked with in all my years as an actress. A lot of us feel that we'd do John's film for nothing. We're so proud of what he's done, and he's in touch with what's going on out here. When you live on West Adams [in Los Angeles] and you experienced the riots firsthand, then you realize that underneath, it's what John showed us in *Boyz N the Hood*."

As Weaver and the other cast members go through take after take, one can see that her resolve is slipping. When Singleton calls out "New Deal," Weaver gets a moment to compose herself. "The initial shock of hearing my own brother had died from drugs was so strong," she explains. "But in this role, John wants me to be real contained, and it's hard, it's hard not to cry."

Dressed in a robe, with a headful of haircurlers, Weaver smiles sweetly when Singleton walks by and gives her a hug. "I used to want to play only characters that are beautiful, sexy," says the fortysomething Weaver. "But working with John has showed me that there's beauty in simplicity, there's beauty in no makeup. There is beauty in an old robe, just like there is in a tight, short skirt. He makes me feel beautiful even though I'm stripped down. I hope the pressure of being a fabulous role model to our people doesn't get to John. It's just that you look at him and you say, 'I can do this. I can do anything.' "

After the next take, when Singleton yells, "Great!" Shakur comes running over to the director's chair. "I think we should do it one more time, John," he says, sarcasm dripping from his voice. "The eggs weren't hot enough in that one." Shakur laughs, and Singleton does too. And in a rare show of male bonding, the two hug. Shakur is notoriously impatient. Singleton is a notorious perfectionist. But at the heart of it, they love and respect each other.

July 2, 1992

We're at the corner of Eighteenth and Fillbert in Oakland, shooting at night. This is the old Black Panther territory, and the production is located only a block from where Huey Newton once lived. In fact, Newton's wife visits the set.

In this scene, Justice, Lucky, Chicago, and Iesha roll into Oakland and find that Lucky's cousin has been murdered. At the top end of the street, Singleton and the makeup artists confer over the corpses. "John, how do you want these dead bodies to look?" Singleton thinks for a second and says, quite unscientifically, "Well, he got hit with an automatic weapon, so there's a whole lot of blood."

A crowd of spectators have assembled and are already proving hard to manage. This is also Tupac Shakur's hometown, and the street teems with neighborhood people, out to see the local guy who hit the bigtime. There is extra security, but the crowd far outnumbers them. In a attempt to quiet them down, Singleton appeals to them personally, asking for their help and their silence. The crowd simmers down, and the long night breaks into daybreak without incident.

"It's difficult out here," explains Shakur, looking around the neighborhood he has since left behind. "We don't get anything out here. In L.A., they shoot movies every day. There's nothing out here. We don't even get concerts. Nothing but dope and liquor stores. We never get our voices heard. The shit you're putting up onscreen is our lives. When that dead body on set gets up and walks away, you know some real dead bodies will follow it."

July 3, 1992
It's a Wrap

*I*t's the last day of the shoot. The scene being shot today is a deceptively simple one: Lucky drops Justice and Iesha off at the Lakeside Motel, where they meet up with Jessie and her crew. Easy enough, but it's a night shoot. At five-thirty in the evening, the cast and crew still have twelve long hours ahead of them.

Throughout the evening, people exchange phone numbers and addresses, talking about what they will do tomorrow, when their lives are their own again. In his trailer Singleton talks about his upcoming family reunion. "I've got to go see my family in South Carolina. I love them, but I hate it because my grandmother Audrey loves to grandstand me in front of all my relatives. She's a diva, and it gives her even more power. She loves to say, 'He's asleep, y'all have to go. But he's here, you can *feel* it.' "

By three-thirty in the morning, amazingly, a few diehard fans line the banister of the Lakeside Motel. But even they are beginning to look sleepy. The crew, for some strange reason, is wide awake. "It's the rush of the last night—pure adrenaline," explains Yon Styles, a PA and good friend of Singleton's. People talk and make periodic raids on the Craft Services table for caffeine-laden soda and the sugar rush of chocolate and candy.

The shot is as follows: It's a close-up of Lucky, and Justice is off-screen. Lucky blames her for Kalil's death, saying that if she hadn't made them stop, they would have gotten to Oakland in time to save him. Singleton decides that there should be tears in Shakur's eyes, but he knows that it's too late or too early to ask the tired actor to produce them naturally. Alvechia Ewing, head of makeup, pulls out a Visine-like bottle marked "Tears," and the desired effect is easily achieved. The takes look good, and with "tears" still flowing from Shakur's eyes, Singleton raises Shakur's arm and cries out, "Ladies and gentlemen, say good-bye to Tupac Shakur." There's a smattering of applause, followed by cheers and cries for the actor to "get lost."

As the sun comes up after the very last take, Singleton cries out, "God is calling. Let's go home. Everybody say good-bye to Ms. Regina King, Ms. Tyra Ferrell, and Ms. Janet Jackson. This is the end of principal photography on *Poetic Justice*."

7
Finding Justice:
From the Diary of John Singleton

Whenever I want to do a new movie, I always start with a certain ritual. I always buy a small three-hole notebook, I buy a new pack of lined notebook paper, then I buy a pack of black Paper Mate pens—not blue, not red.

My original conception of *Poetic Justice* was to do an army film. I was so upset that a friend of mine had been sent to fight in the Persian Gulf, and that once again the United States was fighting a war, sticking its nose where it didn't belong. I originally intended that *Poetic Justice* would be about a young GI's wife named Justice. She would marry a guy who was recruited from South Central Los Angeles and they would go off to live on an army base in Japan, or the Philippines or the Northwest. He would spend all his money on his truck and not in supporting his family. It was basically about those two. He would end up getting mad at one of his CEOs and punching him out, and he'd be sent to jail. Justice would send him poems. Her economic situation was that she has all these babies and no money to take care of them, especially with her husband in jail.

Nevertheless, this didn't work out. I tried to do it, but I couldn't write it without the proper research on living on an army base.

One thing I always do is write "Idea: . . ." or "Dialogue: . . ." One day I sat down and wrote:

Idea: Justice does the hair of some of the other army wives. In *Poetic Justice,* I want Justice to fix people's hair. She does perms, weaves, etc., just for extra money.

Then on January 3, 1991, I wrote:

I've been thinking about changing the setting of *Poetic Justice* to a beauty supply store on Crenshaw involving the lives of three girls. The film will show their interaction with men, their families, etc., kinda like *Mystic Pizza.* Justice is still a poet, she reads poetry in the beauty supply store.

Idea: A girl has been involved with a guy who's been selling drugs. They're sitting together in the car, and some guys come by and shoot him in the head from a driver's side window. It comes out of nowhere. They're just talking and cooling it. He has just confessed his love for her.

DIALOGUE: 'Cause I'm a woman, phenomenally. Phenomenal woman, that's me.

With this, I had the opening for the movie.

1/7/91

Yesterday was my twenty-third birthday, the same number as Michael Jordan. I think it's a sign of luck. I woke up at 4:30 this morning, yeah me. I came up with the backstory for *Justice*—now she's working in a beauty salon and supply store on Crenshaw Boulevard, she is also studying cosmetology at the local beauty college. She is haunted by the death of her boyfriend two years earlier. Her former lover was an up-and-coming dope dealer. They were looking at a movie in a drive-in theater. Two guys walked by and shot him from the driver's side. He was murdered before her eyes. The film they were watching was a romance, the clips of which will be played back periodically, David Lynch style. I want to deconstruct the romance genre, do something different.

Dialogue for boyfriend: You know I really, really appreciate you and all. I know I really trip and shit sometimes, but you know how I feel, don't you? I treat you right, don't I? I really appreciate you sticking by me when I went to county, specially since nobody in my family did. (Then he gets it, after he says, "I love you.")

Two years later, the film opens with a poem called "Same Ol', Same Ol'." As we introduce Justice in images at work, school, on the street, and at home, looking at BET [Black Entertainment Television] and writing a poem, she falls asleep.

Idea for Background in *Justice*: Mighty Mouse, the bullfight cartoon, where the mouse woman sings . . .

Poetry moves the narrative forward.

Key ingredients in this film: sex, poetry, romance, gangsters, music, comedy, drama.

1/9/91

Tonight I'm going to meet with Fatima, a friend of mine that I met at various parties around town I've been attending. She is a hairstylist, around the age of Justice. Fatima is also a former cosmetology student. I'm gonna try to pick her brain for some ideas on *Poetic Justice*.

A buddy of mine, V-Dub, used to work at the post office. And he told me when he used to have to drive mail from Los Angeles to Las Vegas, they'd bring along girls sometimes. That got my head going. It's the funniest thing. What sort of girls would do that? They have to be straight-up homegirls. They made the prime love interest a postman.

It's funny because the girl doing hair makes more than the guy at the post office. It also shows the economic disparity between black men and black women in America.

Idea: In the salon, a girl is cutting another guy's hair and he looks at Justice and says, "Damn, she's fine. She got a boyfriend?" The girl says, "She doesn't want to go out with nobody."

It would be nice to have a scene where Maya Angelou plays a palm reader who reads Justice's palm.

It became a real trip with the whole idea of a road trip with these two guys and these two girls. The male character talks the whole movie about his cousin and Oakland. When they stop in Oakland to see his cousin, it turns out his cousin was shot the day before. We even need a scene where he talks to his cousin on the phone.

Justice and the postman can't stand each other. At one point, she even gets out on the road and says, "Fuck you, I'll walk home." She starts walking, and the postman starts to drive away. Her girlfriend starts going crazy. Cross-cut between the guy driving and Justice walking.

He thinks for a moment, then he ends up going back for her. Dissolve and the truck is alongside of her, then he has to convince her to get back into the truck.

Idea: It would be cool to try to incorporate the way economic disparity plays a part in black relationships.

1/11/92

Idea: Justice walks down the street; in the background a couple of brothers are being shaken down by the cops. Also, I'm thinking about making Janet Jackson, Justice. She'd be good if she can act.

Justice's internal troubles are another cause of her trouble getting along with the postman, on the way up to Oakland. The mail guy has a kid, a baby by the girl he got pregnant when he was sixteen, seventeen. After work, he goes by her house to give her some money from the check he just cashed. She got another nigga there that starts talking shit. This becomes a topic of discussion between him and Justice.

As you can see, the way the scenes are forming, I wrote them down in paragraph form in my diary.

Back from a Sunday excursion with Baha Jackson, the kid who played Doughboy in *Boyz N the Hood*. I took Baha and one of his friends to the Slawson Swap Meet. I got a hat embroidered, it reads: South Central Cinema, my new motto. I got a new idea for *Poetic Justice* where Justice and her girlfriend are in the swap meet talking about—what else?—men. This will start off with the camera looking at and reading signs that say "Nails," "Purses," etc. Then we tilt down to their backs where they're talking. Also do a reverse angle of them walking from the front. The shot ends when they come to a stand that sells fake hair for weaves. Justice's friend buys some hair for some braids.

DIALOGUE: You should be patronizing black business. [Reply:] I patronize black businesses. I bought some conditioner from Chuck's beauty supply yesterday.

Idea: Justice goes on the trip because her psychic tells her to go. Psychic: "You make bad choices in men." Maya Angelou.

We see Justice talking to her psychic as we cross-cut with the mailman taking his baby away. He takes the baby away from his child's mother to be raised by his mother.

DIALOGUE, MAILMAN: We're going to go see Grandmama.
PSYCHIC: You will meet a man of purpose, honor, of warmth and strength.

I wrote a poem, "Same Ol', Same Ol' ":

SAME OL', SAME OL'

The circle is the same
The ultimate father is at work.
Time.
He wears on me, guiding me everywhere and nowhere.
To and fro, work and school and then home.
Same ol', same ol'
It has been two years since my heart stopped beating.

Now I know why I'm making movies and not a poet. This is definitely not my strength. I got to find a new way to do this.

1/20/91

Good news. Spike called me and he's coming into town tomorrow. He wants to hook up with me. That's cool, because we never have really had a chance to talk. He knows I admire his work. It should be exciting.

On another note, I came up with an idea on how Justice and the mailman meet. She gets into the truck.

MAILMAN: What's up?
JUSTICE: You work at the post office?
(He looks at her funny, like that's a stupid question.)
JUSTICE: You got a kid?
MAILMAN: Why?
JUSTICE: Because I don't go out with niggas that got kids.
MAILMAN: Who says we was dating?
JUSTICE: I just thought I'd let you know that.
MAILMAN: Oh, you got a kid?
JUSTICE: Why?
MAILMAN: Cause I don't date bitches that got kids. (and he starts up the car).

Character note: The mailman character is a wannabe rap artist. He's good, but he doesn't have a focus yet. The experience of meeting Justice and his cousin dying, helps him realize that his purpose as a rapper lies in telling stories about the streets.

When he gets to Oakland, his auntie gives him the recording equipment owned by his cousin. He goes to his cousin's wake and talks over the dead body. This should be an intimate scene. He finds his voice, his niche.

DIALOGUE: I'm a government employee—I can do anything I want. I got benefits, credit union, my shit is set.

As it is, I want Ice Cube as the mailman. I need a scene reminiscent of *Five Easy Pieces* with Ice Cube doing what Jack Nicholson did: He wants his sandwich done his way.

Idea: Justice reads *Jive* and *Black Romance* and those other cheap-ass magazines.

1/24/91

I've got a new idea for a character in *Poetic Justice,* her name is Aunt Jessie. She's the owner of the beauty supply and salon Justice works for. Jessie takes Justice under her wing like a mother. She is the ultimate hootchie momma: complete with the hair, nails, and clothes. Fendi like a motherfucker. With this character, I can nix the idea of having a spiritual reader or psychic. It is Jessie who talks to Justice about making bad choices in men and the types of men she'll eventually meet.

Jessie's boyfriend is a high roller who launders money through the beauty supply shop. Jessie is in her late twenties, early thirties, and is as fine as hell. Oh yeah, I also want a hair show in Oakland. That is Justice's motivation for going up north. Her friend invites her on the drive up and she declines. Then when the crunch time comes, her car breaks down. She doesn't want to use her credit card, and all her friends are all gone, have left. She has no choice but to go on the trip.

The first act happens in South Central L.A., the second act happens on the road, the third act happens in Oakland and L.A. That's the whole breakdown.

I want a shot of the mail truck overhead, bass booming from the truck, we see the Pacific Ocean and rolling green hills.

2/1/91

Tuesday was a good day. I showed *Boyz N the Hood* to the studio, that's Frank Price, Marvin Antonosky, Stephanie Allain, and a few other Columbia people. Quincy Jones was there too. I sat next to Cube during the screening. He laughed all the way through and cried on all the right parts. All in all, the studio is happy. Now we have to get ready for a preview screening. . . . Here's a list of ideas of character names for *Poetic Justice*: J-Bones, Peaches, Precious, Justice, Lucky, and Pookie.

Idea: When we first see Jessie, she asks Justice to read her a poem. Justice says she left her notebook in the car.

Today I started the writing of *Poetic Justice.* I only wrote one page today. Tomorrow I'll try to finish the opening scenes, then get into the "Same Ol', Same Ol' " sequence. I'm also going to buy some three-by-five cards to block out scenes with. If I can hold to the old rule of three pages a day, five days a week, then I can finish the script in two months. This is the same rule that got me through school, so I guess it can apply to the real world also.

I want Joe Torry to play J-Bone, a mailman who goes and picks up mail from the beauty shop. He goes back to the post office where we meet Lucky. [What ended up happening was those scenes were reversed.] I want Joe Torry to play this role so bad. The mail bag goes into the truck and back to the post office where it's picked up by Lucky. Lucky is put back on drive detail by his supervisor, that's why he has to go to Oakland.

The first image in the "Same Ol', Same Ol' " montage is we come down on Justice at Markell's grave. She places some flowers on his grave and walks away. Dissolve to different images of South Central. I'm still trying to write some poetry for *Poetic Justice.* "Same Ol', Same Ol' ":

the leaves of summer flow
seasons come and seasons go

love will wither and love will grow
same ol', same ol'

I want to have the Jessie salon scene open with Iesha, Justice's friend, getting her braids done. I changed Peaches to Iesha because of the Another Bad Creation song, "Iesha." Also, I knew a lot of Ieshas in elementary school and junior high school, and they always end up being cute.

Iesha talks about her other friend who got beat up by her boyfriend, saying the girl wears sunglasses now. The other women give her feedback: "Shit, I wouldn't take that shit, girl." "Yeah, that's cool, just go to sleep."

Subplot: J-Bone and Iesha are a real volatile couple. Sometimes they're lovey-dovey and sometimes they fight. J-Bone is an abusive boyfriend. At one point, he starts kicking Iesha's ass and Lucky has to jump in. While the couple fight, Lucky has flashbacks of his mother getting beat by his pops. Lucky and J-Bone fight and argue. Lucky ends up leaving him on the road. This ends up making Lucky look real good with Justice. I don't want to make Iesha the typical victimized woman. In truth, she's the castrating bitch that downgrades her man at every turn. She has nothing good to say about J-Bone, not even sexually. Basically, Iesha is the same as many other black American women: a perfect feminine nightmare that might have conjured up Shaharazad Ali. I just have to remember not to make her unsympathetic. Regular brothers who see this film will automatically side with J-Bone. Tha sisters should be on Iesha's side. Having this conflict is keeping in tune with my goal of making this a nontraditional romance.

JUSTICE: Damn, you just telling everybody's business.

IESHA: Yeah, I'd tell your business too if you had something worth telling.

Note: J-Bone has been changed to Chicago, a brother from Chicago who's a sharp dresser, but no brain. He has a fade, and he wears Chicago Bulls and Bears gear all the time. And Air Jordan up the yang.

3/15/91

Today I spoke at the ABET (Alliance of Black Electricians and Technicians) brunch. It was cool because I spoke about nepotism. I summed it up by saying nepotism isn't bad if it's black nepotism.

On another note, I really need to get myself on a regular schedule with my writing. I'm only on my seventh page of *Poetic Justice.* Tomorrow, I'm turning over a new leaf. I'm going to wake up at six or seven and write at least three pages of the new script. I should do this every day now that I have time. The picture's done, got to get another one in the hopper.

3/21/91
3 A.M.

Tonight I got to page twelve on *PJ.* I'd like to get to page fifteen by Sunday. I have to remember after Lucky gets dissed by the ladies in the salon, we go with him to the post office and then to the projects. Somewhere between the two we have to go back to the salon where Justice is finishing braiding Iesha's hair. They talk about life and how they used to go out together, but now they don't 'cause Justice's life has changed. Mention is made of Iesha's boyfriend, Chicago, and the trip up north. The hair show is Monday, this is Saturday, the first day in the film.

3/22/91

I'm on my way back from New York. I read over my first twelve pages of *Poetic Justice,* and I know it's the hype. I really need to crack the whip on this one to finish it before June to go into preproduction by July. This writing my own poetry shit ain't working. I've been reading some more of Maya Angelou's poems. I think we should average three poems per act, with the second act having more poems because of its length.

Idea: Justice and Iesha do "Phenomenal Woman" together in front of Lucky and Chicago. They learned the poem when they were eighth graders at Audubon Junior High School.

Idea: In the projects, I got to have a small-time dealer counting out one-dollar bills like my aunt Susan's boyfriend used to do. The brother counts out ones so it'll make him look like he has a lot of money. He's an old friend of Lucky's, and they have babies by the same female.

4/5/91

I think I've come up with a good ending to *Poetic Justice.* In the last five minutes of the film, Lucky goes on his regular route, which brings him to the hair shop. Things are as normal. Jessie sees him and cuts her eyes toward Justice. We should have a shot like this starting on Jessie, then quick pan over to Justice, who looks up. Cut to Lucky, who walks up. Scene is just like the beginning. Lucky says, "Y'all didn't get nothing but bills." Lucky turns to walk out after he and Justice look into each other's eyes, then he walks out. Justice runs out to Lucky to ask him to lunch at 1 o'clock at the Crenshaw Cafe. Then at 12:55, Justice is waiting in a seat at the Crenshaw Cafe. She receives compliments from guys that pass by. One man asks if she wants to buy some T-shirts. We will build up the tension between 12:55 and 1:00. Then it is 1:03, and Justice almost can't take it anymore. She gets up to leave, and he comes up from behind her. They say a couple of things. "You hungry?" says Lucky. "Yeah," Justice says. "Really hungry." They sit down to lunch as we cut to a view of them from across the street. The End.

Poetic Justice was the first movie I wrote in my professional career. It didn't take me two months, as I originally planned. I started in February and finished in August. This was because I was busy with the editing and release of my first film, *Boyz N the Hood.* I ended up having to do publicity, take the film to Cannes—distractions I didn't have the luxury of having when I was in college! In school, reading scripts always helped me to learn how to write one. I hope film school students who read this book will similarly get something out of this. Notice I have notes in my script on camera angles and how I'd like to shoot things. This is because I also direct my scripts. So read on, and enjoy. But remember that the script is only a blueprint to the film. There are some things in the script that didn't get shot or ended up being cut from the film. There are things in the film that aren't in the script—these were improvised and brainstormed on set. Peace Out.

John Singleton
South Central Cinema
Dealing A New Hand

8
Postproduction

*i*n a small, dark room on the first floor of the Capra Building, John Singleton and Bruce Cannon, the film editor of *Poetic Justice*, sit and talk. Cannon, an attractive thirtysomething man with a ready sense of humor, worked with Singleton on *Boyz N the Hood*. The two know each other well. They speak to each other in half-sentences, whispering numbers and times back and forth, without prologue or niceties:

"Eleven minutes and forty-three seconds."

"You gonna just have beats, or is it gonna be a song?"

"Kalil's song—go from the nails, to the head, to Iesha."

The relationship between a director and his editor is very special. A director counts on an editor to be a second set of eyes: to choose the best takes, to cut the right scenes, to make the movie flow. Cannon explains that it's not a job for the impatient. "You go through the film once and make little changes," he says. "You go through it again, you make more little changes. Then you keep going through it until it's completely refined."

Singleton and Cannon watch the film on a twenty-inch screen, the size of a small TV. Reels of negatives feed the images onto the screen—as high-tech as filmmaking can be, these reels and this screen resemble nothing so much as an oversize Viewmaster. Cannon explains how the film is slowly but surely being cut down to viewing length. "We're down to fourteen reels from sixteen," Cannon explains. "*Boyz N the Hood* was twelve reels. I have a feeling this will be on twelve, too."

Singleton and Cannon begin editing the scene that had been shot for the screen test—Lucky and Justice's first meeting. It's been seven months since that tense first day when Singleton, the actors, and a preliminary crew gathered for the screen test. Everyone was still nervous then, unsure of what lay ahead. Now the actors and the crew are all gone, leaving behind the fruit of their efforts: walking, talking images captured forever on celluloid.

Is editing easier than the actual shooting process? Is the painstakingly detailed work easier to manage than the day-to-day squabbles, mishaps, and dramas of a film set? "Definitely," says Singleton. "Editing is *a lot* easier than shooting. It's less stressful. It's about positioning shots around. I've got enough coverage on everything"—coverage being a desired number of takes—"that I can pull out the shots I want."

"Mace."

Cannon stops the shot freeze-frame as actor Tupac Shakur mouths the word "Mace." Turning to Singleton, Cannon says, "I think we should go wide here. It's the kind of word that lends itself to wideness." Day in and day out, the editing process continues. Slowly. Shot by shot.

October 5, 1992
Sacramento

a long line of moviegoers is assembling outside a generic multiplex in the central California city of Sacramento. This multiracial group, consisting mainly of teens and twenty-somethings, have assembled for the first test screening of *Poetic Justice*.

For the audience, it's a free movie. For Singleton, it's more than a little nerve-racking. The audience is here to view the rough cut of his movie. It is *only* a rough cut, but it will be judged and assessed all the same. What if they don't *like* it? What if they don't *get* it? If nothing else, it will be a learning process. It's still early enough in the editing process to make changes.

The *Poetic Justice* posse includes not only Singleton but Stephanie Allain, the studio's creative executive in charge of the project; Michael Nathanson, President of Worldwide Production; Mark Gill, Senior-Vice-President of Publicity and Promotion; Sid Ganis, President of Marketing and Distribution; Steve Nicolaides; Dwight Williams, Associate Producer and Director of Development; Bruce Cannon and Assistant Film Editor Margaret Guinee; and Cassandra Butcher, Unit Publicist.

The movie is being screened in Sacramento instead of Los Angeles in hopes of getting a more average, nonindustry-affiliated audience. It is also hoped that here up north, the media will be less likely to try to sneak into the screening. There's already been one prominent gossip item on the film: On the *Joan Rivers* show that morning, not only was the Sacramento test screening mentioned, but Rivers said the movie was allegedly too long. Only a rough cut, the movie is far from what it will become—in terms of length or anything else. Needless to say, though, this bad buzz has not put the executives or the filmmakers in the best of moods.

Once the test audience is seated, Singleton and his group take their seats toward the back of the theater. There is a hush of anticipation as the house lights dim, then the bright burst of color as the movie begins. From the very first scene at the drive-in, the audience responds positively *and* loudly. When Justice and Markell (played by rapper Q-Tip) start kissing, the teenagers swoon, poking each other and shouting at the screen. At different points throughout the film, there is laughter and clapping. Singleton is visibly pleased, more caught up in the audience's reaction than anything else. These are his peers. These are the people he makes movies for.

Still, there are some obvious rough spots in the film. By the third or fourth poem, the youthful—and clearly nonliterary—audience is screaming "Another poem!" as if they were trapped in a boring English class. They also seem distracted by the beautiful scenery along Pismo Beach, Big Sur, and Highway 1. "Where's that?" some people call out. It becomes clear that even though these kids live in California, they haven't been outside the borders of their own communities. It is as Singleton has said; "There are people in South Central who have never been to the beach, even though it's only a few miles away." As Justice walks through the field of zebras, the audience guffaws at what they see as pure fantasy. It is too far from their world, their imaginations are too constricted by issues of race and class to accept the beauty of the California coastline as the setting for a John Singleton movie.

When the film is over, Singleton and his group leave the theater as the audience fills out response sheets, also known as "the cards." A few minutes later, an independent marketing group tallies the response behind a closed door. Singleton is anxious, knocking on the door and asking to be let in. "Just a minute, John," calls out Nathanson, who is in the room with the marketing group.

When Nathanson emerges, the news is good: an overwhelmingly positive response. Clearly, the audience enjoyed the film, and it touched many of the viewers personally. But there was also criticism: namely, the zebra scene, which repeatedly came under fire. The audience cited it as the scene that they liked least and found the least believable. "Zebras in California?" they asked, although Hearst Castle, which once had a whole field of zebras, is located only a few miles down the coast from Sacramento. Some of the other responses included:

> "The movie is packed with stars! But the main thing is this movie took us out of our everyday environment and showed us there is more of the world out there."
> "I would say it is a good movie for young black couples because it describes some of the problems in their relationships. It is a very real movie. Better than *Boyz N the Hood.* Go J.S., get busy."

"The movie was suprisingly funny. I was very surprised at how well Janet did."

"It had so many deep and meaningful moments. There were some scenes that you really had to pay attention to, such as the poetry by Maya Angelou and the scene where the Last Poets talk about revolution and the idea of black women respecting themselves."

Again and again, the audience wondered "What happened to Chicago?" proving that Joe Torry's brush-toting, wannabe loverboy character had left his mark! Overall, it seemed that the audience liked the movie, felt it moved too slow in parts, and unequivocally didn't get the zebra scene. Weeks later, Singleton will make the difficult decision to cut the zebras—one of his favorite elements of the film. "It's hard," he says, his voice filled with emotion. "It was one of the most difficult things I had to do. But it kept going above people's heads. But now the movie is tighter." Then, as if to cheer himself up, he says, "It'll go on the laser disc—there's *always* the laser disc."

December 1, 1992

*t*he newly elected president, Bill Clinton, invites Maya Angelou to write a poem for his swearing-in ceremony. It had been sixteen years since a new American president had commissioned a poet to write a poem for his swearing-in; the last time had been in 1977, when James Dickey read a poem for the inaugural of Jimmy Carter. Before that, Robert Frost had moved the masses with a reading of his poem "The Gift Outright" at the swearing-in of John F. Kennedy.

Clinton's invitation to Dr. Angelou was an honor of the highest order. The fact that Dr. Angelou is both black and female, many citizens understood as symbolic of the changing face of leadership. The fact that Dr. Angelou appears in *Poetic Justice* and that it is her poetry that moves the film elevates the project to a whole new level.

January 20, 1993
Washington, D.C.

*J*ohn Singleton, along with scores of prominent Americans from the arts and the media (including James Earl Jones, Sidney Poitier, Whoopi Goldberg, and Oprah Winfrey) gather for the swearing-in of the forty-second President of the United States—William Jefferson Clinton. Dr. Maya Angelou stands on the stage with President Clinton and reads her inaugural poem "On the Pulse of the Morning" in her deep, rich voice, with the carriage of royalty and the storytelling cadences of a wise African *griot*.

Singleton enjoys himself at the MTV Inaugural Ball and at the various fetes, dinners, and luncheons on and around Capitol Hill. When he began writing *Poetic Justice* and first decided to use the poetry of Dr. Angelou, he had no idea that she would be so thrust into the public's eye, so prominently honored on this eve of change. But it was instinct that he had trusted throughout the making of *Boyz N the Hood*. With *Poetic Justice* as well, his instinct about Dr. Angelou had been right on target.

"Maya Angelou's writing the inaugural poem ennobles the film, it classes up the poetry and the public conception of the character as a poetess," says Steve Nicolaides. "The best thing in that last spring, when we were shooting the family reunion, there were something like eighteen kids acting as extras. I went out and got all these copies of her books, and she read to them in that magnificent voice; then she signed books for all the kids. Now they have something that's important and socially signficant."

"Maya Angelou's involvement in the film lends the stamp of a literary touch," says Stephanie Allain. "She's deified in the black community, in terms of young, black women. Now she's been tapped by the president as the spokesperson for the arts."

January 23, 1993
Culver City, California

*I*n the Busby Berkeley Theater, there is a movie-size screen facing two rows of people. In front of each person, there is a panel of controls, knobs, and dials. If it weren't for the people's civilian clothing, it would seem like a scene straight out of *Star Trek*. The first row of people, however, are sound mixers: Bill Benton, the music mixer; Sergio Reyes, the dialogue mixer; and Bob Beamer, the head of special effects. The second row of people are the filmmakers and their team: Singleton, Nicolaides, Cannon, and sound editor Greg Hedgepath.

"This is the final dub—sort of," explains Cannon. "All of the popular music that you hear will be replaced by original music that John is having recorded for the soundtrack. We started two weeks ago with sound effects only. We went through all twelve reels concentrating on, just listening to sound effects: helicopters, sirens, footsteps. For the most part, the sound editors come in and create the aural world behind the picture from scratch. Then we went through and heard dialogue with the replaced ADR. Automatic Dialogue Replacement, also known as looping, is dialogue that is rerecorded for clarity or improved delivery. Janet had a lot of looping to do—we had her do all the poems again."

The things that most moviegoing audiences take for granted— dialogue that matches an actor's lip movements, atmospheric sounds that don't overpower the spoken word—is, in and of itself, a science. "It's a hard process," explains Nicolaides, "because you have to have the ability to change sound, to blend it smoothly. But like all abilities, it's also a curse because it's all electronic. It's as exploratory and technically diagnostic as a doctor trying to figure out what's wrong. That's what the art of mixing is all about."

The copy of *Poetic Justice* being played on the screen is black and white, and if it weren't for the 1990s hairstyles and clothes, you might think it was an old movie. "It's cheaper this way," says Singleton, sounding more like a cost-conscious producer than a typical spendthrift director. "You make dupe prints to work with. Black and white costs less. They're not the same quality because they break easily when you work with them. They need to be expendable."

On the screen, Lucky and Angel curse each other out. The profanity, just like that in *Boyz N the Hood,* is *colorful,* to say the least. Singleton sits with a laptop computer on the desk in front of him; during breaks, he works on the script for his next film. He looks up at the screen, at the ruckus and cursing, and laughs. "I have no cursing in my next movie," he says. "No *shits,* no *fucks.* A lot of racial slurs—*cracker, nigger.* But that's about it." Nicolaides pipes in, " 'I was born the son of a poor, black sharecropper,' " quoting his favorite line from Steve Martin's *The Jerk.*

Back on the screen, Lucky, J-Bone and a gangsta are knocking the living daylights out of one another. Greg Hedgepath explains how they recorded the sounds of someone getting beaten up: "You put a mike on a pole, see? Then you cover the mike with a boxing glove. Then you swing the pole and hit a 150-pound side of beef." Everyone gets interested, asking, "Really?" Singleton laughs. "Wow, that's funny." Although all the guys in the room are in the business, it seems there is always something new to learn. The magic of moviemaking never fails to impress those who are in love with the craft.

During the editing process it becomes clear that perhaps Justice and Lucky get together too easily. Filmmakers believe in happily-ever-after endings, but there has to be a process for two people to fall in love believably. Late last fall, Singleton decided to do pickup shots with Lucky and Justice that would ease the flow of their relationship. "We shot two scenes in two days," says Nicolaides. "The first scene is Justice in her bedroom, making the decision to stop wearing black and gray all the time, to give up the ghosts she's been mourning for. Since the zebra scene is no longer in the film, the poem 'Phenomenal Woman' is now in this bedroom scene, and it's wonderful. The second scene, which was *my* idea, is Lucky in the garage, plugging in his cousin's music equipment and thinking about Justice. It makes the end of the movie believable. The way it was before, you just don't believe that he comes in the next day in a good mood and gets back together with her. These new scenes show that part of what the movie is about is giving up your anger, giving up your instinct to pull back."

During the fight scene with Lucky, J-Bone, and the gangsta, a Felix the Cat cartoon plays on the TV screen. It is, of course, no coincidence. Singleton asked for that cartoon specifically, and rights had to be purchased. "It's the details that make a film what it is," says Singleton. "That Felix cartoon is so funny," says Cannon, who has seen this reel a thousand times and *still* finds humor in it. "It adds so much to the scene. It takes the edge of the violence when the fight starts. But then the crescendo in the cartoon grows as the fight escalates."

As Singleton and Cannon discuss the existential qualities of Felix the Cat, the sound mixers are putting the "fight sounds" into the fight scene: "What do you think? We thumping them too much?" asks one guy. "No, that sounds good to me," says another. "If we're gonna go for it, we should go for it."

As Lucky grabs Keisha and leaves Crystal's house, the screaming and fighting continue full force. "It always blows my mind," says Nicolaides, "how well adjusted this little girl is and how nice her mom was. How could you bring this four-year-old to work and hand her over to a bunch of twenty-year-olds yelling 'Fuck you' and 'You asshole'? We saw her again when we did pickup shots, and she was the same sweet girl."

February 1, 1993
New York City

*a*fter viewing the movie, Q-Tip is back home on the East Coast. Here, Q-Tip who plays Markell, talks about Singleton, *Poetic Justice,* and the art of film:

As a director, I saw that John has a lot of insight, he has a lot of excitement in what he sees, his vision. So much so that the way he conveys it is different from the normal person. Like a good prize fighter has a good left hook, what John has going for him is good dialogue. He'll never go wrong with that.

As a person, you can see that John is compassionate, compassionate for the people and for where he's come from. The best thing about John is that he's a regular kid. He called my house and he was talking to my mom, saying, "Yes, ma'am." He's just a regular kid doing movies.

The only difference between making a movie and cutting an album is the fact that there's a camera in front of you, the audio-visual. Doing music videos helps you as an actor-musician, so you know the environment of film, you feel more comfortable.

Poetic Justice is so different from *Boyz N the Hood* because it is a love story. This is more from the girls' perspective although it's another coming-of-age movie. You either gonna like *Justice* or you gonna hate it. There's gonna be no in between. I liked it.

Justice didn't remind me of girls in my neighborhood because I'm from New York. In New York, girls aren't afraid to tell you how they feel if you vex them. There's all that game shit out here, fast-talking and getting over. L.A. is more laid back.

Soundtracks ain't nothing but a tool to make more money for both parties involved—the film company and the record company. What really matters is the score. Stanley Clarke's soundtrack is cool. Of course, I could've done better. (Just kidding.)

John *is* the first filmmaker of the hip-hop generation. He grew up on what hip-hop was saying, what hip-hop was doing. He grew up with the culture, so he's gonna have that hip-hop sensibility.

February 15, 1993
Culver City, California

*I*t's been almost three years since a film school kid with a powerful script and the *cojones* to match walked into Stephanie Allain's office. In that short period of time, they've gone from being adversaries to creative partners, from being strangers to being friends. In the process, they've now made two movies together. Here, Stephanie Allain talks about the film and its creator:

It's interesting because I think at a certain point during post-production, the filmmakers and the producers bond, and you don't hear from them much. Then they come out of reclusiveness and they show us the picture. The first time we saw the film, we were really surprised. There were so many good things, and the audience response was overwhelming. Clearly, though, there were some things we felt needed trimming and adjusting. Then it became a question of talking to John and getting him to make the changes that we felt, and the audiences felt, would improve the film—without intruding on his own vision. Luckily, John was able to incorporate the various suggestions into the film in a way in which he felt comfortable. Postproduction has been incredibly positive in that way. We feel like we've gotten everything we needed on this movie, and I think John feels like he was able to hold on to his vision.

On *Boyz N the Hood,* everybody was an enemy. John was just trying to preserve his vision. That's what it took to get that movie made. He hadn't solidified in his creative space, and he was learning as he went along—and rightfully so. This time he'd already achieved some success, and he knew he had his creative autonomy. So this time he listened more, and he could more easily incorporate any comments into a creative process. I didn't have to walk on eggshells. I was freer to bring what I could do to the table. Artistically, he was ready to interact more and elevated the whole project.

I think that in the beginning, it remained to be seen if Janet could pull this off. Based on the footage we saw early on and her ability as a performer within the music arena, we were quite optimistic. But clearly, she went beyond the call of duty. She delivered as an actress, in my opinion, in incredibly surprising and pleasing ways. Part of the reason is she's a real person, and she has real experiences she can call upon. Scenes where she cries, for example. It's impossible to ask an actress to cry real tears for five takes in a row. But Janet does it—it's incredible. She has an innate ability to connect with her inner emotions that is really amazing. So it all worked out.

For me, in my last viewing of it, what I realized is that it's more than a love story. It's a movie about what the arts can do for you. This is especially important in the inner city, where funding for the arts is being cut in public school. I think the movie shows how the arts—poetry, language, music—lift us up and how we can incorporate the three R's into a life that makes sense and is challenging. For me, the movie is about how the arts can save your life—that's an incredible mature message. How you can save yourself from madness through the arts, whether you leave the inner city or whether you stay. And I think Maya Angelou's involvement just elevates that message.

I'm not worried about how the movie will compare with *Boyz N the Hood.* I think *Poetic Justice* speaks for itself because it's not an urban drama. So right there, off the bat, it's a different type of movie. It's a romance that is very different from *Boyz.* John's first movie was clearly *boys* in the hood. This title character is a woman. On a certain level, it'll be hard to draw comparisons for that reason alone.

Obviously, it's the same filmmaker. The positive aspect of that is that the film starts in South Central, a territory John has proven he knows well. But what I think we want to say is that this is from the guy who brought you *Boyz N the Hood,* but this is a whole new world. So we hope to bring back the *Boyz* audience, but also bring in a strong women's audience with this romance.

On a lot of levels, I think *Poetic Justice* is a better film—more complex, more mature. It's not as black and white in terms of good and evil. I think John and the studio are just going to have to be tough and say, "This is another movie. Please judge it on its own merits."

Vivien Scott, vice-president of A&R at Epic Records was not only instrumental in introducing American audiences to the rude-boy rhythms of ragamuffin music by signing dance-hall artist Shabba Ranks, she also collaborated on such successful Epic soundtracks as *Singles* and *Honeymoon in Vegas.* It was to this young dread-locked music executive that Singleton brought the task of creating a soundtrack for *Poetic Justice:*

"I thought *Poetic Justice* was very funny. It was very touching and it was very sad. It pulled every emotion out of me—except for anger, that's the only emotion I didn't have! I thought Janet was incredible—I thought she *looked* just—what's the word? *Voluptuous.* My favorite scene in the movie was when Janet is lying on the floor in her living room, listening to Stevie Wonder in the dark. I thought that was very touching. You could feel her loneliness.

When I saw the movie, I knew the soundtrack needed a street element. I think the demographics are going to be young. When I say young, I don't mean twelve or thirteen. I mean sixteen, seventeen, eighteen. But it's not a hard movie, it's not *Boyz N the Hood,* it's a love story. So you'll get the love element from our R&B artists like Babyface and Miki Howard, and you'll get the street element from artists like TLC and Gang Starr. I should say that the artists are all tentative. We're in various stages of negotiation and there will only be ten or twelve tracks on the soundtrack, so we'll have to cut a few songs. Right now, the artists we'd like to work with are Babyface; A Tribe Called Quest; Karyn White; Arrested Development; Digital Underground; Diamond and the Psychotic Neurotics; Toni! Tony! Toné!; Pete Rock and C. L. Smooth; Snoop Dog; Super Cat; TLC; Keith Washington; a new group called Sister; and Tupac.

How important is a soundtrack to a movie's success? It depends. I think this movie is so strong that it'll sell regardless. But we're putting the soundtrack out a month before the movie, in June. So when the movie comes out, these kids are going to be *dying* for it, because you know, the soundtrack is going to be *dope.*

When John Singleton was looking for a composer for *Boyz N the Hood,* he knew exactly whom to call: composer Stanley Clarke. Singleton had actually met Clarke backstage at the *Arsenio Hall* show, minutes before Clarke was scheduled to go on. "You're going to work with me on my picture," Singleton told the composer, who remembers his reaction being something like "Sure, kid." Later, Clarke would wonder if perhaps he had been a little rude. Obviously not, because Singleton *did* call him to work on *Boys* and again on *Poetic Justice.* Here Clarke gives the score on composing for film:

I've actually been composing music since I was fourteen, fifteen years old. I started out playing piano, then bass. I can also play some drums. I play the recording studio, as they say.

Six years ago, a friend of mine was directing *Pee-wee's Playhouse,* this show that came on TV on Saturdays, for kids. They had a show on childbirth that they wanted some unusual music for. I was acting in something else that the director was doing—I was playing a bass player in some Barry Manilow special. And he said, "Well, you know, I also do this *Pee-wee's Playhouse* thing. Would you like to do the music for this childbirth episode?" I did that show, and I had a lot of fun with it. Then that episode was up for an Emmy, and I thought, "This is pretty great." The fact that I *wasn't* a film composer made my work different, because I was fresh coming in. So it got noticed. Basically, after that, it was a matter of sticking with it. I got an agent, and I would go do interviews for scoring jobs. I've been doing it ever since.

I felt very close to the subject matter of *Boyz N the Hood*— the father-son bonding, the role of black men and how that relates to society—it was nice to see a film focusing on these issues. There were basically two layers to the score we did for *Boyz*—the hip-hop music, which you don't hear much of and the actual underscore, which is what brings out whatever emotion you're trying to communicate. John and I would sit and watch the movie, talking about how the music could enhance the scene: "You could pump this scene up with some violins." or "Let's put some tension here with the music." Sprinkling magic dust is the only way I can describe scoring a movie.

One of my favorite scenes in *Boyz N the Hood* is when Doughboy is taking revenge for his brother's death—the traditional thing to do is to highlight it with strings, thriller music. Instead, what we did is put a slow, hip-hop bass drum under it with very few instruments. Basically what we composed was a death march, which made you feel the sadness of it. Doughboy has to kill somebody because his brother was killed, then somebody will kill Doughboy—and basically the killing never ends. John really liked that sadness in the death march. It brought out something that wasn't even in the actors' heads. Sometimes you can score against the scene, putting in ideas and emotions that aren't even there.

Normally, when you see a scene with young black people, it's just rap music. I actually resent that because it's very thin. Just because someone is fifteen, sixteen years old, wearing their baseball cap backward, doesn't mean that they don't feel loneliness or beauty, emotions you can't express with an 808 bass drum. In *Boyz*, there were scenes with Ricky and his mother, and there was this sweet, almost sappy music to show how much she loves him. Normally, they would just put in some congas and bongos like the old *Shaft* movies, which I resented. *Boyz* was scored as if Robert De Niro or any other major actor was up there on the screen.

This is even more true in the case of *Poetic Justice*. It's a deeper film than it might have been had someone else directed it, or done the music, or produced it. There's a lot of emotion in *Poetic Justice* and it's pulled out with the music. A good score should really pull it out. When people come to a theater, they don't come to experience some cold, heartless thing. People like to feel things on a visceral level where you don't even need the dialogue—you hear the music and you see the faces and you feel "Oh man, this is a drag," or "This is something happy."

Poetic Justice was more difficult to score than *Boyz* for a number of reasons. There are more characters, and I think the story is more complex. I'm hoping the end result will seem like a simple story; sometimes the most simple, beautiful things are very complex at the core. The score is kind of the threat that runs through the film. I was kinda lucky. In scoring, you can be the greatest technician and have the most knowledge about music, but there's a bit that's all luck where you have to wait for that melody to come into your head. So basically I waited for that melody, and luckily, it came.

John has a lot of insight about music in a film. He may not think he does, but he does. He knows what he wants the music to do. If for the rest of his life as a director, he can hold on to that, the score will always work. The music is sort of the emotional glue that's in any film, that something that makes you go through the film. Before the music, *Poetic Justice* was difficult to stick with. You didn't *feel* everything watching it one or two times, you had to look at it many times. When we scored the film, we tried to create a thread, that emotional glue, so the average guy off the street doesn't have to search for the point. The movie is about this girl Justice, she's a poet, and once I found her theme—everything else was icing on the cake.

I think that in the scenes where Justice is reading her poetry, there was a missing link. With poetry, the understanding really depends on the recipient. I might read something and get one meaning. You might read something and get a totally different meaning. With younger kids, who may not have read a lot of poetry, even getting the tone is an important level of understanding. What I did was, whenever she recited this poetry, I had a particular music that had this feel that anybody could get on any level. A person could listen to it, not even speak English, and know she's feeling something. A guy who didn't have a lot of education could hear the music and the poetry and say, "Man, she's deep." That's important, you don't want too many points in the film when it's just flat, that a viewer is getting nothing from the moment. Now the music helps the viewer to understand what she's feeling.

The poems take you out of the film, but not too far—just enough to give the film some depth. Before the score was added to *Boyz N the Hood,* some people found the movie hard to understand. I remember there was a guy at a screening who manages this group that was thinking about being on the soundtrack. Before the score, he said, "Man, what is this film about?" Later, when it was finished, it was as clear as a bell. With any creation—film, writing a song, anything—those last details make a big, big difference. What I like about John's films is that everything's important—nothing's just there. It all means something.

February 1993
Los Angeles

as the rites of postproduction continue, Singleton and his crew put the finishing touches on *Poetic Justice.* At the same time, every spare second, Singleton is busy on his laptop— writing his next script. "One thing you gotta know," he says. "At this point in the game, I'm here, I'm grounded. But my mind is onto the next movie. I'm printing out the script now."

Allain explains that this is to be expected. By the time *Poetic Justice* is released in theaters, it will be old news to its writer-director. "You pour yourself into a film every day for eight months," explains Allain, "then there's nothing left. He's done his job. His creative process, in terms of the story, is over. Being driven, being a writer-director, I think it's natural that he's eager to start putting that energy into his next project."

Watching the pure intensity of Singleton's splintered focus—editing *Poetic Justice,* working on the score, listening to tracks for the soundtrack, in addition to writing the script for his next film—it is hard to believe he is only twenty-five years old. One looks at the body of work he is amassing, the way he has touched people and the many things that he still has to say, and it brings to mind what Dr. Maya Angelou said about Singleton: "I saw at once the intelligence of the man. Everybody is born with talent. They may not know it, they may not show it, but they are born with it. But it's the rare person who has the intelligence, the discipline, the forthrightness, and the perseverance to architect a dream. I could sense this in him."

POETIC JUSTICE

AN ORIGINAL SCREENPLAY BY

John Singleton

POEMS BY

Maya Angelou

REVISED
Final Shooting Script
March 25, 1992
WGAw: #473171
New Deal Productions
From L.A.
South Central Cinema
Dealing A New Hand

COLUMBIA LOGO

TITLE CARD: ONCE UPON A TIME IN SOUTH CENTRAL LOS ANGELES

We hear voices: one male, the other female. From the tone of their speech and the accompanying music, we can tell we are entering a romantic scene.

FADE IN:

1 *INT. FANCY NEW YORK APARTMENT—DINING ROOM—NIGHT*

Where we see a romantic scene played out between a man and a woman. Both are white. The couple have just finished a candlelit dinner.

BRAD

> You like your wine? Want s'more?

She nods her approval.

PENELOPE

> Mmmmm you're good. Candles, dinner, wine. What's next?

He grins.

BRAD

> Let me set the mood.

He goes over to the stereo to turn it on. The Isley Brothers' "Between the Sheets" emanates from the speakers. Brad crosses to the couch and into a position in which to kiss Penelope. He does, and the sound of "Between the Sheets" is invaded by the remix of A Tribe Called Quest's "Bonita Applebum."

2 *EXT. COMPTON DRIVE-IN THEATER—DUSK: SFX*

Two lines of cars wait to enter the drive-in. The heavy bass sounds of hip-hop music mingle in the air with that of the many window speakers that play the movie. In the background we can see the couple in the previous scene kissing on a large movie screen. An LAPD helicopter flies overhead, transcending us into the next shot. Welcome back to South Central Los Angeles.

3 *INT. COMPTON DRIVE-IN THEATER—DUSK: SFX*

Overhead we see a shaft of light coming from the drive-in's projector. As we move past a few cars, their inhabitants are all in various throes of sexual foreplay. Some are kissing; others are actually making love. All the windows are steamed up. We hear the voices of the females as the men grunt, groan, moan, and beg over their bodies. Love is in the air.

CAR #1

Don't bite me so hard! You gotta be more gentle.

CAR #2
(softly)

Use your tongue. Just use your tongue.

CAR #3
(with heated passion)

Ohhhh! Oh, yes, ohhh! Oww! I'm sticking to the seat.

We come to last car, whose windows are crystal clear.

Things are just beginning to heat up between the couple inside the car. The woman is an "around the way" honey with soft brown skin, full brown eyes, and nice delicious full lips. This is Justice, who at seventeen is still looking for her place in the world.

The lucky man kissing her is her boyfriend, Markell, a small-time drug dealer and former gangsta. Justice reluctantly accepts his advances, but she ain't having it.

There is a window speaker, from which the sound of the movie filters into the car.

MARKELL

C'mon, let's get in the back seat.

JUSTICE

No, Markell, why can't we just watch the movie?

MARKELL

'Cause it's boring.

He goes to kiss her again. This time, it's a nice, long, juicy powerhouse kiss that causes the Richter scale to jump two points. Justice appears obviously affected. She asks the inevitable question.

JUSTICE

Markell, do you love me?

MARKELL

Of course I love you.

> JUSTICE

Why? Tell me why you love me.

> MARKELL
> *(looks around)*

Now?

> JUSTICE

Yeah, right now.

There is a pause. He thinks.

> MARKELL

Okay, I love you because you *too* fine.

> JUSTICE

Is that it?

> MARKELL

Yeah.

Justice looks dissatisfied.

> MARKELL

Can I have some sugar? Some butter? Some sweets?

> JUSTICE

No, not yet. Get me some popcorn.

Markell's face drops.

> JUSTICE

Pleazzze?!

Markell relents and gets out of the car. He takes two steps, turns on a heel, and leans into the car again.

> MARKELL

Hey, Justice! I was just thinking. I also love you 'cause when I was in tha county jail, you wrote me a lotta sweet poems.

Justice grins. Markell smiles and blows her a kiss good-bye.

4   INT. COMPTON DRIVE-IN CONCESSION STAND—NIGHT

There are only a few customers in line; all are Black or Hispanic. Markell gets in line, and time slows down. We notice the abruptness of the popcorn popping like gunshots, the sound and motion of the gurgling Orange

CONTINUED:

4 CONTINUED

Bang machine, and two thugs who stand in the corner talking to each other.

Markell seems noticeably nervous at their presence.

THE COUNTER

Where Markell finally arrives at the front of the line.

THE CORNER

Where one of the two thugs looks across the room at Markell. For a moment it looks as though he recognizes Markell. He turns back to continue to talk with his friend. A fight breaks out in another corner, and everyone's attention is drawn in that direction.

BACK TO COUNTER

Markell completes his transaction amidst the mayhem and walks away, popcorn in hand.

In the corner, the thug looks back toward the counter. On his face we see he now recalls where he has seen Markell before.

5 INT./EXT. COMPTON DRIVE-IN—THE CAR—NIGHT

Markell comes back to the car, glancing behind his back every so often.

> **MARKELL**
> (looking over his left shoulder)
>
> I think I saw these fools that Pete and I got beef with.

Markell turns to notice that Justice is not in the passenger seat. Justice leans up from the back seat to kiss his cheek and tenderly run her fingers around Markell's neck and shoulder.

We notice her long fingernails. Markell laughs and places the popcorn on the dashboard.

Our attention is drawn to the passenger window, where the drive-in speaker hangs. Romantic movie music flows into the car. On the driver's side the window is open. Suddenly, a pistol is placed next to Markell's head.

Time slows down. The gun is fired. Justice screams. The popcorn scatters, and the passenger window breaks from the traveling bullet. Time resumes.

Justice's screams turn to a whimper. There is blood on her hands. The drive-in speaker has now fallen on the passenger seat. We hear the romantic movie playing in the background.

OVERHEAD

As we PULL UP and away from the car. There are people running and screaming in every direction, and cars are leaving. These sounds overlap into . . .

5A *EXT. STOCK*

TITLE CARD: POETIC JUSTICE: *The sun rises behind the logo.*

DISSOLVE TO:

6 *INT. INGLEWOOD CEMETERY—DAY*

Where we come out of the leaves of a tree to see a garden of stones, concrete symbols of souls long past. There is one lone figure standing before a grave. We recognize this person as Justice. We also hear Justice speak in voice over. Over the following images she recites the first of many poems that move this story forward. BURN IN: TWO YEARS LATER

JUSTICE (V.O.)

"Alone. Lying, thinking. Last night. How to find my soul a home. Where water is not thirsty. And bread loaf is not stone. I came up with one thing. And I don't believe I'm wrong. That nobody. But nobody can make it out here alone."

DISSOLVE TO:

7 *INT. PACIFIC BEAUTY COLLEGE—DAY*

We move past many women. All of them are dressed in white smocks and are standing over the heads of other women who are seated in reclining beauty chairs. We hear the instructor giving a lesson in hair coloring. We end on Justice listening attentively and primping the hair of the woman in her chair.

JUSTICE (V.O.)

"Alone, all alone. Nobody, but nobody. Can make it out here alone. There are some millionaires with money they can't use. Their wives run round like banshees. Their children sing the blues."

DISSOLVE TO:

8 *EXT. PARKING LOT—DAY*

Where Justice puts some model heads into the trunk of her car.

9 *EXT. CRENSHAW BOULEVARD—DAY*

We see a CRENSHAW *sign up close go past the frame, left to right.*

MONTAGE OF IMAGES

We see various images of life in the Crenshaw district of South Central Los Angeles. Some are static; others are hand-held traveling shots, docu style.

10 EXT. LIQUOR STORE—DAY

There are images of people protesting a Korean liquor store, some protestors flash signs that read BUY BLACK/RECYCLE BLACK DOLLARS.

11 EXT. DONUT SHOP—DAY

We see a Cop come out with donuts and coffee for himself and his partner.

12 EXT. LEMERT PARK—DAY

A group of young men are curbside being interrogated by the LAPD. Nearby a brother with a video camera begins to record. He is chased away by tha police. In between some of these images, we SUPERIMPOSE the heads of some women being done. Over these images we continue to hear Justice's voice reading poetry. She is driving to work.

JUSTICE (V.O.)

"They've got expensive doctors, to cure their hearts of stone. But nobody. No nobody. Can make it out here alone. Alone, all alone. Nobody, but nobody. Can make it out here alone. Now if you listen closely, I'll tell you what I know. Storm clouds are gathering, the wind is gonna blow. The race of man is suffering, and I can hear the moan. Cause nobody. But nobody. Can make it out here alone."

We see Justice's car pull to the curb. It is a 1992 Honda Accord, complete with nice rims and tinted windows. The license plate reads 2 FUNKY.

13 INT. JUSTICE'S CAR—DAY

JUSTICE'S NOTEBOOK
Where we see Justice write the last stanza of the poem.

JUSTICE (V.O.)

"Alone, all alone. Nobody, but nobody. Can make it out here alone."

She closes her notebook. The cover reads NOTES OF A POETIC JUSTICE.

14 EXT. CITY STREET—DAY

Where Justice exits her car. She uses her automatic lock system, which sounds off "armed" when it locks. As she walks up the street, we see the same brothers established in the previous montage on their knees, with their hands behind their heads. Justice walks past them without acknowledging their condition.

15   *INT. JESSIE'S BEAUTY SALON AND SUPPLY—DAY*

Hair, nails, curlers, and combs. A woman picks up a phone and says, "Jessie's Beauty Salon and Supply." We have invaded this place on Friday, the busiest day of the week. We see many women of various ages, shapes, and sizes receiving hair care from different stylists.

No two heads are the same. Our attention and ears are drawn to the loud voice of one young woman who sits on the waiting couch flipping through a Black hair magazine. She has short-cut hair and eyes, nails, and temper of a Siamese cat. This is Iesha.

She is talking to Heywood, who is a spiritual person. He is so cosmic that his sexuality is often questioned. Nearby at another booth is Dexter, another male stylist who is very straight. His dick has guided him into the world of cosmetology.

HEYWOOD
(over images of nails, hair, etc.)

I know whatcha mean. I don't understand some of these women. I don't see how they can allow themselves to be so disrespected! My body is my temple! And a temple should never be defiled. Especially not in this case. I love myself.

Dexter shakes his head in shame at Heywood. He is massaging the head of one fine-ass sistah. She smiles. Dexter suavely bends down and says, "You like that don't cha." She nods in approval.

IESHA

Yeah, well, he just did my girl *all* wrong. She's as 'fraid as a cat. Got her going around wearing sunglasses, and you know how she like braggin about her pretty green eyes. So you know what's up with that. Top it off, she still in love with the nigga.

Justice walks in.

JUSTICE

You telling everybody's business.

IESHA

Yeah, I'd tell your business too if you had somethin to tell.

JUSTICE

You ready?

Iesha nods a yes.

CONTINUED:

15 CONTINUED

JUSTICE

You got your hair?

Iesha holds up a bag of synthetic hair. Justice walks toward her station, saying "Hello" to the other stylists on the fly.

16 INT. THE BABY ROOM—DAY

Where we notice a large playpen with four babies. All are dressed in Baby Guess, Air Jordans, and Fila. One baby plays with a beeper that goes off as he puts it in his mouth. This is the Baby Room, where the women leave their children when they get their hair done. Start this shot off with a fine-ass sistah with a baby in hand walking over to the crib.

THE DOORWAY

Where we see a little boy about twelve years old standing in the middle of these children. This is Baha, the errand boy of the shop. Baha sits playing a Sega Game Gear, looking up from time to time out the window and at the fine women that pass by. Some of the older children attempt to distract him from his game.

BAHA

Stop! Quit!
(*looking out the window, then goes to the doorway*)

Here she comes!

THE SALON

Where all the stylists and customers turn. They know what that means.

17 EXT. JESSIE'S SALON—DAY

We see a hand with keys in the frame. The owner of these keys presses a button, which turns on the car alarm. The license on her car reads MS. BOOTE. At leg level we swing around to walk toward the salon. In front of the door stands a Panhandler with a sign in hand.

PANHANDLER

Good morning, Jessie. Could you spare some change?!

JESSIE (O.S.)

Hell, naw! And get your dirty, smelly, unemployed ass out from in front of my shop.

We move past the Panhandler and toward the front door of the shop.

17A *INT. JESSIE'S SALON—DAY*

BACK TO DOORWAY

*Where we see Jessie open her Fendi purse to send Baha on an errand.
Since we are at chair level, we notice her shapely bottom half. She got
much ass! IDEA start on her purse being opened, then PAN over to Baha
as we hear Jessie offscreen.*

JESSIE (O.S.)

Baha, do me a favor, baby, and go to the liquor store get
me a Honey Bun and a pack of—

BAHA
(taking the money)

Big Red. Yeah, I know.

WIDER

*As we see Baha take off for the store and Jessie turned around calling to
him.*

JESSIE

And bring me back my change!

*She turns back around, and we see her face. Jessie is the owner of this
shop. She is the queen of the hootchies in tha hood. Her attire puts the E
in ethnic, as she is wearing the hottest, most expensive outfit that can be
bought at the Fox Hills Mall. She takes off her sunglasses, and we can see
her face.*

JESSIE
(in a good mood)

Good morning, everybody.

ANOTHER ANGLE

*As Jessie walks across the room and to the corner. All the women in the
shop are looking at her funny.*

JESSIE
(sweetly)

What?! What?
(vicious)

What y'all looking at? I know I'm fine, but damn! Get back
to work.

THE SALON

Where everybody goes about their business.

CONTINUED:

17A CONTINUED
THE SINK

Iesha's head is in the sink. Justice is shampooing and conditioning her hair. Iesha's eyes are closed to keep the suds from stinging them.

JUSTICE

Just let that conditioning sit for five minutes.

IESHA

Where you going? You not gonna talk to me?

JUSTICE

No, I wanna go over here and talk to Jessie. It's a five-hour job anyway—you might as well just chill.

Justice walks away.

IESHA

All right, then, just play me like a biscuit. Hair all wet, cold.

THE COUNTER

Where Justice joins Jessie, who is busy checking the receipts of the morning.

JUSTICE

So.

JESSIE

Yeah.

They both start laughing. A Delivery Man arrives with boxes of shampoo. A few sistahs throw him an interested eye. Jessie is checking him out also.

JUSTICE

So he's out, huh? Y'all got buckwild last night? Where'd y'all go?

JESSIE

Could you put 'em over there? Snooty Fox Motor Inn.
                    (to the stylists)

Y'all make sure to fill out them receipts!

JUSTICE
(laughing)

They still got them red walls?

JESSIE

Yep, mirrors on the ceiling. Same ole, same o'. They been
filling out them receipts?

JUSTICE

Yeah.

JESSIE

What you know about mirrors on the ceiling? When the
last time you been there?

JUSTICE

Snooty Fox? Don't remember.

17B *INT. JESSIE'S BEAUTY SALON—DAY*

DOORWAY

Where we see a brother, Rodney, come in with this woman.

RODNEY

Hey, my girl need her hair and nails done.

JESSIE

She got an appointment?

RODNEY

Naw.

HEYWOOD *(O.S.)*

She ain't got no hair, either!

*Some people laugh. We see the Woman. She got about as much hair as a
snap.*

JESSIE

Make an appointment.
          (lights a smoke, touches Justice's hat)

Why you keep wearing these hats? What you hidin?!
Ooow, keep it on.

JUSTICE
          (pulling her hat on)

Stop.

JESSIE

You need to let me do somethin to that head of yours.
Man, I'm tired. Got a poem for me today? Lord knows I
need one.

CONTINUED:

17B CONTINUED

JUSTICE

I left my notebook in the car. I'll get it in a bit.

JESSIE

When *you* gonna get a man? Asking all these questions about mine. You still in mourning? Sportin black, don't make time to do your own hair. Lookin tore up from tha floor up. You can always tell when a woman ain't givin up no coochie.

JUSTICE

I like black. Besides, I don't have no time for no man right now.

JESSIE

See, your problem is you make bad choices in men. You don't know how to pick 'em.

CUT TO:

18   EXT. STREET—DAY

Where we come down out of the sky to see a small U.S. Postal Mail jeep turn in the street and come to the curb. We hear the heavy bass beat of hip-hop coming from the jeep.

JUSTICE (O.S.)

Look who's talking.

19   INT. POSTAL JEEP—DAY

Inside the jeep a hand presses the stop/eject on the recorder and flips the tape.

19A EXT. CITY STREET—DAY

THE GROUND

Where the jeep door opens and a pair of sharp Nikes come out. We travel up to reveal the face of a young Black brother, twenty-two years, well built, rough looking, a close fade under a cap that reads U.S. MAIL.

This is Lucky. Not your everyday postman, but just another hard-working young South Central brother trying to make that hard-to-come-by daily dollar.

ANOTHER ANGLE

As Lucky gets his bag and walks toward the salon entrance.

> **PANHANDLER**
> (singing)

Hey, hey wait a minute, Mr. Postman! Mr. Postman, got some spare change?

> **LUCKY**

Naw, muthafucka, but I gotta spare stamp so you can mail your ass a job application!

> CUT TO:

20 *INT. JESSIE'S SALON—DAY*

Where Lucky enters. His eyes take in the sight of all these fine, beautiful sistahs. This is his favorite part of his route. One or two women pass in front of him.

ANOTHER ANGLE

Lucky makes his way to the counter, where he gives the mail to Justice, who is organizing the outgoing mail. Jessie sits nearby.

> **LUCKY**

Y'all didn't get nothing but bills.

Lucky looks at Justice, trying to make eye contact, which she skillfully avoids. JUSTICE'S P.O.V.: Lucky's hands pull out mail and place it on the counter. 36, 48, f.p.s. Justice is licking stamps and placing them on outgoing envelopes. Lucky notices her sexy tongue.

> **LUCKY**

Why you always looking so mad? You too fine to be looking so angry. . . . You must ain't got no boyfriend 'cause you always angry!

Justice finally looks up. Blank eyes. Blank face. No interest whatsoever. Then her face breaks out into a mischievous smile. She looks Lucky up and down, checkin him out.

> **JUSTICE**
> (with attitude)

What do you want? What do you want from me?

> **LUCKY**

Well, I think you kinda fly. We could start with your number.

> **JUSTICE**

Come here.

Lucky looks around.

> CONTINUED:

20 CONTINUED

> **JUSTICE**
> *(sexy)*

Come closer. I want to whisper somethin to you.

Lucky leans in closer.

> **JUSTICE**
> *(coolly)*

Let's cut to the chase. What do you *reeaally* want? . . . You wanna smell my poonani?

Lucky is taken aback. Surprised.

> **LUCKY**
> *(smiles)*

. . . Uhh, yeah. Here?

> **JUSTICE**

Wait a minute, baby.
> *(turns to Jessie, loud)*

Jessie! He said he wanna smell my poonani!

> **JESSIE**
> *(coolly, smoking)*

Really.

> **JUSTICE**

Yeah. Should I let him smell it?

> **JESSIE**

Yeah.

Jessie coolly walks from behind the counter and comes face to face with Lucky. She leans in close to his face and blows air into his face. Lucky is surprised. Justice and Jessie start laughing.

Justice hands Lucky the outgoing mail and walks across the shop to attend to Iesha's hair. She laughs her ass off.

Lucky coolly closes his mailbag and walks out of the salon. Jessie looks at his exit and then in Justice's direction. She just smiles in amusement and puts out her cigarette. Same ole, same o'.

21 EXT. JESSIE'S SALON—DAY

Lucky exits the salon, retaining his cool despite being dissed.

John bonding with his cast (clockwise from lower right):
Janet Jackson, Regina King, Joe Torry, Tupac Shakur.

Justice with her first love, Merkel, before his tragic death.

Lucky tries to bust the rap, but Justice isn't having it.

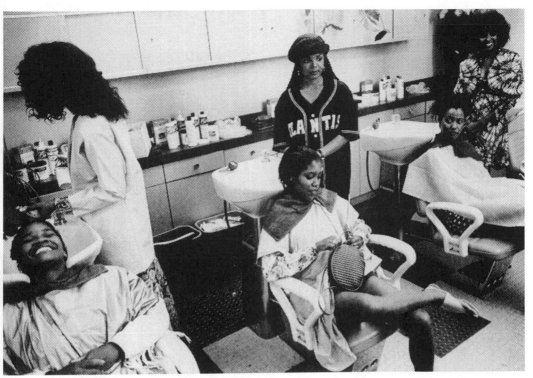

The girls in the salon.

Justice still in mourning.

John has a quiet moment with Janet.

Super-macho Dexter (Keith Washington) and gender-bender
Heywood (Roger Smith), who are usually at each other's
throats, take a break from their bickering.

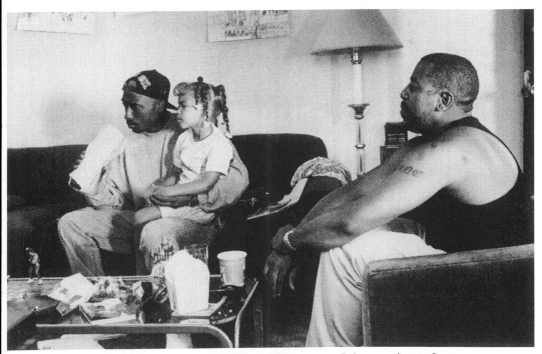

Lucky, his daughter Keisha (Shannon Johnson), and
J-Bone (Tone-Loc) sit together and watch cartoons.

John in charge. Film school was never like this!

Back to their roots: Janet, John, and Joe with the musicians and dancers in the African marketplace scene.

The director and his muse.

Sometimes making a movie is like sitting on top
of the world.

The calendar girls: Aunt April (Ernestine Reed), Aunt May
(Norma Donaldson), and Aunt June (Maya Angelou).

Poet Maya Angelou, a true Renaissance woman, inspired everyone on the set with her eloquence and humor.

Justice, Iesha, Chicago, and Lucky hit the road.

Justice and Lucky have stopped fighting long enough
to realize they actually like each other.

Chicago doesn't know it yet, but Iesha is starting to get bored.

It wasn't all fun and games, really: It just looks that way.

Justice and Lucky are heading toward Oakland, but they keep getting distracted along the way.

"No Smoking" means nothing to Jessie (Tyra Ferrell). She always does as she pleases.

The girls arrive at the hair show. You can't tell these sisters that they're not fierce!

Justice finds the poetry in her life by opening herself
up to love again.

Behind the scenes with John: Some of the women who made it happen (clockwise from bottom left): Creative Executive Stephanie Allain, Unit Publicist Cassandra Butcher, Location Manager Elisa Ann Conant, Casting Director Robi Reed, Lead Hairstylist Pauletta Lewis, Veronica Chambers, Assistant Production Coordinator Sherri G. Sneed, Wardrobe Assistant April Hunter, Second Assistant Director Simone Farber, Lead Makeup Artist Alvechia Ewing, and Script Supervisor Dawn Gilliam.

LUCKY
(under his breath, looking back)

Crazy Black bitches.

The Panhandler comes nearby. Lucky reaches into his pocket and gives him a quarter.

LUCKY

And don't smoke it. Here, take a stamp too.

He hops into the jeep and drives off.

DISSOLVE TO:

22   *INT. SOUTH CENTRAL POST OFFICE: CENTURY BOULEVARD—DAY*

A TIME CLOCK

CLOSE:

A second hand flows past the frame.

The minute hand is steady.

The hour hand clicks to 4:30 P.M.

A time card is placed in. Someone is checking out.

THE HALLWAY

Where we see Lucky is the one checking out. We PUSH IN to him as he takes his card out and places it in a slot on the wall. He then goes in his pocket to pull out an envelope.

THE ENVELOPE

As it is opened, we can barely see that it is a paycheck.

ANOTHER ANGLE

As Lucky notices the amount of the check. He looks frustrated. Offscreen we hear the clock tick once more. Lucky looks around to see if anyone is watching. Then he hits the clock, breaking the glass.

23   *INT. BATHROOM—DAY*

A DUFFEL BAG

Being stuffed with a postal uniform. A hand pulls out a baseball cap.

24   *EXT. BATHROOM—DAY*

Where Lucky emerges in more comfortable clothing. As he walks up the hall and into . . .

25 *INT. THA SORTIN ROOM—DAY*

We start on a large CLOSE UP of George Bush's face. Suddenly, it is hit with many darts. Maybe a shot on dart P.O.V., as in Robin Hood.

WIDER

Where we see that we are in a Sorting Room. This is the place where mail is sorted by ZIP code. There are eight guys at work. Three are brothers; the other five are Hispanic. Chicago and a Mexican dude, E.J., are playing darts.

CHICAGO

You see that? I tore that muthafucka's nose up!

E.J. goes up to the dartboard, to which they have taped a picture of George Bush.

E.J.

Yeah that was nice!

Lucky comes into the room.

LUCKY

Y'all need to get y'all asses to work before y'all get fired!

CHICAGO AND E.J.

Fuck you.

LUCKY
(gestures to Chicago)

What up, souljah?

Chicago walks toward Lucky. E.J. looks a little left out.

CHICAGO

What's up? Hey you know they put two more Buddha heads on mail carrier. Still got me waiting, sorting with tha Mexicans.

We see E.J. in the close background nearby, sorting mail with an open ear.

E.J.

Hey, Chicago, don't be talking bout Mexicans! I kick your ass. At least *we* got a country.

CHICAGO
(whispers)

I'm on Oaktown Run tomorrow. Getting a truck ready. Wanna go?

LUCKY

Yeah.

E.J.

Y'all going to Oakland?

Lucky cuts him a dry look that reads "Mind your own business."

CHICAGO

Cool. You gonna bring a yamp?

E.J.
(now in the middle)

What's a yamp?

LUCKY

A *young tramp.* You mind?

E.J. calls Lucky a "Puto!" and goes back to sorting mail. Lucky and Chicago walk away and talk.

LUCKY *(O.S.)*

And get them ZIP codes right.

ANOTHER ANGLE: MOVING

LUCKY

I dunno. Why don't you get that crazy hoe you go wit to hook me up?

CHICAGO

I'm on it. You call your cousin K-Dog?

LUCKY

Naw, not yet. I hadda find a way up there this weekend anyway.
(with pride)

Gotta work on our music thang. It's cool, we gettin' paid to go. Gotta go, Loc.

Lucky goes to leave.

CONTINUED:

25 CONTINUED

CHICAGO

Where you goin?

Lucky turns.

LUCKY

Why you need to know? You ain't my bitch! I'm off!

DISSOLVE TO:

26 *EXT. THA PROJECTS—DAY*

WIDE

As Lucky comes to the curb and gets ready to exit his car. In the far background, we see and hear another car coming up.

27 *INT. GANGSTA RIDE—DAY*

From the inside of the car, we roll up on Lucky getting out of his car. We get the feeling something drastic is gonna happen. 36, 48, f.p.s. Time slows down. Lucky turns around just as the car stops.

ANGLE

On Lucky, as he turns and attempts to see who is in the car. It turns out to be some of his old friends.

LLOYD

What's up, Lucky?

LUCKY

What up, nigga? What y'all doing?

LLOYD

Looking for a nigga to jack.

In his lap we see a gun.

LUCKY

Ya'll need to jack that cracka Darryl Gates.

BACKSEAT GANGSTA

Who's that?

Everybody just turns and looks at him. He shrinks back into the back seat.

LLOYD

Yeah we gonna jack him too. Goin up to City Hall later today. . . . Remember Derek?

LUCKY

Yeah. He live over there.

(points)

LLOYD

Not no more. Got his ass caped out yesterday. . . . We gonna get tha niggas that got him.

Lucky nods.

LUCKY

Well, later.

LLOYD

All right. Peace.

Lloyd smiles ironically.

LUCKY

Yeah, peace.

They drive off. Lucky turns and walks into tha projects.

28   *EXT. J-BONE'S PORCH—DAY*

Lucky walks up to a porch where we see a tall, slender, light-brown brother wearing no shirt and smoking a joint. This is J-Bone, Lucky's old friend.

So close are they that they have children by the same woman. J-Bone is standing on his porch enjoying the afternoon sun and a cool Santa Ana breeze. We hear a jet fly overhead. We hear a fly-ass beat flowing from someone's apartment window.

J-BONE
(in greeting)

Mr. Postman! Working muthafucka!

LUCKY

Don't start! Whatsup, J-Bone.

J-BONE

Want some Thai bud?

LUCKY

Naw. Can't fuck wit that.

They pause for a moment. J-Bone's attention has wandered across the way.

CONTINUED:

28 CONTINUED
ACROSS THE WAY

We see an Old Woman toiling in her garden. In the projects older folk respect their small spaces by making them as comfortable as possible. Some playing children run through this shot.

BACK TO PORCH

J-BONE

Hi, Ms. Jackson. . . . She hate my ass.

MS. JACKSON

Looks up toward J-Bone. Her face does not register the slightest hint of a positive response to J-Bone's greeting. In fact it says, "Go to hell." Ms. Jackson tells one of the kids, a Young Boy, to go inside. Upset and reluctant, the boy complies with his grandmother's wishes.

THE PORCH

LUCKY

Heard 'bout Derek.

J-BONE

Yeah, Derek. D-Dog! Crazy muthafucka, huh? Ain't that about a bitch?
                    (reminiscing)
. . . Anyway, so you here to check on Keisha, huh?

They start walking.

LUCKY

Yeah, I'ma give Angel some money to buy her some clothes.

J-BONE

Awww, muthafucka, you don't need to do that. I'll get her some clothes. Take her to the Slauson Swap Meet, Fox Hills Mall, get her what ever she need.

LUCKY

Naw, you don't need to do that.

A crack addict walks toward J-Bone. He makes a quick transaction.

J-BONE

Ain't no thang. . . . It ain't like I ain't got the money. Besides, she call me Daddy sometimes anyway.

J-Bone walks on ahead. Lucky seems a little miffed.

They walk upstairs to Angel's apartment.

29 *INT. ANGEL'S PLACE—DAY*

Where Lucky and J-Bone enter. There are two small children on the floor watching television. One is a girl, the other a boy. The girl is six years old, and the boy is four. This is Keisha and Antonio.

On the screen are afternoon cartoons.

> **LUCKY**
>
> What you mean she call *you* Daddy?

> **J-BONE**
>
> Just what I said.

> **LUCKY**
> *(gestures to his child)*
>
> Hey, little girl!

Keisha runs up into her daddy's arms.

> **LUCKY**
>
> Who's your daddy?

Keisha timidly points to Lucky, who smiles and looks at J-Bone.

> **LUCKY**
>
> That's your son, this my daughter. Don't you be forgetting.

> **J-BONE**
>
> Well, I'm her second daddy, since they came from the same hooka.

As if on cue and "on cue," we see a young woman of about twenty-two enter the room. Her face looks like that of someone who is entering the throes of what will be a hard life. Despite this, she retains a beautiful but very uninnocent look. This is Angel.

> **ANGEL**
>
> What y'all two fools talking 'bout?

> **LUCKY**
>
> Talking 'bout your yamp ass.
> *(takes a drink, then takes a second look at her)*

CONTINUED:

29 CONTINUED

We notice the unusual color of her lipstick and her nervous twitching.
Angel begins rearranging things on her already-cluttered-up coffee table.

LUCKY

What you cleaning up for? Place look fucked up!
Normal! . . . You ain't been basing, is you?
(to J-Bone)

Has she?

J-Bone doesn't say anything.

ANGEL

No, I ain't, and neither one of y'all is my husband, so y'all
can't tell me shit.
(darts back toward the bedroom)

ANGEL'S P.O.V.: MOVING BACK AWAY FROM LUCKY

LUCKY

You know what I told ya ass bout that!

The bedroom door is slammed shut.

Lucky lets his little girl out of his lap and loose.

LUCKY

Told her if she start doing that shit, I'm gonna take
Keisha to live with my momma.

J-BONE
(looking at cartoons)

She all right, Lucky. Believe me, I'd know.

LUCKY

Yeah.
(takes a swig, then places his forty on the table)

I gotta stop drinking this shit. Fuckin wit my brain.

From outside someone calls J-Bone. He reluctantly leaves the cartoons to
sell some more crack.

Lucky starts to take notice of all the clutter on the coffee table. Downstairs,
J-Bone makes a transaction. We see a piece of a crack pipe under the hair
of a Black baby doll. This catches Lucky's attention. Lucky picks it up and
notices Angel's lipstick is on its tip. He looks from J-Bone outside toward
the bedroom. Then he gets up and walks in that direction.

29A *INT. ANGEL'S PLACE—DAY*

THE BEDROOM

Where we see Lucky opening the door. Inside Angel is just covering herself up after being with a gangsta. Lucky closes the door.

IDEA: Start shot of Lucky opening the door then PAN OVER to reveal Angel and the Gangsta surprised then PAN back to Lucky's reaction and he CLOSES the door.

29B *INT. ANGEL'S PLACE—DAY*

THE HALLWAY

As Lucky takes a moment to think. He walks off.

THE LIVING ROOM

Lucky picks up Keisha.

> ### LUCKY
>
> C'mon, we gonna go see Grandma. Your momma tripping.

Suddenly, Angel bursts from the bedroom, cursing and talking shit.

> ### ANGEL
>
> Who the fuck you think you is? You don't tell me what the fuck I can do! Who the fuck I can see!

29C *EXT. ANGEL'S PLACE—DAY*

OVERHEAD

Outside, downstairs, J-Bone begins to take notice of the storm brewing in the apartment. He looks up toward the noise.

29D *ANOTHER ANGLE: ON CRANE*

Where J-Bone runs around and up the stairs as we CRANE UP with him and past the front of the apartment to see Lucky and Angel, perfectly framed in a window, arguing up a storm.

INT. ANGEL'S PLACE—DAY

BACK TO LIVING ROOM

As Lucky and Angel go at it. Lucky has Keisha in hand. J-Bone enters the apartment and comes in between the two of them.

> ### LUCKY
>
> Fuck you, bitch! How you gonna be fucking some nigga while my little girl around here?!
> *(to the guy)*
>
> What you looking at, nigga?

CONTINUED:

29D CONTINUED

GANGSTA #1

Hey, Bone, you better tell this muthafucka to get outta ma face before I get my strap!

J-BONE

Lucky! Lucky, calm down, G!

LUCKY

Naw, fuck her yamp ass!

GANGSTA #1

Who is this muthafucka?

Lucky throws the Gangsta a funny look. Then, breaking the first rule of the street, he turns his back on him to continue arguing with Angel.

GANGSTA #1

What you looking at, punk? Mark ass, nigga!

Gangsta #1 sucka-punches Lucky. And they both start a big fight in the middle of the small apartment. J-Bone joins the fight, on Lucky's side.

J-BONE

Hey, hey!

Lucky and J-Bone kick his ass. Tha Gangsta is out cold. From the fire and light in Lucky's eyes, we can see shades of his previous life. He and J-Bone stand back to admire their handiwork. Outside we can see a crowd has gathered from the noise.

LUCKY

Aw, shit! I just got offa work. I don't need this shit. C'mon, Keisha. Later, Bone.

Lucky walks off, daughter in hand.

30 EXT. ANGEL'S PLACE—DAY

As Lucky, daughter in hand, quickly emerges. Behind him Angel throws a verbal arsenal of dirty insults and threats such as "Fuck you, nigga!" "You don't make no money, anyway!" "How you know she your baby?" etc. As Lucky walks, we lower Angel's voice and hear another one of Justice's poems.

JUSTICE *(V.O.)*

"In a time of secret wooing.
Today prepares tomorrow's ruin.
Left knows not what right is doing.

My heart is torn asunder.
In a time of furtive sighs.
Sweet hellos and sad goodbyes.
Half truths told and entire lies.
My conscience echoes thunder."

DISSOLVE TO:

31   *INT. JESSIE'S SALON—LATE AFTERNOON*

As we see Justice standing over her notebook reading a poem to Iesha while putting the finishing touches on her head. The salon is nearly empty. Jessie is sitting at the counter. Heywood is on the phone.

JUSTICE

"In a time when kingdoms come.
Joy is brief as summer's fun.
Happiness, its race has run.
Then pain stalks in to plunder."
(*closes the notebook*)

So what you think?

IESHA

It's pretty. What you call it?

JUSTICE

"In a Time."

Iesha's beeper goes off.

IESHA
(*looking at her beeper*)

Uh-oh, Chicago paging me.

Iesha gets out of the chair and goes to the receptionist's phone.

Heywood is on the phone. His face is so serious. Jessie quickly points Iesha in the direction of the pay phone on the wall. Iesha sighs and walks that way.

JESSIE

You need some change?

IESHA *(O.S.)*

No.

Justice begins cleaning up her station.

THE COUNTER

Where Heywood gets off the phone. From the look on his face he has heard some terrible news.

CONTINUED:

31 CONTINUED

JESSIE

What'd they say?

Heywood crosses over to the couch, where he sits with his head down. Jessie goes over to console him.

THE WALL PHONE

Where Iesha is on the phone with Chicago.

IESHA
(with attitude)

What you want? Ah, huh. Ah, huh. Yeah, I'm wit it. We got a hair show to go to up there anyway.

CHICAGO *(O.S.)*

Bring one'o your friends too. A *fine* one.

IESHA

What you mean, a fine one? You trying to say I got ugly friends?

Justice and Iesha make eye contact. Both smile. Suddenly in the background on Justice, we see and hear police lights converge on some brothers across the street. This catches Justice's attention.

BACK TO COUCH

Where Jessie is still consoling Heywood. Behind them out the window are the police.

JESSIE

What the hell they doing now?! I'm as glad as hell we getting outta here tomorrow.

JUSTICE
(walks up)

What's wrong?

Heywood gets up and walks away. Jessie stands.

Justice joins Jessie at the window. Both stand in profile. Red and blue flashes of light flow across their faces. There are people leaving the shop throughout this scene.

JESSIE

You got your styles together for tha Oakland Show?

JUSTICE
(demure)

Yeah. I'ma play with Lisa and Gena's heads. If they like it, they like it. If they don't, they don't.

JESSIE

So you riding with us? You know we got us a little caravan going.

Justice nods. Jessie notices the stress on her face.

JESSIE

Justice. I know I ain't your momma. Hell, I ain't *even* old enough to be that. But we pretty close, and sometimes we talk like sisters. I just gotta tell ya, baby . . . you gotta move on. . . . A man ain't nothin but a *tool*.

You got to know when to take 'em out tha box and when to put 'em back in. And if ya lose one—well, you just . . . go get another. . . . Take a chance, do somethin different for a change. There's always another man somewheres out here.
(looks out the window)

You gotta know sometimes you gonna lose one.
(matter of factly)

Like a blow dryer or a good brush. What I gotta do? Play Momma to everybody in this shop?

Justice thinks, looks down for a moment, then out the window once more.

BACK TO THE STALLS

Where we see Dexter, Heywood, and four other stylists: Maxine, Colette, Lisa, and Gena.

DEXTER

Where's my blow dryer! I'm tired of all my shit disappearing alla time!

HEYWOOD
(coolly)

Calm down. Calm down. Here it is. I borrowed it for a wrap I had to do this morning.

DEXTER

Heywood! Why you always borrowing my shit without asking?!

CONTINUED:

31 CONTINUED

HEYWOOD

I asked you for it this morning, and you said yes. Why are you crying over it like a bitch?

DEXTER

Who you calling a bitch? If anybody's a bitch, you a bitch!

HEYWOOD

Excuse me? You wan some? Maybe you forget I was Golden Gloves. You catchin me on tha wrong mutha-fuckin day.

MAXINE

All right. All right. Dexter! As much as you talk and you borrow everybody else's stuff alla time.
(*looks over his tools*)

Like my brush right here.

Maxine walks away. As she does, we notice the round beautiful fullness of her boo-tay. Her hair is dyed blood red.

DEXTER

I was gonna give it to ya, Maxine, I just got dis—trac—ted. Mmm-mmm.

HEYWOOD

Shit, I was wrestlin champ at Crenshaw High School.

JUSTICE'S STALL

Where she and Iesha meet up once more. Iesha begins playing with her new braids in tha mirror.

JUSTICE

So what your new man talking bout?

IESHA

He want me to go onna *run* with 'em.
(*starts scrutinizing her hair*)

This is good now. I don't haveta be messing around with it. Just walk out tha house—ya know.

JUSTICE

Yeah. What's a *run*?

IESHA

Oh, you know what a run is.

Iesha keeps fixing her hair. It is apparent that she is luring Justice's curiosity. Justice takes the bait.

JUSTICE
(pulls Iesha's hand away from her head)

No, I don't. And stop messing with it. What's a run? He ain't no slanger is he?

IESHA

A run . . . is, well, it's like this. You really wanna know?

Justice gives her a frustrated look.

IESHA

Well, you know my boyfriend Chicago, right?

CUT TO:

32 *EXT. THE POST OFFICE—DUSK*

Where we see Chicago point at a truck and sign a rec order. "That one," *he says. He is brushing his head with a flat brush and arguing with an* *Oriental co-worker.*

IESHA (V.O.)

You know he work at the post office and all. The one on Century and Van Ness. Well, every so often he and his friend at work, they have to drive up to Oakland in this mail truck, see.

32A *INT. JESSIE'S SALON—DUSK*

BACK TO SCENE

IESHA

You listening?

JUSTICE
(her interest apparently lost)

Yeah.

In the background the other stylists are leaving. A few of them say good- *bye to Justice before they go. Justice resumes cleaning her station. Her* *interest in Iesha's proposal is lost.*

CONTINUED:

32A   CONTINUED

> IESHA
> *(attempting to persuade)*

Well, we get in this mail truck and we drive up the coast, get drunk, eat Mexican food, and just have a good time. It's fun!

> *(seeing no effect)*

You ain't having it, huh?

> JUSTICE

No, I'm not. That is *too* to the curb. How am I gonna look like riding in some mail truck? What you doing seeing some mailman, anyway? You know they don't make no money! What he gonna do for you? Mail your bills for free?!

Iesha folds her arms in defiance of Justice's comments.

> IESHA
> *(frustrated with Justice)*

How come you don't ever wanna have no fun no more? Girl, the world is just one big place waitin for us to go out and fuck up in it. You gonna end up being a straight spinster.

We see Justice's face. She is definitely looking more hardened.

Iesha pulls a wad of money out of her pocket and gives it to Justice.

> IESHA
> *(walking out)*

Later. Thanks. You a Straight Buster!

Jessie comes up.

> JESSIE

What she all mad about?

> JUSTICE

Nuthin.

We hear on the salon's radio the beginning of "What You See, Is What You Get!"

> JESSIE

Listen, meet us at my place at eight o'clock tomorrow. Come on, let's close up.

We PAN over to reveal Heywood dancing. He goes over to Jessie, and they start to dance. Justice is left standing alone.

                                                              DISSOLVE TO:

33 *EXT. JESSIE'S SALON—DUSK*

As we see Justice, Jessie, and Heywood close the shop. Justice pulls the iron gate closed and secures its front. Jessie locks the locks. A car cruises by, and we hear some bumping sounds of hip-hop music coming from the inside speakers as well as the voices of some brothers shouting out compliments to these two beautiful sistahs. We also hear Heywood go on about how he loves himself, how life is beautiful. He tells Justice, "See, that's your problem, Justice. You don't love yourself."

                                                              DISSOLVE TO:

34 *INT. JUSTICE'S HOME—NIGHT*

It looks as though it was decorated by her grandmother, which in fact it was. We notice a portrait of an elderly woman with similar features as Justice. There are also more than a few clocks around, one grandfather clock and a large twenty-four-hour sandclock are prominent. Justice has nothing but time on her hands. The air is full of ticking mingled with the sound of the outside streets. We dissolve through these images and slide into . . .

35 *INT. BATHROOM—NIGHT*

We START outside the doorway and SLOWLY MOVE IN, invading Justice's privacy. Justice is busy rolling her hair in the mirror. She is alone. She looks at her face in the mirror. She is a mess. She lets her mind wander as she looks at the cold tile floor. Suddenly, Justice thinks she hears some-thing. PAN from mirror to her face as she hears the sound.

36 *INT. HALLWAY—NIGHT*

Where Justice quietly stalks. She is nervous as hell. The sounds of the clocks become more prominent as she moves forward. Justice's P.O.V. moving forward, as she walks down the stairs.

THE DOORWAY

Where Justice stands. Someone is on the other side. We hear a slight scratch, then silence. Quiet tension. This is broken up by the sound of a friendly meow. Justice opens the door, and a big white cat enters.

JUSTICE

White Boy! C'mere.

She picks him up. Pets him, then he pulls away with a screech and runs offscreen.

                                                              CONTINUED:

36 CONTINUED

JUSTICE

Yeah, you just like a boy. I should have you fixed.

THE LIVING ROOM

Where Justice picks up the remote control to turn on the television. On the screen is Bet's Midnight Love. There is a montage of romantic R&B videos. A flash of static and we . . .

CUT TO:

37 *INT. IESHA'S APARTMENT—NIGHT*

We see Iesha and Chicago do a smooth, close, sexy Ragamuffin dance. We hear some Ragamuffin music in the background.

37A *INT. JUSTICE'S LIVING ROOM—NIGHT*

BACK TO JUSTICE

Justice seems dissatisfied. She turns the television off.

Across the room we see Justice sitting at the piano. She looks bored.

CLOSE

On the piano keys as Justice presses a low-note key. The sound transcends us into the next scene.

DISSOLVE TO:

38 *INT. JUSTICE'S LIVING ROOM—NIGHT*

As we see Justice looking through a collection of 45 records. She picks out one.

THE RECORD PLAYER

As the record begins to spin. The first few bars of Stevie Wonder's "I Never Dreamed You'd Leave in Summer" float into the air.

JUSTICE

As she begins to groove to the music. She walks toward the kitchen.

38A *INT. JUSTICE'S HOME—NIGHT*

VARIOUS ANGLES

Of the empty rooms within the house.

38AA *INT. JUSTICE'S KITCHEN—NIGHT*

Where she makes popcorn. Pours it in a bowl, then pours tabasco sauce on it.

38B   EXT. JUSTICE HOME—NIGHT

THROUGH THE WINDOW FROM OUTSIDE

From a voyeuristic P.O.V. we see Justice grooving to the music and eating her popcorn. She picks up a candy bar off a table.

38C   INT. JUSTICE'S HOME—NIGHT

BACK INSIDE

Justice stops dancing, candy bar in her mouth. She looks around for a moment and then into a mirror. Everything seems fine, then out of nowhere she bursts into tears. She cries a few tears for a few seconds, then wipes them away.

THE TELEPHONE

Justice picks up the receiver and enters some digits.

39   INT. IESHA'S APARTMENT—NIGHT

We see a pair of lips that turn out to be a telephone as Iesha picks up the receiver, and we follow it to reveal her and Chicago in bed together. Iesha lies on her stomach with Chicago on top. Tha skins are definitely on. Chicago is wearing nothing except a Chicago Bulls fisherman's cap. Ragamuffin music is playing in the background mon.

> IESHA
>
> Who dis? Oh, what's up, girl? You change your mind? . . . Somethin wrong?

40   INT. JUSTICE'S HOME—NIGHT

> JUSTICE
>
> No. No, girl, I just wanted to talk.

40A   INT. IESHA'S APARTMENT BEDROOM—NIGHT

BACK TO IESHA

> CHICAGO
> (whispers)
>
> Get off tha phone. Get off tha phone.
> (louder)
>
> She busy!

CONTINUED:

40A CONTINUED

IESHA

I'm talking to *my* friend, you mind?!
(*rolls her eyes and reaches into a bag of Fritos*)

Listen, J, I'm kinda busy. Could you call me back later?

JUSTICE *(O.S.)*

Yeah.

Iesha hangs up the phone.

CHICAGO

Finally.

IESHA
(*getting up*)

What you mean? You wasn't doing nuthin anyway!

41 INT. JUSTICE'S LIVING ROOM—NIGHT

Where she sits. Her eyes wander around the room and then rest on her cat across the way. The cat looks back at her, then turns around and walks away into the hallway. Justice shakes her head. Then her eyes settle on something else.

THE COFFEE TABLE

Where we move up on her notebook.

JUSTICE

As she wipes a few more tears away and reaches for her notebook.

42 INT. LUCKY'S HOUSE—NIGHT

A NOTEBOOK

As we see it being opened. Its pages are ratty. We notice its pages are colored with children's drawings: a family, a dog, a house.

THE LIVING ROOM

Where we see Lucky lying on the couch like a potato watching television. In the foreground Keisha lies on the floor drawing in her notebook.

ON TELEVISION

Is one of those Tom Foo Infomercials. He's that Chinese guy who sits on a boat with a lot of pretty women (all white) and says, "You can be rich too." We can't tell if Lucky is looking at this or is lost in his own thoughts. He mumbles a rhyme about Black business versus Korean exploitation.

KEISHA

As she looks at the screen. We hear a helicopter go overhead as its spotlight flows into the room. Keisha reacts to it with indifference and continues to draw. Lucky calmly cuts his eyes in that direction. The light gets his attention and prompts him to get up and make a phone call.

LUCKY

Operator? Yeah, give me Oakland, please. Area code 415.

43   *INT. COUSIN KALIL'S SOUND LAB: OAKLAND—NIGHT*

Where we travel past a ringing phone and some sound equipment to reveal a picture of a young man. Our attention settles on his eyes. This is Lucky's cousin, Kalil.

SUDDENLY WE HEAR THE SOUND OF GUNSHOTS.

43A   *INT. LUCKY'S LIVING ROOM—NIGHT*

BACK TO LUCKY

He takes his ear away from the phone and looks in the direction the shots were coming from. There is some question as to which end of the telephone the shots came from.

CLOSE

On Lucky's face. He looks up in the direction of the gunshots and down on the floor.

THE FLOOR: LUCKY'S P.O.V.

Where Keisha is rolled up in a ball.

LUCKY
(hanging up phone)

Go to bed.

Keisha gets up and goes toward the bedroom.

Lucky looks at her exit, then goes toward the window and looks outside the blinds. On the TV in the background is the Life Alert commercial, "I've fallen and I can't get up." We see Lucky through the blinds in the foreground and the TV in the background.

THE DOORWAY

Where a woman enters. She is a short, medium-size woman, with a pretty but hardened face. The light in her eyes says she still has some humor left. This is Annie, Lucky's mother. She has a bag of groceries in hand.

CONTINUED:

43A CONTINUED

LUCKY

Hi, Momma! Need some help?

ANNIE

Just like you to offer help when I only got one bag. . . . So are you going up north to see Kalil this weekend?

LUCKY

Yeah, look like we finally gonna get this music thing going. Tryin to hook somebody up to listen to these tapes—so I won't haveta be doing this post office shit no more.

ANNIE

Don't be cursing around me. Who you think I am, one'a your friends? Be glad you got an honest job. And don't be wearing out your welcome, going to Oakland every other weekend. You know how your Aunt Audrey can get!

LUCKY

It's not even like that, Momma.
(sighs in frustration)

THE KITCHEN

Where Annie enters and begins to load the refrigerator up with goods. Lucky comes into the background.

LUCKY

Keisha's here.

Annie begins to glow with the mention of her grandchild.

ANNIE

Really? How's my grandbaby doing?

LUCKY

She fine. I want her to stay here, for good.

Annie reacts to this.

LUCKY

Angel been fucking up bad. Basing.

A pause. Silence. Neither of them says anything. Lucky begins to walk back toward the living room.

> ### ANNIE
>
> Are *you* gonna take care of her?

Lucky turns around. He thinks.

44 *INT. KEISHA'S ROOM—NIGHT*

CLOSE

On Keisha in bed under covers.

CUT TO:

> ### LUCKY
>
> Yeah.

He walks away.

44A *INT. LUCKY'S LIVING ROOM—NIGHT*

BACK TO THE LIVING ROOM

Where Lucky gets closer to the television and turns on the Sega Genesis Joe Montana Football Game. He begins playing.

> ### ANNIE *(O.S.)*
>
> Well, you just remember, that's your baby. I'm done rais-
> ing kids! You need to quit playing them video games and
> figure out what you gonna do with your life. Time ain't
> forever!

LUCKY'S FACE:

As we MOVE into his face as he plays. We hear bass beats get louder and louder, then boom! We smash cut to . . .

45 *INT. JUSTICE'S HOME—MORNING*

MONTAGE

Of Justice preparing to go on the trip to Oakland. The music we hear comes from her living room stereo.

46 *INT. JUSTICE'S BEDROOM—DAY*

Where she throws her Louis Vuitton luggage bag. Several articles of clothing follow into the bag.

47 *INT. JUSTICE'S LIVING ROOM—DAY*

THE TABLE

Where Justice arranges her cosmetology tools by order of preference and priority. We hear her mumble "I need this, and this, and this."

48 *INT. JUSTICE'S HAT ROOM—DAY*

Where we see Justice look around in a room full of hats. She picks up a baseball cap with her name JUSTICE *on the front.*

48A *INT. JUSTICE'S LIVING ROOM—DAY*

ANOTHER SETUP: THE LIVING ROOM

She runs frantically into frame. We quickly MOVE into her as she turns around and thinks for a moment.

49 *EXT. JUSTICE'S HOME—DAY*

THE FRONT PORCH

Where Justice fills a large dog bowl full of Meow Mix cat food. Her cat comes into frame at her feet and begins surveying this feast. When Justice goes back inside, her cat is joined by no less than eight other neighborhood cats.

49A *INT. JUSTICE'S HOME—DAY*

Justice turns off the stereo and grabs her keys.

50 *EXT. JUSTICE'S HOME—THE FRONT WALKWAY—MORNING*

Where Justice walks in a quick hustle toward her car. She turns off the alarm with a key-chain button. The car shouts out in an electronic voice, "Disarmed!"

ANOTHER ANGLE

As Justice tries to start up her car. It won't start. She hits the dashboard in frustration and thinks for a moment.

51 *INT. JUSTICE'S HOME—DAY*

THE KITCHEN

Where we see Justice on the telephone. We hear the phone ringing on the other end.

52 *INT. JESSIE'S APARTMENT—DAY*

JESSIE'S ANSWERING MACHINE

Which clicks on. We hear some smooth R&B music, then Jessie's voice. Over this we see the following images.

JESSIE *(V.O.)*
(sexy voice)

Hi. This is *me.* If you don't know who *me* is, then you have no business calling *me.*

THE LIVING ROOM

Where we see Jessie's meticulous but uniquely furnished apartment. Her place is just like her: polished, and all about the look.

JESSIE *(V.O.)*

If you *do* know who *me* is, then you can do *me* a favor.

JESSIE'S BEDROOM

Where we see her large ornate bed. What tales it could tell if it could speak.

53 *EXT. JESSIE'S APARTMENT—DAY*

Where we see Jessie leaning up against her car, a 1992 Lexus. She takes the last toke of her cigarette and throws it on the ground and extinguishes it with her sharp-ass shoes. In the background we hear Heywood say, "We been waiting for half an hour. She ain't coming! Let her catch up!"

Jessie gets in the car and drives away as Justice's voice clicks in on her machine.

JESSIE *(V.O.)*

Leave *me* a message. Okay? Thank you.

JUSTICE *(V.O.)*

Jessie, it's *me*, Justice. You there? Well, I'm running a little late. I'll . . .
        (she decides it's futile)

Shit!

53A *INT. JUSTICE'S HOME—DAY*

BACK TO JUSTICE'S HOME

ANOTHER ANGLE

As she hangs up the phone. She thinks for a second, then dials some more digits.

JUSTICE

Iesha? What's up, cow?

54 *EXT. JUSTICE'S HOME—DAY*

Where Justice and Iesha walk past Justice's car.

IESHA

I'm telling you, girl, you gonna have fun. There ain't nothing like this.

Justice gives her car a kick and the alarm goes off. She quickly turns it off with her key.

As they walk out, we follow with them until we let them cross and are on their backs to reveal the truck, which is a 1990 Ford-made U.S. Mail truck. It is all white with the government seal painted on both its sides. Justice stops in her tracks.

JUSTICE AND IESHA

As Justice takes in the sight of the truck. Iesha is all smiles, in contrast to Justice's discomfort.

JUSTICE

I don't believe I'm doing this.

IESHA

C'mon, we gonna have fun.

They walk toward the truck, and we see Lucky in the front seat. Lucky switches his U.S. Mail cap to a more comfortable Sox hat. He smiles at Justice. Offscreen we hear Chicago in the back of the truck.

CHICAGO *(O.S.)*

Muthafucka say that girl from Ethiopia! That bitch from Compton! How she gonna be from Ethiopia and have a kid named Lammar?

LUCKY

She look it, though.

Justice walks back to Iesha on the side of the truck.

JUSTICE

I don't know about this.

IESHA

Why you gotta be a buster? C'mon, take a chance for a change! Cow!

55 *INT. THE TRUCK—DAY*

Where Lucky looks back at Chicago.

CHICAGO

She fine, Loc.

LUCKY

Humph, I know that hoe. Crazy ass. She work in a beauty
shop on Fifty-fourth.

THE PASSENGER DOOR

*Where Justice and Iesha get into the truck. Lucky goes back into his
quiet, cool, unassuming mode. Iesha is all smiles as she does the introduc-
tions.*

IESHA

Lucky. This my friend Justice. Justice, this is Lucky.

JUSTICE
(with attitude)

Hi.

LUCKY

Whatsup.

THE BACK SEAT

Where we see Iesha and Chicago.

IESHA

And you know Chicago already.

CHICAGO

Whatsup, baby.

IESHA

Baby? Well. Let's go.

Lucky starts up the engine.

56 *EXT. THE TRUCK—DAY*

We see the front of the truck: Ford symbol all up in our faces.

We PAN past the U.S. Mail symbol.

57 *INT. THE TRUCK—DAY*

Lucky shifts into first gear as we TILT UP and he smiles at Justice.

JUSTICE

Who is not amused. She puts on sunglasses.

58 *EXT. THE TRUCK—DAY*

WIDE

As we see the truck turn in the street to make a U.

59 *EXT. CRENSHAW BOULEVARD—DAY*

Where we see the truck go up the street and end on a Crenshaw sign. They are leaving their part of the city.

60 *INT. THE TRUCK—DAY*

From inside we see the overpass of the 10 freeway come up.

INSERT

The 10 freeway West.

A TRAFFIC LIGHT

Which we hear and see turn red.

61 *EXT. CORNER OF ADAMS AND CRENSHAW—DAY*

Where we see the truck come to stop.

THE TRUCK

Where Lucky waits for the light. He looks over on the other side of the street.

THE BUS STOP

Where an Old Woman gets her pocketbook stolen.

BACK TO LUCKY

Who makes an expression that reads "Oh, well." There is no shock on his face. That's the way of the world, as Earth, Wind and Fire says.

62 *INT. THE TRUCK: BACK—DAY*

Iesha and Chicago affectionately play with each other. Iesha gives him a couple of love taps.

> ### CHICAGO
> *(laughs)*
>
> You can't make your mind up whether you wanna kiss me or hit me, huh? That your way of saying you like my ass?

> ### IESHA
> *(jokingly)*
>
> I don't.

> ### CHICAGO
> *(makes a muscle)*
>
> Feel that. Feel that muscle. That's man stuff.

> ### IESHA
>
> That ain't shit.

Chicago grabs one of her breasts.

> ### IESHA
>
> Oww, shit! Muthafucka, don't be grabbing my tittie like that!

ANGLE ON JUSTICE

Who glances behind her back at Iesha and Chicago and then into the side-view mirror once again.

62A *OMIT*

TIME SLOWS DOWN

63 *EXT. THE TEN FREEWAY—DAY*

MONTAGE OF ROAD SIGNS

Of various signs along the 10 freeway. At first we go past signs that read LA CIENEGA, CENTURY CITY/BEVERLY HILLS, *then we begin to read* 405 NORTH SACRAMENTO. *Different shots of the truck traveling between dissolves.*

64 *EXT. DESERT HIGHWAY—DAY*

We start on a car as it comes in the other left-hand lane, and as it goes past, we WHIP PAN with it to reveal the truck. Lucky and Justice are in the front seat. Justice is obviously bored out of her mind.

Lucky adjusts his vision from the road to her in an attempt to grab her attention.

65 *INT. THE TRUCK—DAY*

Lucky is driving. He looks at Justice out of the corner of his eye.

Justice is looking out at the road. Her face is concealed behind sunglasses. We cannot tell if she is lost in the scenery or in her own world.

THE BACK

Where Chicago and Iesha are asleep. Iesha is cradled in his arms.

FRONT SEATS

Where there is virtual silence. All we can hear are the sounds of the engine, the road, and other passing cars. Lucky attempts to break the ice.

> **LUCKY**
>
> You kinda quiet, huh?

Justice doesn't say anything.

> **LUCKY**
>
> Guess so.

> **JUSTICE**
>
> Don't have nuthin to say.

> **LUCKY**
>
> Why you so mean? What you got to be so mean about?

Justice remains silent. She continues looking out the window.

> **LUCKY**
>
> Oh, so you one of them angry *bitches*, huh? A feminist.

Justice turns around. Lucky has gotten her attention.

> **JUSTICE**
>
> What did you call me?

> **LUCKY**
> *(matter of factly)*
>
> I said you a *mean bitch.*

> **JUSTICE**
> *(taking off her glasses)*
>
> No, nigga! You don't call me no bitch! You don't know me! You don't know nothing about me!

LUCKY

I know you a bitch! Look at the way you actin. I been trying to act all courteous and shit, and I gotta call you a *bitch* to even get your damn attention!

JUSTICE

Fuck you, I ain't no *bitch*, I am a Black woman! I deserve respect! If I'm a bitch, yo momma's a bitch!

LUCKY

You a bitch! We ain't talking about my momma! We talking about you! Think you too fine to talk to nobody! L.A. bitches! I'm tired of 'em!

Justice is fuming now.

JUSTICE

Let me out!

LUCKY
(coolly)

Where you gonna go, huh? Where you gonna go?

JUSTICE

Fuck you! I'll walk!

66 *EXT. ROADSIDE—DAY*

Where we see the truck pull to the side of the road. The passenger door opens, and Justice gets out, bag in hand.

LUCKY

Get tha fuck out then, bitch! Walk your àss home! It'll do them big-ass thighs of yours some good anyway! Cottage cheese legs!

Justice turns, fuming mad. The last thing you should joke about with a woman is her weight, even if she has a nice body.

JUSTICE

I better not *see* your ass around L.A. 'cause I'm gonna get some niggas to *fuck you up!*

THE BACK OF THE TRUCK

Where Iesha wakes up from the sound of Justice and Lucky arguing. She mumbles, "What's going on?!"

CONTINUED:

66 CONTINUED

JUSTICE

They gonna fuck you up!

LUCKY

Fuck you, bitch!

JUSTICE

Fuck you up!

This exchange goes on one more time, then Lucky cuts it off by abruptly closing the passenger door in Justice's face.

Iesha pokes her head up front.

IESHA

What you doing!? What's happening? Where my girl at?!

LUCKY
(shifting into first gear)

I'm leaving that bitch!

IESHA

Leaving her! You can't just leave my friend out here in the middle of nowhere?! Chicago! Chicago, wake up!

67 *EXT. DESERT ROAD—DAY*

From on HIGH we see the truck get back on the road and drive off as we COME DOWN to reveal Justice. She is pissed off beyond pisstivity!

68 *INT. THE TRUCK—DAY*

Where we see Lucky driving. He is pissed off also. He is thinking heavily about his actions.

IESHA (O.S.)

Chicago! Lucky left Justice! Lucky left Justice!

CHICAGO (O.S.)

So what! I'm trying to sleep!

IESHA (O.S.)

But he left her! He left her out in the middle of nowhere!

Chicago comes up close to the back of Lucky's head.

CHICAGO *(O.S.)*

Lucky. What's up, G?

Lucky sighs and looks into his side mirror.

WIPE:

69 *EXT. DESERT ROAD—DAY: MINUTES LATER*

Justice is in the foreground, and the truck is following along in the background. Iesha is trying to convince her to get into the truck.

IESHA

C'mon, Justice, get in the truck. Ain't you kinda hot? Lucky said he'd apologize.

LUCKY

Looks at Iesha. His face is about as nonapologetic as you can get. Ain't no apologies jumping off today.

IESHA

C'mon, Justice. J!
      (sees something)

Justice walks past a big diamondback rattlesnake. She is so mad, she doesn't even notice it. Iesha plays it off and continues to call Justice.

IESHA
(turns to Lucky)

Justice! She get kinda stubborn sometimes. Stop the truck.

The truck stops, and Iesha gets out. Chicago gets into the front seat.

WIDE

As we see Iesha get out of the truck and walk over to her friend. Lucky exits the driver's side and goes to the back of the truck.

THE BACK OF THE TRUCK

Where Lucky opens the wide doors to let Justice and Iesha into the back.

Justice and Iesha come around the corner. The latter holds a consoling arm around her friend's shoulders. Justice and Lucky come face to face.

JUSTICE
(looks up and then with a mean face)

You still gonna get fucked up!

Iesha smiles and tries to laugh it off.

CONTINUED:

69 CONTINUED

*The two women climb inside. Lucky begins to close the door, but not before
giving his comeback to Justice's threat.*

LUCKY

Frankly, my dear. I don't give a fuck.

70 *INT. ROADSIDE—THE FOREST—DAY*

HOOTCH MONTAGE

71 *INT. JESSIE'S CAR—DAY*

We see a pair of nails being filed with a nail filer.

*A compact mirror, where we see eye shadow being applied to a beautiful
brown eye.*

A PAIR OF NAILS

*Are being painted bright red. The hand is brought up to reveal they belong
to Colette. She admires her handiwork.*

71A *EXT. ROADSIDE—THE FOREST—DAY*

HEYWOOD

Walks up looking through the viewfinder of a small videocam.

VIDEOCAM P.O.V.

*Where we see Jessie in the foreground standing next to her car. In the far
background we can hear the rest of their party off in the woods. We should
get the idea some of them are taking a leak.*

JESSIE

It's not on. You gotta push the button.

HEYWOOD *(V.O.)*

What button?

JESSIE

The red one.

HEYWOOD *(V.O.)*

Oh, this button.
  (*pushes the button and the word REC flashes on the
      screen in the left-hand corner.*)

It's on. Showtime!

Jessie proceeds to act a fool and show off in front of the camera.

JESSIE

Well, here I am. It's me.
(*coolly poses on her car and takes a toke of her cigarette*)

In the wilderness. The wild blue yonder.

In the background we can see Dexter come out of the trees zipping up his pants. He calls back in the trees to one of the women.

DEXTER

Hey, Maxine! I think I saw a snake back there. You better hope it don't bite your big ass!

JESSIE

They gettin close to nature.
(*laughs*)

Heywood laughs too, offscreen. He drops the camera.

WIPE:

72 *INT. THE TRUCK—DAY*

Where Lucky and Chicago ride along in the front seat. Chicago is driving with one hand and brushing his head with the other. Chicago starts humming a few bars of a song. Lucky joins in with a bass beat from his mouth. We soon recognize the theme from Sanford and Son.

73 *EXT. THE ROAD—DAY*

We see the truck drive along.

74 *INT. THE TRUCK—LATER*

CHICAGO

I'm telling ya, it was *him*. Saw 'em in the liquor store.

LUCKY

Which one?

CHICAGO

J and B on Manchester?

LUCKY

. . . You out your mind!

CHICAGO

He had the beard, tha voice, everything. He bought a forty of Red Bull.

CONTINUED:

74 CONTINUED

> **LUCKY**
>
> You saw Marvin Gaye in the liquor store, buying a forty?
> You stupid muthafucka!

The truck makes a funny noise.

> **CHICAGO**
> *(brushing his head)*
>
> It's thirsty. Pull the second tank.

Lucky pulls a knob. The car makes another weird noise. Chicago and Lucky look at each other, bewildered.

BACK OF TRUCK

Justice and Iesha look at each other. Justice is making shapes with a piece of string.

> **LUCKY**
>
> Empty. I thought you filled 'em.

> **CHICAGO**
>
> I thought you did.

Lucky gives him a look that reads "You stupid muthafucka."

> CUT TO:

75 *EXT. ROADSIDE COFFEE AND GAS—DAY*

Where we see the truck pull into one of the stations. In the background we see an eighteen-wheeler semi truck pull into the other side.

ANOTHER ANGLE

As Lucky hops out of the truck. He walks toward the back of the truck, just as Iesha and Justice open the back doors. We hold on them for a moment.

> **IESHA**
>
> Good, now I can get me some liquor!

They walk past as we follow them and end on Chicago.

> **CHICAGO**
>
> Hey, hey, don't get crazy now!
> And buy me a forty and some Cheetos!

The girls walk on. Iesha waves off Chicago.

LUCKY *(O.S.)*

You need to put her in check! C'mon, let's hurry up. Try
to stay on schedule for a change. Fuck that CP time!

THE PUMP: OPPOSITE SIDE

A foot steps out of the cab.

*A pair of gloves are taken off, revealing worn callused hands. The same
hands unscrew the cap off the truck's massive gas tank.*

THE SIDE OF THE GAS PUMP

THE PUMP

*Where we see Lucky's hand grab the handle. Another hand grabs at the
same time.*

LUCKY

Looks up to see.

A large white Trucker. Checked shirt, suspenders, big leather boots.

There is a short moment between Lucky and the Trucker.

LUCKY

You mind?

*The Trucker nods, indicating that he doesn't. He continues to study
Lucky.*

OPPOSITE SIDE OF THE PUMP

Where Lucky inserts the nozzle into the tank and begins to pump the gas.

CUT TO:

76 *INT. ROADSIDE COFFEE AND GAS—DAY*

THE FREEZER

Where Iesha is selecting liquor.

IESHA

I gotta have my Gordon's and Socko. Justice, check that
freezer, see if they got some Super Socko. . . . Hey, they
don't have Old E! Y'all don't have no Old English?

THE COUNTER

*Where the cashier throws his hands up, indicating that they don't carry
it.*

CONTINUED:

76 CONTINUED

> JUSTICE

Girl, don't you know they don't sell that outside of Black neighborhoods?

> IESHA

Oh yeah, I forgot. Oh well, Chicago gonna have to settle for a Miller Light.

> JUSTICE

Don't get too crazy now. You know how you get when you drink. You heard what your man said.

> IESHA

Chicago?! I don't listen to him. He ain't my daddy!

> JUSTICE

He's supposed to be your man, though.

> IESHA

Sheeehit! I got him sprung! I be making that fool stutter. You know he start stuttering when he lying and shit.

> *CUT TO:*

77 *EXT. ROADSIDE COFFEE AND GAS—DAY*

CLOSE: CHICAGO

> CHICAGO

Now, now, now, wait, wait, wait, see, see, see!

ANOTHER ANGLE

> LUCKY

Money?! You give her money?!

> CHICAGO

Just sometimes. I like my woman to have tha best.

> LUCKY

You getting played! How much o' that coochie she be giving up?

77A *EXT. ROADSIDE COFFEE AND GAS—DAY*

BACK TO STORE

IESHA

I don't hardly have to do nothing. I be rationing it to 'em.

JUSTICE

Rationing tha booty!

(laughs)

77B *EXT. ROADSIDE COFFEE AND GAS—DAY*

BACK TO PUMP

CHICAGO

Aw, nigga, I be knocking that shit out every other day.
She can't get enough o' me.

77C *EXT. ROADSIDE COFFEE AND GAS—DAY*

BACK TO STORE

IESHA

That nigga is weak! Ain't got no rhythm! Plus, he a
preemie! You know what a preemie is? Two-minute bro-
tha.

Justice laughs.

77D *EXT. ROADSIDE COFFEE AND GAS—DAY*

BACK TO PUMP

LUCKY

You paying for it!

CHICAGO

Wait, wait, wait!

LUCKY

Naw, nigga, you can't say shit! You paying for it! Paying
for tha poon!

He glances across the pump.

THE TRUCK

Where the Trucker stands patiently with his arms folded.

LUCKY

Be done in a second, cuzz.

The Trucker waits. Arms folded.

77E EXT. ROADSIDE COFFEE AND GAS—DAY

BACK TO STORE

JUSTICE

Is at the counter.

JUSTICE

You got everything?

IESHA

Yeah. So what you think of Lucky?

JUSTICE

I don't. Look.

She points to a display where we see some toy water guns.

IESHA

Oooow!

The cashier has finished. He has a total.

CASHIER

That'll be $15.35.

Justice walks back over to the counter.

JUSTICE *(O.S.)*

I got it. Iesha, pick up some o' those blow bubbles, too.

CUT TO:

78 EXT. ROADSIDE COFFEE AND GAS—DAY

Where we see Justice burst out of the store laughing. She turns and begins squirting water at Iesha. We travel with them back to the truck as Iesha playfully squirts Chicago. He starts running after her. He catches her, and they affectionately play with each other. The contrast of their play to the tension between Lucky and Justice is apparent. They share a quiet, uncomfortable glance. Justice gets into the passenger seat.

LUCKY
(to Chicago and Iesha)

Get in tha truck! We don't have all day! Shit! I gotta be somewhere.

He walks around the side of the truck.

THE PUMP

Where the Trucker begins pumping his gas.

79 *EXT. ROADSIDE COFFEE AND GAS—DAY*

Where we see the truck take off once more.

80 *INT. THE TRUCK—DAY*

THE BACK

Where Iesha and Chicago are kicking it. Chicago looks bored. Iesha is mixing the gin with the Super Socko.

IESHA

Drink some o' this.

She hands him the Super Socko. Chicago takes a squig.

IESHA

Drink some more. To the middle.

Chicago takes a couple more drinks. He checks for the level of Socko left. Iesha takes the bottle back and fills it with gin. She then proceeds to shake it up.

CHICAGO

Lemme have my forty.

He looks in the bag.

IESHA

They didn't have no Old E.

Chicago looks frustrated.

Iesha has finished her concoction. She samples her work. Taking a small sip from the bottle.

IESHA

Mmmmmm.

She passes the bottle to Chicago, who takes a sip. Over their drinking we hear Justice's voice.

JUSTICE (V.O.)

"Love is a juice with many tastes. Some bitter, others sweet. A wine which has few . . ."

81 *INT. THE TRUCK: FRONT—DAY*

JUSTICE'S NOTEBOOK

Where we see her hand write.

JUSTICE *(V.O.)*

" . . . few . . . vineyards."

Justice is lost in thought. Where to go from here?

LUCKY

Takes notice of her writing out of the corner of his eye.

JUSTICE

Notices Lucky looking at her periodically. She takes particular notice of his dirty nasty fingernails.

JUSTICE

Your fingernails are dirty.

Lucky looks at his fingernails. He seems kinda self-conscious and moves his hands to another part of the steering wheel.

LUCKY

What you writing?

JUSTICE
(a beat)

Stuff.

There is an uneasy space of time between them. They look at each other out of the corner of their eyes. They almost make eye contact.

82 *EXT. THE ROAD—DAY*

Where we see the truck zoom up the road and into the distance.

DISSOLVE TO:

83 *INT. THE TRUCK—DAY*

THE BACK

Where Chicago and Iesha settle in the back seat letting the liquor take its effect.

CHICAGO

Say you love me.

                    IESHA

Why?

                   CHICAGO

Cause I *said* so!

                    IESHA

That's what you wanna hear, huh?

                   CHICAGO

Yeah.

                    IESHA

Really? Good.
                    (gets up, stretches her arms)
You're so dumb. The more I teach you the dumber you
get.
          (does a double take and smells the air)
Mmmmm. S'mthing smell good.

THE FRONT: FROM THE OUTSIDE: DRIVER'S SIDE

Where Lucky and Justice sit.

                   LUCKY

What's that smell?

Justice samples the air with her beautiful nose.

                   JUSTICE

Barbecue.

Chicago comes up front.

                   CHICAGO

Y'all smell that?

                   LUCKY
           (his eyes catching something)
Yeah.

FROM THE INSIDE OF THE WINDOW

We see a sign which reads JOHNSON FAMILY REUNION.

                    IESHA

What this?

                                        CONTINUED:

83 CONTINUED

JUSTICE
(with open eyes)

Oh shit! Look!

ANOTHER ANGLE

As we see a virtual ocean of Black faces in the distance. There is a gathering of some kind going on in a large park by the side of the freeway. We start on this image, then PAN over to reveal the truck moving forward.

84 *EXT. THE TRUCK—DAY*

As we travel alongside the truck as we see it in relation to the reunion. Note Three Levels: Truck in f.g./Trees in m.g./People in b.g./Characters speak in Long Shot.

CHICAGO

C'mon, we gonna get some barbecue.

LUCKY

We can't stay long, man. I gotta get to Oakland. Why niggas always gotta be thinking about eating?! You eat too much anyway. That's why you head so big. Hair look like taco meat.

85 *EXT. THE TRUCK—DAY*

As the truck stops and everybody gets out and walks toward the gathering of people. Iesha lags behind and takes the last couple of sips from her drink. She takes one long last hit.

86 *EXT. THE JOHNSON FAMILY REUNION—DAY*

WIDE

As we START on Lucky, Justice, and Chicago, and Iesha running to catch up. They are walking forward just as we SWING behind them and CRANE UP to reveal a banner that reads JOHNSON FAMILY REUNION.

MONTAGE OF IMAGES

We see people talking, playing games, some hugging, reunions between relatives, old mixing with the young, some dancing and a lot of food being cooked. This is the Johnson Family Reunion. We emphasize this last image of food being cooked.

LUCKY AND CHICAGO

Look at each other. Their intentions are obvious.

IESHA

Catches up as we PULL BACK with her, to reveal all four of them.

IESHA

What y'all gonna do?

CHICAGO

We gonna eat.

JUSTICE

This ain't your family!

LUCKY

We Black. They don't know that.

ANGLE

Where we see a brother who is walking through the crowd obviously drunk. He is about thirty years old and has a beard. He is also talking very loud greeting everyone around him. Everyone around seems to be amused by his antics. He is known as Cousin Pete.

COUSIN PETE

My cousins! My cousins! I'm with my family! My family!
  (sees a couple of fine women standing together)

Mmmm, how you doing? We related, huh?

The woman nods yes.

COUSIN PETE

Oh, really? Well, you know, third removed don't count.
  (laughs and moves on)

The crowd parts to reveal him as he walks toward the foursome.

COUSIN PETE

My cousins! My cousins! What's up, cousin? You got a pretty girlfriend here. Y'all make a good couple.

JUSTICE'S FACE

As she reacts to being called Lucky's girlfriend.

COUSIN PETE

What's your name, cousin?

LUCKY

People call me Lucky.

CONTINUED:

86 CONTINUED

COUSIN PETE

With a lady like this, I'd say that too. What's your name, sweet li'l West Coast thang?

JUSTICE

Justice.

COUSIN PETE

Justice? You mean like the law, huh?

JUSTICE

Yeah.

COUSIN PETE

How you get a name like that?!

JUSTICE

It's a long story. This is—

IESHA
(putting on airs)

Iesha. And this is my *husband*, Chicago.

We see subtle eye contact between Iesha and Justice.

CHICAGO

How you doing?

LUCKY

Yo, ah—cousin, what's your name?

COUSIN PETE

Just call me Cousin Pete. I want y'all to meet some family.

They begin to walk, Cousin Pete leading the way.

ANOTHER ANGLE: MOVING BACK

As Cousin Pete begins introducing Lucky, Justice, Iesha, and Chicago to the Johnson family. He introduces a few relatives, then we switch to a P.O.V. shot and we GO PAST their faces and see them as he says their names. We end on three old ladies sitting at a picnic table.

COUSIN PETE *(V.O.)*

This is Aunt Jessica, Uncle Herb, Aunt Aida Pearl, Uncle Fred and his wife Wilma, Cousin Isaac, Cousin James, Cousin Kwame, the Kids, I don't know all of they names, and sitting here is Aunt June, Aunt May, and Aunt April.

THE BENCH

Where three old women sit: Aunt April, Aunt May, and Aunt June. From their faces we can tell they are full of opinions.

COUSIN PETE

So y'all just enjoy yourself,. and have fun.

Iesha and Chicago go to sit down on the bench across the table from the three old women. Iesha sits in Chicago's lap.

LUCKY

That food looks good.

COUSIN PETE

Don't it? Go on, help yourself.

Lucky and Justice walk toward the tables with food.

ANGLE: MOVING BACKWARD

On Iesha and Chicago

IESHA
(with sarcasm)

Goodbye. Don't they make such a nice couple?

JUSTICE

Turns and throws Iesha a nasty look and continues walking with Lucky.

BACK TO TABLE

Where Iesha and Chicago settle. They are both thoroughly amused by the game they are playing. The both of them then turn to notice

THE STERN FACES OF THE THREE OLD WOMEN

We PAN past the stern faces of Aunt April, Aunt May, and Aunt June. We rest on June's face as she speaks.

AUNT JUNE

Are y'all in love?

IESHA AND CHICAGO

Look at each other.

IESHA

Yeah.

AUNT JUNE

Do you know what love is, child?

CONTINUED:

86 CONTINUED

IESHA

No.

AUNT MAY

How can you be in love if'n you don't know what it is?

IESHA

That's just how things go.

The three women are quiet for a moment.

AUNT MAY

Are y'all married?

IESHA

Yeah.

AUNT APRIL

You young. How long you been married?

IESHA
(looks at Chicago)

Six months.

Aunt June's hawklike eyes probe Iesha.

AUNT JUNE'S P.O.V.

We see Iesha's hand on Chicago's shoulder. Then we TILT UP to reveal her face. She looks at her hand searching for a ring.

IESHA

Oh, I don't wear it alla time.

WIDE

Of the table. You could cut the tension in the air with a knife.

AUNT JUNE
(to Chicago)

You don't mind if she don't wear your ring?

IESHA
(answers for him)

No, he don't mind.

AUNT MAY

I think he can answer for himself. If he's a *real* man. A real man always answers for himself.

CHICAGO
(a beat)

No. No—I don't mind.

The three women shake their heads. One says, "Shoot, my husband kill me if I didn't wear no ring."

CUT TO:

87 *EXT. THE JOHNSON FAMILY REUNION—DAY*

THE FOOD TABLE

Where Lucky is filling his plate with food. Justice is nearby. Next to her is a woman with a baby. The woman is trying to fix a plate of food and hold the baby at the same time.

JUSTICE

Damn you greedy.

LUCKY

Gotta eat to live.

Justice notices the woman having trouble juggling baby and plate.

JUSTICE

You need help?

WOMAN

Thank you.

Justice takes the baby in her arms.

Lucky looks at her out of the corner of his eye and continues surveying the food.

JUSTICE

Aww, she's so cute.

We see the baby's face. She is a black angel.

LUCKY
(with sarcasm)

You be seeing them professional men, huh? Doctors, lawyers, pharmacists.
        (tastes something, then adds)

Street pharmacists?

Justice looks at Lucky, then down at the baby.

CONTINUED:

87 CONTINUED

> **LUCKY**
>
> Ah huh, I knew you was like that.

Justice says nothing.

The Woman finishes fixing her plate.

> **WOMAN**
>
> Here, I'll take her.

> **JUSTICE**
>
> She's beautiful. What's her name?

> **WOMAN**
>
> Her name is Imani.

The Woman walks off to a table and sits with another group of relatives.

> **JUSTICE**
>
> You got a kid?

> **LUCKY**
>
> Why?

> **JUSTICE**
>
> 'Cause you look the type.

Lucky begins to walk.

ANOTHER ANGLE: WIDE TRAVELING

As they walk together and talk. In the background we see kids playing, and some old men throwing horseshoes, etc.

> **LUCKY**
>
> What's the type?

> **JUSTICE**
>
> Dunno, you just look like—like—

Lucky looks at her for a second, stops walking, and walks on.

> **LUCKY**
> (changing the subject)
>
> Anyway! You got any kids?

> **JUSTICE**
> (vehemently)
>
> Hell, naw. I don't like kids.

They arrive at some chairs and sit down.

LUCKY

Don't look like that to me!
> *(looks around)*

This is good. You ever been to one a' these?

JUSTICE

No. I don't have a lot of family. The family I have ain't that close.

LUCKY
> *(looking around)*

Well, I never seen this many Black folks in one place where there wasn't no fight. Hmmm. . . . Now what about these street pharmacists you *useta* go out with?

JUSTICE

Yeah, I only went out with one. . . . He was my first boyfriend—my first love.

LUCKY

So you was out for tha money, huh?

JUSTICE

No. Just 'cause somebody does a certain something for a livin don't make 'em a bad person. Some people don't choose their path in life. They let other folks write their story. Most of them in jail now.
> *(adds)*

There's some fine niggas in jail.

LUCKY

You used to count his money?

JUSTICE

Yep.

LUCKY

Write letters to 'em while he was inna county jail?

JUSTICE

Mmmm-huh. That's right.

CONTINUED:

87 CONTINUED

LUCKY

You used to send 'em naked pictures while they in jail too?

CLOSE: JUSTICE'S FACE

JUSTICE
(a beat)

You getting too personal. . . . Oh what do you know. You don't even keep your nails clean!

She gets up and walks away.

Lucky just looks at her, grins, and shakes his head.

DISSOLVE TO:

DIFFERENT IMAGES

Kids playing. Two little boys fight and are broken up by Cousin Pete, who says, "Y'all family. Don't fight."

OLD MEN THROWING HORSESHOES.

Some young people are dancing. A few older folk join in on the fun.

Lucky and Chicago playing a game of spades with Cousin Pete and another man.

Iesha going to an ice chest to get a Bacardi Cooler.

Justice playing with some children. The three old women sitting like statues.

Lucky and Chicago winning a hand, then starting the game up again. Cousin Pete shouts out, "Awright then, let's play for money, play for money!"

Iesha getting another drink.

Justice resting on the beautiful green grass as a little girl puts a flower in her hair. Suddenly, she turns to notice something.

One of the old women taps another as all three direct their attention toward

Iesha, who is talking to some brother, a fly-looking Johnny Gill type. There is definite interest in both their eyes.

Justice looks from this sight over toward Chicago.

THE CARD TABLE

Where Chicago notices this also. He is pissed. Offscreen, someone asks him to deal his hand. He does so, never taking his eyes off of . . .

IESHA AND JOHNNY

We PAN from Iesha's drunken smiling face to the handsome face of Johnny.

THE OLD WOMEN

Are having a field day. All three of them are talking away and looking out the corner of their eyes.

JUSTICE

Gets up from the children and walks over toward Iesha.

WIDE

As Justice approaches Iesha and Johnny.

JUSTICE

I gotta talk to my friend for a second.

BACK TO CARD TABLE

Where we MOVE IN on Chicago's face.

LUCKY

Looks at Chicago and then over toward Iesha.

BACK TO SHOT

Where Iesha pulls away from Justice and goes back to talking with her new friend.

CHICAGO

Gets up and throws his entire hand down. We PAN OVER to Lucky, who takes off his hat and scratches his head.

LUCKY
(under his breath)

Oh, shit!

WIDE SHOT

As Chicago walks into the shot toward Iesha and Johnny. Iesha looks over at Chicago nonchalantly. She doesn't even acknowledge his presence. Chicago grabs her arm. Iesha pulls away and tries to resume her conversation. Chicago pulls her again, and Iesha walks away toward the parking lot.

CONTINUED:

87 CONTINUED

Johnny tries to interfere and Chicago pushes him. She begins cursing loudly, making it more of a scene than it already was. Chicago and the brother get into a fight. Several family members attempt to break it up.

JUSTICE

Is embarrassed. She looks over at Lucky.

LUCKY

Looks back at her. Their eyes meet.

LUCKY
(to the card group)

Y'all don't mind if I take some food to go, do you?

THE TABLE

Where the old women sit.

AUNT JUNE

Humph, that ain't gonna last long.

CUT TO:

88 *EXT. THE ROAD—DAY: OVERHEAD ON CRANE*

As we see the empty road, then ZOOM as the truck goes up into the distance. We hear Iesha and Chicago arguing.

89 *INT. THE TRUCK—DAY*

LUCKY

Is driving once more. He taps his fingers on the steering wheel and looks over at

JUSTICE

Who looks at him shakes her head and looks out the window.

THE BACK

Where Chicago and Iesha are going at it. Swinging insults like swords.

CHICAGO

What's your muthafuckin problem, huh? What's your muthafuckin problem? Why you disrespect me like that, huh?! Why you disrespect me?

IESHA

Fuck you! You don't *own* me!

CHICAGO

Fuck you, bitch! Fuck you and your pussy!

IESHA

If I'm a bitch, why you wit me, huh? Why you wit me?!
Leave, then! Step tha fuck off! 'Cause I ain't in the busi-
ness of keeping niggas when they don't wanna be kept!
All that talkin—do it while you walkin.

THE FRONT

Justice is fed up. She looks over at Lucky.

JUSTICE

Pull over.

90 *EXT. REST STOP—DAY*

Where the truck pulls over in line with a row of ten-wheelers.

91 *INT. THE TRUCK—DAY*

THE BACK

CHICAGO

Why we stopping?

IESHA

Good, I gotta pee.

CHICAGO

'Cause you drinking too much! That's your goddamn
problem. You an alcoholic bitch!

They continue arguing back and forth.

91A *EXT. REST STOP—DAY*

THE PASSENGER DOOR

Justice hops out of the truck and goes toward the back.

THE BACK

Of the truck, where Iesha (bottle in hand) opens the door.

JUSTICE
(coolly)

C'mere. I gotta talk to you.

*Iesha faintly sees the anger on Justice's face but is not aware that it is
directed toward her.*

CONTINUED:

91A CONTINUED

IESHA
(sweetly and drunk)

What's wrong, J? Lucky talking shit again? I'ma fuck
him up! Where he at?

*Justice lures Iesha out to the middle of the parking lot. The latter is
holding her stomach. A few truckers walk past to notice the two girls
arguing.*

*Iesha begins to convulse, then she throws up on the ground. She calmly
and coolly accepts a tissue from Justice, then says . . .*

IESHA

What's the problem?

Justice grabs the bottle out of Iesha's hand.

IESHA

My drink!

JUSTICE
(smashes the bottle on the ground)

This is the problem!

(pushes Iesha in anger)

You acting like a stupid bitch, Iesha! A stupid, alcoholic
bitch! I'm tired of seeing you get drunk! That's why I
don't go nowhere with you—'cause you get crazy! You
just like my damn . . . momma was.

*Iesha looks at her angry friend as if stunned. Actually, she is drunk.
Iesha sways back and forth as if in a daze. She begins crying.*

IESHA
(crying)

I'm sorry.

Justice's anger gives way to compassion. She hugs her friend.

WIDE SHOT

As they hug each other and an eighteen-wheeler pulls out and away.

ANOTHER ANGLE

As the large truck goes past, to reveal the women once more.

JUSTICE

It's all right. It's all right. You my girl and all, but you
gotta chill on the liquor.

Iesha continues to cry, mumbling in a drunken tone about how much she values Justice's friendship: "You helped me when I had that abortion," etc. Crying gives way to sniffles, and Iesha tries to regain her composure. She turns around to see . . .

REVERSE ANGLE

THE TRUCK

Where Lucky and Chicago sit by the front of the truck. Chicago is looking at Iesha.

IESHA'S FACE

As she wipes her tears away and stands up straight. She looks in her Fendi bag to pull out some tissue, maintaining her dignity in front of the men.

IESHA

I gotta pee.

Justice looks at her friend and almost cracks a smile. They walk off toward a restroom.

JUSTICE
(playfully)

Cow.

IESHA

You a cow. Cow! Mooo!

BACK TO TRUCK

LUCKY

I'm telling you she's crazy, Loc. You better get ridda her.

CHICAGO
(upset)

Damn man, I gotta piss. I 'ma go over here and piss in the field. Get my nuts close to nature and shit.

As they walk off.

DISSOLVE TO:

92 *EXT. JUSTICE'S HOUSE—SEVEN YEARS EARLIER—DAY*

We see an early-model 1980s car pull up the driveway. Out the passenger door springs a twelve-year-old Black girl. This is Justice, seven years younger. She runs toward the house. The driver of the car is Geneva, Justice's grandmother.

CONTINUED:

92 CONTINUED

GENEVA

> Girl, you better come on back here and help me with these grocery bags!

THE STEPS

Where Young Justice reluctantly shrugs her shoulders and walks back toward the car.

93   *INT. JUSTICE'S HOUSE—THE KITCHEN—DAY*

Where Justice and her grandmother put away the groceries. Geneva snatches a box of cookies out of Justice's hand.

GENEVA

> You'll spoil your dinner. I'm making ox tails.
> *(calls out)*
> Alfrieda! Frieda! Go tell your mother to come here!

The little girl takes off.

93A   *INT. JUSTICE'S HOUSE—DAY*

THE STAIRS

As Young Justice shoots up the stairs.

93B   *INT. JUSTICE'S HOUSE—DAY*

THE TOP OF THE STAIRS

Justice the adult woman arrives at the top of the stairs.

YOUNG JUSTICE

> Momma! Momma! Nanny want you!

93C   *INT. JUSTICE'S HOUSE—DAY*

AN OFFICE ROOM

As Justice looks in. No Momma here.

93D   *INT. JUSTICE'S HOUSE—DAY*

JUSTICE'S MOTHER'S BEDROOM

No one here.

93E   *INT. JUSTICE'S HOUSE—DAY*

THE BATHROOM

We see Justice walk forth. She slows down as she discovers

ANOTHER ANGLE

As we move toward the body of a woman collapsed on a tile floor of the bathroom.

YOUNG JUSTICE'S FACE

She screams!

93F *INT. JUSTICE'S HOUSE—DAY*

BACK TO KITCHEN

As Justice's grandmother hears her screams.

93G *INT. JUSTICE'S HOUSE—DAY*

THE TILE FLOOR

We see an opened bottle of pills. Different angles of pills on the tile floor. [Idea: Image of Justice's mother's hand open, holding pills, in the background]

OVERHEAD

Justice's grandmother grabs Justice and discovers the body.

ANOTHER ANGLE

As Justice is pulled away. Geneva turns her face away from the horror of Justice's dead mother and into the hallway mirror. Justice covers her face up, then slowly looks at her reflection. The light behind her changes, and we are back into . . .

94 *INT. REST STOP BATHROOM—DAY*

Justice looking at herself in the mirror. A beat. Iesha comes out of the stall behind Justice and taps her shoulder.

ANOTHER ANGLE

As Iesha walks past and we end on Justice.

IESHA

Let's go.

95 *EXT. REST STOP—DAY: MINUTES LATER*

A BENCH

Where Lucky sits eating some leftover barbecue. Music is playing from his small boom box. Chicago is lost in thought. He is visibly shaken by the recent events. He looks out along the road and then down toward the ground.

CONTINUED:

95 CONTINUED

LUCKY

Hey, hey, hey, pick your head up. Don't be a buster! You don't want her to know you upset! Be cool!

CHICAGO'S FEET

Where his shoelaces are untied.

CHICAGO

I gotta tie my shoelace.

LUCKY

Wait, just wait. . . . Leave it untied—it'll look better that way.

CHICAGO

That shit played out years ago.

Chicago bends down to fasten his shoes. Lucky looks at him and shakes his head. Then he looks up to notice

CHICAGO'S P.O.V.: LOW ANGLE

While he is down on his knees, Justice and Iesha walk up. Chicago looks up and sees Justice, who walks away to reveal Iesha. Iesha mumbles the "shake it to the east/shake it to the west" cheer.

WIDE

As Justice sits on one side with Lucky. Iesha puts her arms around Chicago's neck and gives him a kiss.

Justice and Lucky look at this exchange out of the corner of their eyes.

CHICAGO

As he attempts to stay angry in light of this loving treatment. He looks over at Lucky.

CHICAGO
(*uncomfortable*)

Is it good?

LUCKY

Jammin.

Justice looks away, listening to the music.

JUSTICE

This is nice. Who's this?

LUCKY

My cousin Kalil.

JUSTICE
(matter of factly)

He's flowing.

LUCKY

I give him ideas and stuff sometimes. That's who I'm going to see now. We got this music thing going.

CHICAGO
(sarcastic)

It's all right.

LUCKY

Fuck you, bitch. Why you always got something negative to say?! At least the nigga's *creative!*

CHICAGO

I'm *creative!* I know how to dress.

LUCKY

That ain't shit. You just a post-office-working nigga can't even get into the union. What you got?

CHICAGO

What you got? Just cause you in the union don't mean shit!

JUSTICE

Why y'all always fightin? I thought y'all was friends?

CHICAGO

We ain't friends. We just work at the same place.

There is a pause. No one but the air moves. Iesha is restless. She gets up. Sobriety gives way to silliness. She stands and begins stomping on the ground and slapping her legs. She continues to do the "shake it to the east/shake it to the west" cheer.

IESHA
(to Justice)

Remember this?! Audubon Junior High?! "Shake it to tha east, shake it to tha west—it really doesn't matter who shakes the best!"

CONTINUED:

95 CONTINUED

Justice joins in.

The Two Guys just look at them crazy.

CUT TO:

96 INT. THE TRUCK—DAY

Chicago and Iesha poke their heads through the back. Everybody seems to be in a good mood. Iesha is telling a joke.

IESHA

So we up in heaven, right? And it's Judgment Day. And this brother goes up to the gate. The angel at the gate says, "How many times did you cheat on your wife?" The brother says, "I never cheated on my wife." So the angel checks the book and says, "You're right." So the brother rolls on into heaven in a Rolls-Royce. . . . So another brother comes in and he says, "I can't lie. I cheated on my wife once." So the angel checks the book, and he rolls on into heaven in a Cadillac. . . . So then this other brother comes in and he's a straight-up hoe, and he tells the angel, "Well, I can't remember how many times I cheated on my wife." So he goes and rolls into heaven on a bike. So now he's in heaven and he's just pedaling along, and he rolls by the brother in tha Rolls, who is crying. So the brother on the bike says, "Why you crying? You rollin through heaven in a Rolls-Royce." And the brother in the Rolls says, "I just passed my wife on roller skates!"

Everybody laughs.

JUSTICE
(looks at Lucky)

You need to clean them nails. Get a manicure. Plenty men do it. Football players, basketball players. They all come in the shop.

96A EXT. THE ROAD—DAY

LUCKY *(V.O.)*

You out your mind!

Where we see the truck shoot up past a beautiful California backdrop.

97 EXT. ALICE'S RESTAURANT—DAY

Where we see Jessie's Lexus roll up, as well as the other car with the girls inside.

HEYWOOD *(V.O.)*

Finally! I could eat a horse!

JESSIE *(V.O.)*

From the looks this place, they probably have that on the menu.

They get out of the car and walk toward the restaurant.

THE TERRACE: OUTSIDE

Where some bikers sit eatin lunch.

BIKER

So I said, Fuck that! got on my bike—ran 'em over!

He picks up a bottle of Evian and takes a squig.

97A   *INT. ALICE'S RESTAURANT—DAY*

ANOTHER ANGLE: JESSIE'S P.O.V.

As we go into the café on the backs of Heywood and Dexter, who part to reveal a café full of bikers, motorists, and a Waitress. Jessie looks her up and down. The sound of Steely Dan's "No Static at All" flows through the room. There is definitely a bohemian atmosphere here.

REVERSE ANGLE: JESSIE

Checking out the place.

WAITRESS
(instant attitude)

How many?

JESSIE

Seven, please. Smoking section. I gotta have a cigarette.

WAITRESS

There is no smoking section.

JESSIE

I see. Just gimme a seat then.

WAITRESS

You can have that table over there once it's cleaned off.

THE TABLE

Where a man begins setting the table.

CONTINUED:

97A CONTINUED

DEXTER
(to Heywood)

Man, why you always rubbing your stomach?

Jessie playfully rubs Heywood's stomach. The Waitress comes back.

The Waitress begins walking to a table across the room. Jessie and party follow.

DEXTER

Maybe we should go to an AM/PM on the way. I'm not that hungry.

JESSIE

I don't want no frozen food, no chips. I need something *hot* to eat. Besides, these folks need to see some Black people sometimes. Wake 'em! Pick 'em up! Give something interesting to talk about.

THE TABLE

Where they arrive and pick up menus.

Jessie begins to look in a menu as she notices behind her a couple, white, twentysomething, who are arguing.

Everybody else at the table looks over at the couple too. Jessie ignores this and begins to select from the menu.

HEYWOOD

I like this. Healthy food. Good people.

MAXINE

They got avocado salad. I love avocadoes.

JESSIE

Anyway. Make sure we got some tabasco sauce at this table. You know *they* food don't have no taste to it.

She looks in her purse, pulls out a pack of cigarettes, picks one out, and lights up.

ANOTHER TABLE

Where the Waitress takes another order. She keeps looking toward Jessie and Co.

DEXTER

Jessie, you know this is the *non*smoking section.

MAXINE

Look. Look. Girlfriend is tryin to decide whether or not to come and tell you to put it out.

We see the Waitress at the other table. She is definitely looking in Jessie's direction.

JESSIE

She better just keep thinking.

WAITRESS'S P.O.V.

The Waitress begins walking toward Jessie. At the end of the shot she comes to the front of the table, just as Jessie lets out a cool puff of smoke and gives a look as if to say "What the hell you want?"

HEYWOOD

Oh look, baby's got some courage. Here she comes.

ANGLE

The Waitress arrives at the table.

WAITRESS

You have to put your cigarette out. You're ruining the environment.

THE KITCHEN

Where we see Arlo Guthrie flipping burgers on the grill and smokin a joint.

BACK TO SCENE

JESSIE
(ignoring her)

I'm almost finished. Gotta satisfy my nic-fit. Be done in a sec.

WAITRESS

I'm not gonna take your order if you smoke.

JESSIE
(looks up)

Well then, you can just stand there and wait until I finish my smoke.

WAITRESS

You are disturbing other customers.

CONTINUED:

97A CONTINUED

> **JESSIE**
> *(turns around to the other table)*

You mind?

The couple nods they don't mind.

> **JESSIE**
> *(to her entourage)*

You mind?

Everybody at the table nods their approval.

> **JESSIE**
> *(sarcastically)*

Thank you.

The Waitress storms away as if she has been personally insulted.

> **JESSIE**

With her Farrah Fawcett 1977 hairdo. This place is a time warp.

They all laugh loudly.

Jessie continues to smoke.

BACK TO TABLE

> **DEXTER**

I think we should go.

> **JESSIE**

Dexter, calm down. I ain't gonna let you get lynched. This ain't Mississippi.
> *(opens her purse)*

You see that?

We see a .38 pistol inside her purse.

> **JESSIE**

I got it all under control. I don't play. Ask Maxine. You remember what I did to that nigga in Riverside that grabbed my booty?

> **HEYWOOD**
> *(changing subject)*

I wonder what happened to Justice?

> **COLETTE**
>
> I feel kinda bad she had to drive up by herself.

> **JESSIE**
>
> She ain't by herself. She probably with Iesha. Justice—
> now there's a girl who's got some problems.

98 *INT. MONTEREY AQUARIUM—DAY*

UNDERWATER

We see a montage of different beautiful tropical fish.

> **JESSIE (V.O.)**
>
> Don't wanna go nowhere, don't
> wanna have no fun, ain't seeing nobody . . .

*We cut to a dolphin swimming toward frame, then PAN over to reveal
Justice looking through an underwater viewing room.*

> **JESSIE (V.O.)**
>
> I think she need a boyfriend.

Justice looks over toward . . .

LUCKY

Who is looking in another tank. He turns to look at Justice.

98A *INT. ALICE'S RESTAURANT—DAY*

BACK TO CAFE

*Jessie pauses. Thinks. Puts out her cigarette and turns toward the Wait-
ress.*

> **JESSIE**
>
> Hey! Farrah! come over here and take my order!

CUT TO:

99 *EXT. A QUIET CALM BEAUTIFUL BEACH—DAY*

*We see an empty beach, dunes, flat sand. We PAN to reveal the mail truck
parked on the sand. In the distance are four figures.*

*Justice, Lucky, Iesha, and Chicago. No one speaks. Everybody is doing
their own thing. All we can hear is the voice of the Pacific Ocean. Justice
sits on the sand, sifting it through her hands like a funnel.*

We hear her thoughts as she looks out onto the ocean.

CONTINUED:

99 CONTINUED   .

JUSTICE *(V.O.)*

A wise man once said, you should look at the ocean and realize that no matter how famous you are, or how much money you make, you should know that you will never be as important as the ocean. . . . Damn, why didn't I go to college? Grandmomma would roll two times in her grave if she saw me now.

(looks toward Lucky)

Hmmm, he look kinda good. I know he got a kid, though. Look at him. He look like the type that got a baby stashed away somewheres.

Lucky and Chicago are throwing rocks, seeing who can make a rock skip the farthest. We hear Lucky's thoughts.

LUCKY *(V.O.)*

She's kinda cute. Got a nice little frame. Maybe I should get that number, see how that bootie works. . . . I wonder what Kalil's doing?

Iesha is playing in the warm sand. She has dug a hole and has placed her feet into it.

IESHA *(V.O.)*

I wonder if my momma picked up my clothes from the cleaners. . . . Oh, I know what I gotta do when I get back. I gotta call Terry with his fine ass. Ask him to take me shoppin.

Chicago is throwing rocks in the water.

CHICAGO *(V.O.)*

I need to just let her ass go. . . . Fuck it! I can just go and get me another bitch. I'm a good-looking nigga. I got a job. Income. Car. Apartment. My shit is set.

Chicago turns to look at Iesha. Note: Chicago in foreground, Iesha in background.

IESHA

Looks up at Chicago as if to say, "What the fuck you looking at?"

Chicago turns back around to continue throwing rocks.

Iesha turns to Justice.

IESHA

I'ma quit Chicago. His ass is L7 soon.

CUT TO:

100   *EXT. THE ROAD—DAY*

The truck shoots past a beautiful expanse of California farmland.

101   *INT. THE TRUCK—DAY: MOVING*

THE BACK

Where Iesha and Chicago sit. Both look bored. Iesha's legs and arms are folded.

Chicago gets up and looks into a bag and pulls out a couple of letters. He begins to open a few of them. Iesha looks surprised.

>   **IESHA**
>
> You can't do that.

>   **CHICAGO**
>
> Yeah, I can. Just put it in damage pile. It's fourth-class mail anyway.
>
>   *(reads)*
>
> A love letter.

He smells the paper.

>   **CHICAGO**
>
> Obsession.
>
>   *(to Iesha)*
>
> You wear that too. Don't you? I like the way you smell.

Iesha sits across the way. Arms folded.

>   **IESHA**
>
> I don't like the way you smell!

>   **CHICAGO**
>   *(reading letter)*
>
> "I can't wait to see you again. My heart aches with every day that you are gone. I had a dream last night, you were here, with me."
>
>   *(reads on to himself)*

>   **IESHA**
>
> You know you wrong.

Chicago looks up for a moment, then back to the letter.

                                          CONTINUED:

101 CONTINUED

IESHA

I'ma quit you when we get back to L.A. I'm young. I need to be alone for a while. Find myself and shit.

Chicago keeps reading the letter, acting like this isn't affecting him.

Iesha snuggles into a corner and closes her eyes.

Chicago looks over at her sleeping.

DISSOLVE TO:

102 *EXT. AFRICAN MARKET FESTIVAL—DAY*

We see images of dancers on a stage, people shopping at booths, carnival games. The air is alive with the sounds and smells of an African market festival. What follows is a Felliniesque scene on the Afrocentric tip. The sounds of African drums fill the air. Between the dialogue some striking visuals are intercut.

ANGLE

As we see Justice and Lucky walking together. Justice is taking in the sights and sounds of her environment. She is almost childlike but very much an alive woman for once. She is blowing soap bubbles.

Lucky seems lost in his own thoughts.

JUSTICE

What's wrong with you? Why you so quiet now?

LUCKY

Nuthin. I'm just thinking. I like to get out the city. Too much shit going down there. This is the only time I get to think. Or when I'm with my cousin and shit.

ANOTHER ANGLE

Where we notice both Iesha and Chicago are not walking together.

IESHA

I'm getting tired of all this walking, J!

CHICAGO

Me too.

BACK TO JUSTICE AND LUCKY

JUSTICE

So what you wanna do with your life?

LUCKY

Survive. Live. Shit. What you wanna do?

JUSTICE

I'm talking about goals, aspirations, shit like that.

LUCKY

I don't know yet. Music maybe.

JUSTICE

So what does your cousin rap about?

LUCKY

Stuff. Life.

JUSTICE

You sure he don't talk about typical shit?

LUCKY

What you mean typical? Like what?

JUSTICE

Like "I'm bad, I'm tha shit, I'll shoot a nigga in a minute,
I get all the pussy." Stuff like that.

LUCKY

What you write about in that notebook you carry?

They stop to notice.

*A large Black bald muscular brother standing before one of those amuse-
ment things where you hit a peg with a sledgehammer and it goes up to a
certain height. Several spectators are waiting to see the man hit the peg.*

JUSTICE

Poetry.

LUCKY

You trying to say my cousin's shit ain't poetry?

THE STRONGMAN

Hits the peg! It flies up!

JUSTICE *(V.O.)*

It ain't if he just talk about himself. You gotta have something to say. Somethin different, a perspective.

CONTINUED:

102 CONTINUED

The peg hits a bell, under which is written in red letters the word REVOLUTION.

JUSTICE

A voice.

They turn to walk out of the crowd.

LUCKY

What you write about?

JUSTICE

I write about what's in my heart.

LUCKY

And what's that?

(touches her shoulder)

She says nothing.

JUSTICE

I dunno. What's in yours?

LUCKY

I'm still trying to find out.

(notices the fact that he has touched Justice)

CHICAGO

Stands in a crowd. We are looking over his shoulder at Iesha throwing baseballs into holes. She wins a little bear, which brings a smile to her face. When she notices Chicago looking at her, it turns to a frown. Chicago then turns to look in Lucky and Justice's direction.

LUCKY AND JUSTICE

They are interrupted by Chicago's shouting.

CHICAGO
(shouting)

Why do we keep stopping? Don't we have a schedule to keep to?

LUCKY
(shouting)

We got plenty o' time. What you worried about, nigga? We always do this.

CHICAGO

We need to hurry up and get where we got to go. You keep proscratinatin.
> (joking)

You keep trying to gib to that bitch! That's tha problem.

JUSTICE
> (ignoring Chicago)

There's a fruit stand over there.
I wanna get some plums.
> (walks away)

CHICAGO

You can't pull that. She outta your league.

Lucky just gives him a look. Then he turns, and . . .

ANOTHER ANGLE

Lucky and Chicago in a crowd of people. Chicago walks away, frustrated, as we PULL BACK and around to see the source of the drums we have been hearing through this entire scene. It is the Last Poets, beating out the last couple of lines to "Niggas Are Scared of Revolution."

BLACK MAN

"But I'm a lover too! I'm a lover too! I love niggas! I love to see them walk, talk, and shoot tha shit! But there is one thing about niggas I do not love! Niggas are scared of Revolution!"

The crowd applauds.

> DISSOLVE TO:

103 *INT. THE TRUCK—DAY: MOVING*

THE FRONT

Where we see Justice bite into a plum with her juicy lips.

LUCKY

You didn't wash it.

JUSTICE

Yeah, I did.

LUCKY

How?

> CONTINUED:

103 CONTINUED

Justice rubs the plum back and forth between her hands and kisses it up to God.

Lucky looks on in amazement. All that is left is the seed, which Justice holds up proudly. She laughs.

DISSOLVE TO:

104 EXT. GRASSY FIELD—DAY

We see Justice walking toward us through a field. She walks slowly, almost dreamlike. Over this we hear Justice's voice reading a poem. It is "Phenomenal Woman." Suddenly, a zebra (yes a zebra) walks into the shot. First one, then another, then another. Soon there is a herd. Now we know we are in a dream—Until we hear Lucky's voice shout out.

LUCKY
Whatcha you doing?!

WIDE

Where we see the truck at the top of a hill that overlooks a field, in which we see Justice walking among African zebras. Chicago and Iesha get out of the truck and look down. Lucky has the hood up and is checking the engine.

JUSTICE
(shouting)
I wanna pet one of them!

ON THE HILL

IESHA
OOOOH!

BACK TO FIELD

Where Justice pets one of the animals.

LUCKY
They came from that castle over there. Hearst Castle! They have a some kinda private zoo there.

CHICAGO
They musta got out or somethin.

Chicago looks at Iesha. She senses she is being watched, then she looks over at him and walks away. He follows her.

THE ROAD

Where we see the truck by the road with the castle in the background.

Iesha has walked to the back of the truck. Chicago comes around the corner and tries to talk to her.

He tries a smoother approach.

CHICAGO
(smoothly)

So you wanna quit me, huh?

He puts his arms around her waist.

Don't you know how much I *love* you? Can I have a kiss?

She turns around to face him, and they kiss.

CUT TO:

105 *INT. THE TRUCK: MOVING—DAY*

Where Chicago and Iesha are still kissing. They are getting hot and heavy. Iesha is still doing this with some reluctance.

THE FRONT

Where Justice and Lucky sit. They are chummy-chummy now; they talk like old friends.

JUSTICE

My first boyfriend used to get into a lot of shit. . . . He got killed, though. Tried to jack the wrong person.

LUCKY

Tha *jacker* got himself *jacked*!

He laughs. Justice doesn't find it funny.

JUSTICE

He got killed over some stupid shit.

Lucky looks at her.

LUCKY

Then why you date fools like that?

JUSTICE

That's who I fell in love with. Didn't know no better.

LUCKY

What about now?

Justice has no reply. Lucky changes the subject.

CONTINUED:

105 CONTINUED

LUCKY

How many brothers and sisters you got?

JUSTICE

None. My momma didn't have no more kids. . . . She didn't
get a chance to.

*There is a somber moment. Lucky understands, vaguely. They hear a
moaning sound. Justice motions for Lucky to be quiet. She peeks through
the curtain.*

THE CURTAIN

*Where Iesha is now on top of Chicago. Riding him. Slowly she moves back
and forth, her legs around his waist.*

Suddenly, something is wrong. Iesha gets up.

THE BACK

Where we see Iesha looking frustrated.

IESHA

Is that it?!

CHICAGO

Shhh! Give me a coupla minutes.

IESHA
(louder)

Fuck that! You can't even hang that long! Couple minutes
shit my ass!

CHICAGO

Fuck you.

IESHA

You can't! That's the muthafuckin problem!

They begin arguing loudly.

THE FRONT

Where Lucky and Justice listen to Iesha and Chicago going at it.

LUCKY

I'm getting sick of this shit.

JUSTICE

Pull over somewheres.

LUCKY

Here we go again.

CUT TO:

105A EXT. ROCK CLIFF—DAY

FROM OVERHEAD

We see the truck pull to the side of the road. Iesha hops out, closely followed by Chicago. We MOVE slowly with them to reveal they have parked next to a cliff that overlooks the Pacific Ocean and some other rocky cliffs. In the distance we see Chicago and Iesha arguing.

ANOTHER ANGLE

As we see Iesha and Chicago squabble. We cannot hear them shouting at each other over the loud ocean waves crashing among the rocks below the cliff. The wind is blowing with a strong force.

THE TRUCK

Where Lucky and Justice sit. Justice is watching. Lucky minds his own business. He glances at his nails.

THE ROCKS

Where we see the waves crashing against the side of the cliff, eroding its sides bit by bit.

We juxtapose images of the waves to the ballet of Iesha and Chicago arguing. He pulls at her. She pulls away, etc. Their dialogue is drowned out by the sounds of the raging ocean.

Iesha gets fed up and walks toward the truck.

ANOTHER ANGLE

As we come down and follow Iesha. We can fully hear them arguing now.

IESHA

You weak! You a weak-ass punk! Just 'cause work out don't mean shit! Think you buff! I wish I never met your sorry ass! Sorry muthafucka!

Chicago takes his brush out of his back pocket and begins brushing his head. He is trying to maintain his cool because they are now in front of Lucky and Justice.

CONTINUED:

105A CONTINUED

IESHA

Yeah, that's right. Brush that hair. Weak-ass fade! Nigga dick can't stay hard five seconds. Watcha do, take steroids?!

We see Iesha's mouth in CLOSE UP. She continues to lay on the insults as we SLOW DOWN TIME.

Chicago continues to brush his head. He concentrates on looking at Iesha's mouth running a mile a minute.

REAL TIME

IESHA

That's why I'm fucking somebody else!

This catches Chicago's attention. He stops brushing his head, and calmly walks toward Iesha, as we PULL BACK with him to an over-the-shoulder with Iesha.

JUSTICE

Is wondering what will happen next.

CLOSE: ON CHICAGO'S FACE

He is angry.

CLOSE: ON IESHA'S FACE

Who gives him a look that reads, "You ain't gonna do shit!" She continues to taunt him.

ANOTHER ANGLE

Lucky, as he turns away.

LUCKY

Awww, shit!

SLOW MOTION

As Chicago slaps tha shit outta Iesha. Her back is to CAMERA so that we can see the fury in Chicago's face.

ANGLE: SLO MO

Chicago's hand hitting Iesha.

BACK TO NORMAL SPEED

Iesha reels back, then recovers. She touches her mouth. There is blood on her hand. She looks up toward Chicago. We see fire and fury in her eyes, and then . . .

IESHA GOES MUTHAFUCKING CRAZY!!!

IESHA
(shouting and echoing)

Muthafucka!!!!

Iesha charges toward Chicago with fury. Hell hath no fury like a Black woman's scorn.

Iesha and Chicago fight. Each is cursing at the other. To our surprise this is no one-sided battle: Iesha is holding her own. She hits Chicago square on the chin with a wild punch. Chicago reels back in shock and continues fighting.

Justice is going crazy. She doesn't know what to do.

JUSTICE
(to Lucky)

You just gonna let 'em fight?!

LUCKY

That ain't my business.

Wild with frustration, Justice gets out of the truck and walks toward the fighting couple.

Lucky gets outta the truck.

CHICAGO AND IESHA

The tide has turned on the fight—Chicago is kicking Iesha's ass now. She swings a wild punch, and he connects with a direct hit.

Chicago drops back to get his bearings. We see Justice come up in the background. Boom! A foot slams between Chicago's legs.

Chicago grabs his crotch in pain. He slowly turns, then charges Justice. They tumble on the ground, and he reels back to hit her.

LUCKY (O.S.)

Hey!

ANGLE

On Lucky, who walks toward us with anger.

LUCKY

What tha fuck is wrong with you, nigga?! Get the fuck offa her!

CONTINUED:

105A CONTINUED

> ### CHICAGO
> (getting up)

What's wrong you?

> ### LUCKY

What you beating up on females for, dude?! That shit is weak!

> ### CHICAGO
> (pushes Lucky)

Aw, punk. You just saying that shit 'cause you strung out over this bitch! Moralistic muthafucka!

Lucky walks closer to Chicago and socks him in the stomach. He folds like a set of new French doors.

> ### LUCKY

If you was a real man, your shit woulda been straight from tha git and you wouldn't have to hit your girl. Punk-ass.
> (helps Justice up)

Get up. You all right?

Justice murmurs a "yes" and walks over to attend to Iesha. Lucky is left standing alone. He thinks.

JUSTICE AND IESHA

Where Justice helps her friend up. Iesha is scratched. She continues to curse with a bloodied mouth. Iesha pulls away, attempting to continue fighting, only to be restrained by Justice.

> ### IESHA
> (crying)

Fuck that muthafucka! He getting *jacked*! I'ma, I'ma call Dooky, I'ma call Monster Loc! They gonna shoot that nigga. He ain't nobody's daddy!

Lucky looks over at Iesha. He doesn't notice Chicago getting up and charging him.

Lucky and Chicago get into a brawl. They tumble and wrestle, punches are thrown, kicking, all the elements of a good scrap. Lucky prevails.

He gets up.

> ### LUCKY

Fuck you, punk! I'm leaving your stupid ass!

CHICAGO
(coughing)

You can't leave me! We got a job to do!

LUCKY

Fuck this muthafuckin job! My momma didn't have me so
I could work at no muthafuckin post office all my life!
Shit! Catch a bus to 'Frisco. We only forty miles away.

*He walks away. Justice and Iesha are getting into the truck. Chicago
suddenly becomes apologetic.*

CHICAGO

Naw, man. I'm sorry, dude! Yo, we friends, man. Fuck
them hoes! Why don't leave them, dude?! Why you trip-
ping?!

WIDE

*As the truck drives on, leaving Chicago on the road. A duffel bag is thrown
out the window. Chicago continues to shout out at Lucky: "Watch you
doing, man?" and "Stop bullshitting!"*

ANOTHER ANGLE: BACK OF TRUCK P.O.V.

As we PULL AWAY from Chicago shouting at the truck.

We hear Justice's voice over the following images.

JUSTICE *(V.O.)*

"Is it true the ribs can tell the kick of a beast from a
Lover's fist?"

106   INT. THE TRUCK—DAY

THE BACK

Where Justice holds Iesha in her arms. Iesha cries.

JUSTICE *(V.O.)*

"The bruised bones recorded well. The sudden shock, the
Hard impact. Then swollen lids . . ."

THE FRONT

Where Lucky drives alone. He is very upset.

JUSTICE *(V.O.)*

"Sorry eyes, spoke not of lost romance, but hurt."

CONTINUED:

106 CONTINUED

BACK TO ROAD

Chicago staggers a couple of feet, looks around, picks up his brush. He sits by the side of the road and begins to brush the back of his head.

JUSTICE *(V.O.)*

"Hate is often confused. Its limits are in zones beyond itself. And Sadists will not learn that. . . ."

BACK TO LUCKY

Who pulls over the truck in frustration.

THE BACK SEAT: Leave time for voice over, then Justice speaks.

JUSTICE *(V.O.)*

"Love by nature, exacts a pain unequalled on the rack."

Justice looks up from holding her crying friend. She has noticed the truck has stopped moving.

JUSTICE

You all right?

IESHA

Yeah. Why we stopped?

JUSTICE

I don't know.

107 *EXT. THE TRUCK—DAY*

OVERHEAD: ON CRANE

We see Justice get out of the truck as we DESCEND to let her pass, then go back UP to reveal they are on another peak overlooking the Pacific Ocean. We see Lucky sitting on the grass in the far distance. Justice walks out to talk to him.

A blanket drapes her shoulders.

ANOTHER ANGLE

As we see Justice come forward and drop down to sit next to Lucky.

There is a pause. Neither one of them says anything. All we can hear is the sounds of the ocean and the sea gulls. Justice attempts to break the ice.

JUSTICE
(laughs)

They was gonna break up anyway.
(reminiscing)

I remember when I was little and my uncle Leon used to come around and give me and my cousins change. He would go to the liquor store, buy a forty-ounce of beer, then throw us the change. And I'd always ask for the "big nickel." I couldn't pronounce quarter, so that's what I'd call it.
(to Lucky)

Yuk, look at them nails. *Give me your hand.*

Lucky gives her his hand. Justice looks in her pocket and produces a nail file. She begins to file Lucky's nails. Lucky shows his discomfort.

JUSTICE

Anyway, so because of that my grandmother used to say I was always looking for the big nickel. Anything I did—ride a bike, go to school, do somebody's hair—she'd say "Justice! You still looking for that big nickel?" That was before she died.

Lucky looks at the concern on her face.

LUCKY

When she die?

JUSTICE

About two years ago. She left me her house. My mother died when I was twelve. Suicide. She named me Justice cause she was in law school when she got pregnant with me. . . . I'm all alone. I got a cat, though.

LUCKY

Damn.

Justice looks at Lucky's nails. Their eyes meet. They kiss. Justice looks at Lucky's nails. Tilt to nails, clean, filed. Tilt up, they kiss.

108 INT. THE TRUCK—DAY

Where we see Iesha inside. She has cried herself to sleep.

108A   *EXT. THE ROAD—DAY*

THE GRASS

Where Lucky and Justice continue to kiss.

Justice stands up for a moment, looks off into the distance. We hear her thoughts over the following images.

JUSTICE *(V.O.)*

Give me your hand. Make room for me to lead and follow
you beyond this rage of poetry.

Then she opens the blanket up like a cape and surrounds Lucky. They make love.

JUSTICE *(V.O.)*

Let others have the privacy of touching words and love of
loss of love. For me, *give me your hand.*

WIDE

As we see them against the backdrop of the grass and the beautiful Pacific Ocean. The blanket erupts with the ripple of their bodies.

DISSOLVE TO:

109   *EXT. THE ROAD—DAY*

Where we see the truck shooting up the Pacific Coast Highway.

110   *INT. THE TRUCK—DAY*

Where Lucky and Justice ride on. Suddenly something catches Justice's eye.

JUSTICE'S P.O.V.

Off the road she sees a dilapidated empty drive-in theater.

She and Lucky exchange a glance.

DISSOLVE TO:

111   *EXT. WINDMILL VALLEY—DUSK*

We see a windmill. Then another, then another. Then we see a whole hill covered with windmills.

We see the truck coming through the hills. The hills are covered with windmills.

DISSOLVE TO:

112   EXT. THE ROAD—DUSK

We start on the truck coming up the road, then PAN with it to REVEAL a sign that reads YOU ARE NOW ENTERING OAKLAND.

DISSOLVE TO:

113   INT. TRUCK—DUSK

Where Lucky and Justice ride along.

LUCKY'S P.O.V.

Where he sees a big brawl in the street. Docu-style realism sets back in.

BACK TO TRUCK

Justice turns to Lucky and smiles. Lucky just looks at her. Then he lowers the boom.

LUCKY

I gotta tell you something.

Justice turns her attention out the window. She sighs. She can sense this is gonna be something heavy.

JUSTICE'S P.O.V.: Subjective to objective, then reveal Justice.

There is a car accident in the street.

JUSTICE

What? Oh shit, don't tell me you got somethin!

LUCKY

No. But listen—I'm only saying this cause I like you and you should know before anything else happens.

114   EXT. OAKLAND NEIGHBORHOOD—NIGHT

Where we see the mail truck turn a corner and go up a street. In the far distance we can see the red lights of an ambulance.

115   INT. THE TRUCK—NIGHT

Where the flashing lights fall upon Lucky's face. He ignores them and pulls to the curb.

JUSTICE

A little girl, huh? Why didn't you tell me that shit from the beginning?

CONTINUED:

115 CONTINUED

LUCKY

I didn't think it was important. How was I to know we
wuz gonna . . . hold on, let me just check in with my
cousin.

He gets out of the truck.

115A *EXT. OAKLAND NEIGHBORHOOD—NIGHT*

A WALKWAY

*Where Lucky gets out of the truck and walks up to his Aunt Audrey's
house, notebook in hand. He is on cloud nine and in the best of spirits.
People are running past him and down the street toward the ambulance
and police lights.*

BACK TO TRUCK

Where Justice and Iesha emerge.

IESHA
(stretching)

What we doing here? How come we didn't go to the hotel?
Shit, I'm tired.

THE DOORWAY

Where Lucky arrives to notice that it is open. Empty. Dark.

LUCKY

Kalil! Aunt Audrey! Anybody in here!?

He goes in.

ANOTHER ANGLE: NEW SHOT

*As Lucky comes back out and looks down the street. He senses something
wrong. Lucky hops off of the porch and runs with the rest of the crowd
down the street. We follow with him some ways then swing around in
front of him. Lucky pauses in shock. We hear screams. Lucky comes
forward as we move with him to reveal his cousin Kalil on a bloody
stretcher, his aunt Audrey frozen in shock, and a crowd of spectators
standing around.*

Lucky makes his way to his aunt, and they embrace.

CLOSE UP: LUCKY

*As he looks up from his aunt toward the ambulance. In the background
an attendant is trying to get some information from Lucky and his aunt.
They say nothing. Also we hear the various voices of people in the crowd
with a thousand explanations of what happened.*

TIME SLOWS DOWN

JUSTICE AND IESHA

Walk up. Both stand there in shock. We frame up Lucky holding his aunt in the foreground, with the two women in the background.

116 *INT. AMBULANCE DOOR P.O.V.*

Where the door is closed and the truck moves away, revealing Lucky and his aunt still embracing. He leads her toward her home.

DISSOLVE TO:

117 *INT. THE TRUCK—NIGHT*

Lucky is driving. Justice sits in the next seat. Solemn. Iesha is in the back quiet and frozen.

118 *EXT. OAKLAND HOTEL—NIGHT*

We see Jessie come down some stairs and enter some change into a cigarette machine. It takes her change, she hits it a couple of times, and a pack comes out.

THE PARKING LOT

The truck comes into the lot, and Justice and Iesha hop out. Lucky comes around from the driver's side.

Iesha looks as though she wants to say something to Lucky, but she can't bring out the words.

IESHA

You all right?

Lucky has no reaction.

Iesha backs up and reluctantly walks away, leaving Lucky and Justice alone.

LUCKY

Walks over to the front grill of the truck and sits down.

JESSIE

As Iesha walks past her, and she watches and waits to talk to Justice.

JUSTICE

Follows him and sits next to him. She puts her arms around Lucky and tenderly kisses him. She kisses his neck, face, etc. The music gets higher. Everything is romantic, then

Lucky puts his head down then looks back up.

CONTINUED:

118 CONTINUED

LUCKY

I mighta got there on time if I hadn't been fucking around wit you.

He walks away.

JUSTICE
(confused, shocked)

What?!

ANOTHER ANGLE: WIDE SHOT: PARKING LOT: SFX

As we see the truck start up and back away from Justice. Leaving her standing there alone. She walks toward the hotel and Jessie.

JESSIE

You scraping the bottom of the pudding cup now, huh?

JUSTICE
(pissed off)

Know what you talking about before you judge.

They walk on.

JESSIE

Oooh, you even walk different.

Justice just turns to look at Jessie, then she walks on.

DISSOLVE TO:

119 *INT/EXT. THE POST OFFICE—P.O.V. BACK OF TRUCK—NIGHT*

Lucky opens the back door, and we see him and a Dockworker talking. Several workmen begin unloading boxes and bags off the truck.

DOCKWORKER
(filling out a form)

I thought there was supposed to be two of you?

LUCKY

Nope.

DOCKWORKER

Well, see ya next time around.

LUCKY
(taking the form)

I don't think so!

120 *INT. JUSTICE'S HOTEL ROOM—NIGHT*

There is a conference going on. Justice, Iesha, Jessie, and Heywood are present. From the looks on their faces, we can tell what the topic of discussion is: men.

Iesha is holding a cold towel to her eye.

HEYWOOD

Hold it there. It may swell a little. Let me see it.

She takes the towel away. We see her eye. It's a small shiner.

HEYWOOD

Awww, that ain't that bad.

IESHA
(looks at him like he's crazy)

It ain't.

Jessie looks at Iesha's eye.

JESSIE

That ain't nuthin, girl. I got this girlfriend Susan, she got this thing where she don't think a man loves her unless he beats her. Anyway, this nigga went off on her once, and her eyes were so big. You know them Dunkin' Donuts?

HEYWOOD

The big ones with the glaze on 'em?

JESSIE

Yeah, those the ones. Well, you take two of those, put them on both eyes, and that's what she looked like. You young. You gonna learn. Don't fight no man with you fists—you fight him in his wallet. Now instead of swinging on 'em, you shouda gave him some, let 'em go to sleep, reached into his wallet, and took his credit card.

HEYWOOD

And we all woulda had a party!

JESSIE

On him!

Jessie and Heywood laugh. They start reminiscing, uttering past stories. Iesha cuts them off.

CONTINUED:

120 CONTINUED

IESHA

What credit card? That nigga ain't got no credit card!

Jessie turns and stops.

JESSIE

Well, shit then, you is a fool.
                    (laughing and looking at Iesha's eye)

Men ain't shit.

Jessie and Heywood start laughing again.

JUSTICE

That's the truth.

Jessie stops laughing.

JESSIE

Excuse me? I thought you was in love.

JUSTICE

You thought wrong. Don't assume. You assume, and you
make an ass outta you and me.

JESSIE

You were already an ass. Ya'll still gotta lot to learn about
the world.

Justice's face, as Jessie's words sink in.

JESSIE

C'mon, Heywood. Let's go get a drink.
                    (walks away, mumbles)

These little young girls don't know they cuchie from a
hole in the wall. Shit, I just rest and dress, honey. Love
don't live here anymore.

*Justice returns to consoling her friend, but we can tell her mind is miles
away.*

JUSTICE

It ain't that bad.

She helps her with the towel on her eye.

THE DOORWAY

Where Colette sticks her head in.

COLETTE

Is everything all right?

Justice turns around. Iesha is cradled in her arms.

JUSTICE

No.

DISSOLVE TO:

121 *INT. THE SOUND LAB—NIGHT*

Lucky's cousin's makeshift recording studio. We see a four track, a drum machine, a keyboard, two turntables, a large boom box, a rhyme dictionary and thesaurus, and a ton of records.

The walls are covered with the faces of the heroes of hip-hop. Posters of Public Enemy, KRS-One, EPMD, and everybody else who is truly down.

Among the mess Lucky spots a tape that reads LUCKY'S NEW BEATS. *He pops it in the box. We hear the beat. It is a smooth, Loc'd out gangsta groove. Lucky listens for a moment, then presses* STOP *on the box.*

He thinks for a moment, then hits his hand on the desk and stands. Then he sits once more to think. Like "The Thinker."

DISSOLVE TO:

121A *INT. THE SOUND LAB—DAY*

The light changes to a golden hue as a new day arrives, and we see Lucky, who has apparently fallen asleep in the chair. He awakes. He sits up, leaving an afterimage of his sleeping self on the chair. When he stands, it disappears!

He smells the air: Food. We hear children playing upstairs.

122 *INT. AUNT AUDREY'S KITCHEN—DAY*

Where Aunt Audrey is cooking up a storm: A real southern breakfast. We see eggs, bacon, fried chicken, biscuits, etc. Aunt Audrey is cooking to keep her mind off of the death of her firstborn. Also in the kitchen is Uncle Earl, Audrey's brother Tequan, her second son Shante, her daughter, and a few other family members young and old.

AUNT AUDREY
(*manages a smile*)

Morning, Lawrence. You hungry, baby? C'mon over here
and get you somethin to eat.

Lucky goes over to the table.

CONTINUED:

122 CONTINUED

LUCKY

I ain't hungry. I'm too mad to eat.

Audrey has no reply to this.

THE STOVE: A FRYING PAN

Where Aunt Audrey pulls some chicken wings out to drain on some paper towels. She pauses for a moment and attempts not to lose her composure.

UNCLE EARL

Audrey, sit down. Sit down. You gonna wear yourself out.

Audrey sits down across from Lucky. She looks as though she is in a daze of depression. Her gaze finds Lucky.

AUDREY

Lawrence and Kalil useta do music together. They used to make them tapes. They was trying to do something with they lives. Something constructive instead of de-structive.

She laments for a moment.

Shante, check that chicken, baby. Make sure it don't burn.
>   (a beat)

Lawrence, I want—I want you to know you my favorite nephew. Your mother, even though we sisters, we don't always get along. I was always happy you and Kalil were more like brothers than cousins. Family should stick together no matter what.

LUCKY

What you gonna do with all this equipment?

SHANTE
>   (nonchalantly)

Sell it.

LUCKY

What?

SHANTE

We need the money.

LUCKY

Every dollar he made went into that room. Why every time people try to build and do somethin, somebody gotta come along fuck up shit?!

AUDREY

What do you think we should do?

LUCKY

Give it to me. I'll do somethin with it.

SHANTE
(sarcastic)

Like what?

AUDREY
(looks over to stove)

Shante! Turn the fire off. Take them wings out the skillet and drain off all that oil. My blood pressure's bad enough as it is.
(turns back to Lucky)

Anyway, what would you do with it?

LUCKY
(looks around)

Use it.

CUT TO:

123   EXT. AUDREY'S HOUSE—DAY

Where we see Lucky and some of his cousins loading the equipment back into the mail truck. Aunt Audrey gives Lucky a hug before he gets into his truck. Over these images we hear Audrey's voice.

AUDREY (V.O.)

Well, take it then. Just 'cause my baby didn't get a chance to realize his dream don't mean you can't do what you gotta do.

Lucky starts up the truck.

DISSOLVE TO:

123A   EXT. THE ROAD—DAY

Traveling montage on the road. Beautiful sights of California.

> DISSOLVE TO:

124   EXT. THE ROAD—DAY

Lucky's face from outside the truck while it is moving. The truck speeds up, and goes into the distance. We hear Justice's voice: another poem begins.

125   INT. THA HAIR SHOW—DAY

As we TRAVEL through the Oakland Hair Show from a docu-style perspective. Heywood is behind the camera. There are many exhibits on display. We see new products being introduced. Salesmen on different stages peddling everything from mousse to gels to tools. Our attention is drawn to the various hairstyles present and the reactions of the characters to being filmed.

We see Jessie and entourage walking through the crowd having a good time. She is pointing at people and making comments.

Heywood points the camera at Dexter: "Sexy Dex."

Eventually we see Justice. She is attending to Lisa and Gena's hair, as well as the hair of two other women. They are her models, for her hairstyles. There are many other stylists doing other people's heads also. Justice is noticeably nervous at being recorded. She tells Heywood to turn that shit off. End of docu-style.

THE RUNWAY

Where we see the models come forth. Our attention is drawn to their heads as we notice their beautiful intricate hairstyles. The hairstyles are like sculpture.

A TABLE OF JUDGES

Watches the models as they come forth.

126   EXT. THE DESERT—DAY

Where we see Lucky walking along the road in the desert. The truck is nearby in the distance. He is thinking.

126A   INT. THA HAIR SHOW—DAY

Justice lets out a breath.

The Judges begin to talk and review their notes.

> DISSOLVE TO:

AN AWARDS CEREMONY

Trophies are given out to representatives from different salons.

Justice receives a trophy and is congratulated by Jessie and company. She holds it up for all to see. But she is not happy. She smiles an uneasy grin.

126B   *EXT. HIGHWAY—DAY*

We end on an image of the truck going across the horizon.

FADE TO BLACK:

127   *INT. JESSIE'S SALON—DAY*

MONTAGE

We see hair and nails being done. Everything seems normal once more in the shop. A voice changes the mood.

RITA *(V.O.)*

Bitch, if you don't quit staring at me, I'm gonna knock them eyes outta your head!

THE STYLISTS

Look up.

WAITING BENCHES

Where two women sitting across from each other are looking at each other like cats in a fight. The first one is Rita, the second one is Simone. Simone is kinda prissy. She talks to her friend next to her.

SIMONE

I can't even deal wit her skainchie ass! She just better stay away from James.

A HAIR STATION

Where Jessie is doing someone's head.

JESSIE

Hey, hey, hey, why we gotta have this here? Take your shit out in the street. I got enough problems as it is.

RITA
(stands up to leave, looks at Simone)

Yeah, bitch, you can say what you want. But remember this, every time you kiss him, you tasting my pussy!

CONTINUED:

127 CONTINUED
JUSTICE'S STATION

Where she stands attending to a client's head. Her face looks much as it did at the beginning of the film. Only this time she is made up more. Justice finishes the woman's head and begins cleaning up.

THE DOORWAY

Where Rita leaves, and Lucky enters with Keisha in hand. He is dressed in very casual attire. As soon as he enters, his presence is felt by every woman in the shop.

Justice looks up and, noticing Lucky, excuses herself from her client and goes over toward the counter.

LUCKY'S P.O.V.

As we slowly move forward toward Justice. She looks around to see the reactions from the other women.

BACK TO LUCKY

Who reaches the counter and casually leans against it, looking at the other women. His gaze reaches a couple of them, who instinctively look away. He turns to face Justice.

> **LUCKY**
>
> What's up?
>
> **JUSTICE**
>
> Who's this?
>
> **KEISHA**
>
> Keisha.

They shake hands.

> **JUSTICE**
>
> My name's Justice.
>
> **KEISHA**
>
> What's Justice?

Lucky and Justice just smile.

> **LUCKY**
> (motions toward the couch)
>
> Mind if we sit down?

ANOTHER ANGLE

As the party of three all sit down. Simone and her friend sit across from them.

Both women are nosy and attempt to listen in on the conversation between Lucky and Justice.

LUCKY

Ah, mm, well, listen I want you to know I'm sorry. I made a mistake.

JUSTICE

Come closer. I wanna whisper somethin to you.

LUCKY

Get the fuck outta here. I ain't fallin for that shit again.

JUSTICE

Naw, seriously—come here.

They look at each other. Get closer. They kiss. The kiss is initiated by Justice, which surprises Lucky.

THE SHOP

Where Jessie and the rest of the salon look equally surprised.

JUSTICE

Your nails look clean.

LUCKY
(looks at nails)

I wonder why?
(to Simone and party)

What you looking at?

Justice's gaze turns away from Lucky to Keisha.

JUSTICE

What did you do to this little girl's hair?

LUCKY

Nuthin.

JUSTICE

It looks like it. C'mere, little girl.

CONTINUED:

127 CONTINUED

ANGLE

As Justice guides Keisha toward her station. She sits Keisha in the chair and proceeds to analyze what can be done with her hair.

THE COUCH

Where Lucky looks at Justice playing with his daughter's hair. There is a glazed look on his eyes.

LUCKY'S P.O.V.: MOVIN TOWARD JUSTICE

As he/we see Justice skillfully workin on Keisha's hair. We hear Justice's voice over as she says another poem. At the end of the poem, Justice looks up toward Lucky/us. She smiles.

POETIC JUSTICE

Written and Directed by
John Singleton

Produced by
Steve Nicolaides and John Singleton

Starring:
Janet Jackson

Tupac Shakur

Tyra Ferrell

Regina King

Joe Torry

Roger Guenveur Smith

Dina D.

Rose Weaver

Director of Photography
Peter Lyons Collister

Production Designer
Keith Brian Burns

Edited by
Bruce Cannon

Music by
Stanley Clarke

Poetry by
Maya Angelou

Casting by
Robi Reed, C.S.A.

A New Deal/Nickel Production

CAST
in alphabetical order

Simone	**Khandi Alexander**
Aunt June	**Maya Angelou**
Thug #1	**Lloyd Avery II**
Thug #2	**Ché Avery**
Kim	**Kimberly Brooks**
Ticket Taker	**Rico Bueno**
Dina	**Dina Bunn**
Shante	**Maia Campbell**
Policeman #4	**Jeff Cantrel**
Panhandler	**Michael Colyar**
Female Cousin	**Kina V. Cosper**
Uncle Earl	**John Cothran, Jr.**
Policeman #7	**Joe Dalu**
Helicopter Pilot	**James Deeth**
Aunt May	**Norma Donaldson**
Truck Driver	**Kelly Joe Dugan**
Policeman #1	**Judd Dunning**
Last Poets	**Suliamen El Hadi**
E.J.	**Rene Elizondo**
Crackhead	**Benjamin I. Ellington**
Jessie	**Tyra Ferrell**
Lloyd	**Dedrick Gobert**
Mailroom Supervisor	**Clifton Gonzalez Gonzalez**
Gangsta	**Ricky Harris**
Last Poets	**Omar Ben Hassan**
Policeman #2	**Randall C. Heyward**
Maxine	**Miki Howard**
Baha	**Baha Jackson**
Justice	**Janet Jackson**
Policeman #6	**Mike James**
Patricia	**Patricia Y. Johnson**
Keisha	**Shannon Johnson**
Rodney's Girlfriend	**La Keisha M. Jones**

Cop	**Kirk Kinder**
Iesha	**Regina King**
Angry Customer	**Vashon LeCesne**
Beauty College Instructor	**Jennifer Leigh**
Annie	**Jenifer Lewis**
J-Bone	**Tone Loc**
Cousin Pete	**Special K McCray**
Policeman #3	**Mark Miller**
Rita	**Sarena Mobley**
Policeman #5	**Al Murray**
Antonio	**Kahlil Gibran Nelson**
Last Poets	**Jalal Nuriddin**
Penelope	**Lori Petty**
Cashier	**Denney Pierce**
Woman with Baby	**Renato Powell**
Fighting Man	**Jimmy Ray, Jr.**
Dockworker	**Michael Rapaport**
Aunt April	**Ernestine Reed**
Woman on Couch	**Robi Reed**
Angel	**Crystal A. Rodgers**
Lucky	**Tupac Shakur**
Heywood	**Roger Guenveur Smith**
Last Poets	**Daoud Spencer**
Uncle Herb	**Eugene Tate**
Chicago	**Joe Torry**
Gena	**Mikki Val**
Concession Stand Man	**David Villafán**
Cousin Dion	**Dion Blake Vines**
Dexter	**Keith Washington**
Aunt Audrey	**Rose Weaver**
Rodney	**Anthony Wheaton**
Colette	**Yvette Wilson**
Brad	**Billy Zane**

Unit Production Manager	Steve Nicolaides
1st Assistant Director	Don Wilkerson
2nd Assistant Director	Simone Farber
Associate Producer	D. Alonzo Williams
Art Director	Kirk M. Petruccelli
Set Decorator	Dan May
Second Unit Director	Peter A. Ramsey
1st Assistant Film Editor	Margaret Guinee
Assistant Film Editor	Maria Lee Silver
Script Supervisor	Dawn Gilliam
Camera Operator	Anthony Gaudioz
First Assistant Camera	Bob Hall
Second Assistant Camera	Brian LeGrady
Costume Designer	Darryle Johnson
Men's Wardrobe	John K. Lemons
Women's Wardrobe	Shirlene Williams
Makeup	Alvechia Ewing
	Susan A. Cabral
Hair Stylist	Pauletta O. Lewis
Chief Lighting Technician	James R. Tynes
Assistant Chief Lighting Technician	John Sandau
Key Grip	Domenic Giorgio
Second Grip	Robert A. Thomas
Dolly Grip	Michael Giorgio
Stunt Coordinator	Bob Minor
2nd Second Assistant Director	Janice Jackson
Special Effects	Eric Rylander
Production Coordinator	Linda Folsom
Production Secretary	Sherri G. Sneed
Production Accountant	Alison Harstedt
Assistant to Mr. Nicolaides	Judy Alonzo
Assistants to Mr. Singleton	T. David Binns
	Joseph Doughrity
Location Manager	Kokayi Ampah
Assistant Location Manager	Elisa Ann Conant
Property Master	Michael Wilson
Assistant Property Master	Randy J. Gaetano
Construction Coordinator	James J. Ondrejko

Set Designer	Darrell L. Wight
Transportation Captain	James Brown
Transportation Co-Captain	Tim Roslan
Supervising Sound Editors	Tom McCarthy
	Greg Hedgepath
Assistant Sound Editor	Rodney Sharpp
Music Editor	Lisé Richardson
Production Mixer	Robert D. Eber, C.A.S.
Boom Operator	George Baetz, C.A.S.
Re-recording Mixers	Sergio Reyes
	Robert Beemer
	William Benton
Supervising ADR Editor	Bobbi Banks, M.P.S.E.
Foley by	
Craft Service	Stan Saffold
Caterer	Variety Cinema Caterers
Unit Publicist	Cassandra Butcher
Still Photographer	Ellis Reed
DGA Trainee	Evan Gilner
Casting Associate	Andrea Reed
Security to Mr. Singleton	Shorty
Office Production Assistants	Gregg Allain
	Cynthia R. Harris
Set Production Assistants	Randall Heyward
	Rayniece Holmes
	Yon-Allyn Styles
	Dion Vines
	Maurice Williams
Foley & ADR by	Sony Pictures Studios
	Culver City, California
Opticals by	Cinema Research Corporation
Negative Cutter	
Color Timer	Bob Putynkowski
Title Design	Saul & Elaine Bass

SPECIAL THANKS TO:

Gordon Henderson
Moods Magazine
Rex Perry
Astarte
Dudley Products
Johnson Products
Joico Labs
Rene of Paris
Rusk
Sebastian International
Soft Sheen Products
Worlds of Curls

The Major League Baseball trademarks
depicted in this motion picture were licensed by
Major League Baseball Properties, Inc.

"Felix the Cat" courtesy of
Broadway Video Enterprises, Inc.

Film Oakland Mayor's Office
Jeanie Rucker

Los Angeles Film and Video Permit Office

Hollywood Curl Beauty Salon

The People and Businesses of
South Central Los Angeles

Kevin & Money Donen

Ladies and Gentlemen
From L.A.
Black Cinema in Effect
Dealing a New Hand

I.A.T.S.E. Bug

Dolby® Stereo
In Selected Theaters

ABOUT THE AUTHORS

JOHN SINGLETON is the writer and director of *Boyz N the Hood* and *Poetic Justice*. He lives in Los Angeles.

VERONICA CHAMBERS is Senior Associate Editor at *Premiere* magazine. Also a correspondent for BBC Radio 5, Veronica was named one of *Glamour* magazine's Top Ten College Women in 1990. She lives in New York City.